DEVIL'S HAND

by M. E. Patterson

ISBN 978-0-983-84481-5

Published by Digimonkey Studios

Printed in the United States of America

First Paperback Edition

Acknowledgments

Thanks to those who have journeyed with this story at various points along the way: Kurt, Carrie, Kari, Matt, Stephanie, Diane, John, Michelle, the Novels-in-Progress and SlugTribe study groups, and many others.

This book would not have been possible without you.

For Katrina, my light in shadow.

Sway to and fro in the twilight gray;
This is the ferry for Shadowtown;
It always sails at the end of the day,
Just as the darkness closes down.

Rest, little head, on my shoulder so
A sleepy kiss is the only fare;
Drifting away from the world we go,
Baby and I in the rocking chair.

See, where the fire logs glow and spark,
Glitter the lights of the shadowland;
The raining drops on the window, hark!
Are ripples lapping upon its strand.

There, where the mirror is glancing dim,
A lake lies shimmering, cool and still;
Blossoms are waving above its brim,
Those over there on the window sill.

Rock slow, more slow, in the dusky light,
Silently lower the anchor down,
Dear little passenger, say "Good night!"
We've reached the harbor for Shadowtown.

The Ferry of Shadowtown, Nursery Rhyme

1

"THE END TIMES ARE NEARLY upon us! We will all stand in judgment beneath the watchful eyes of our Lord! Come now, to the arms of the King, and repent! Repent for your sins, and you will find everlasting love in the—"

He had only listened to "Eddie Palisade's Hour of Faith" for a few minutes out of sheer curiosity and a certain morbid fascination. Too hellfire-and-brimstone for Trent's taste, but the syndicated radio show was immensely popular with the God-fearing crowd. Trent had found it on three separate stations as he searched the band for some decent music.

Thick drops of rain splattered against the windshield of the rented moving van. Ahead, the flat horizon glowed like a neon tube set in the sand of the south Nevada desert, and beyond stood the hypercolor wasteland of Las Vegas, a neon monstrosity to which Trent had no interest in returning. He looked sidelong at Susan, asleep in the passenger seat, smiling, blonde hair half-covering the pixie-like features of her face. He would do anything for her, though, even if it meant coming back here.

The radio hissed through a patch of white noise and then settled on an oldies country music station, a bit weak in strength, but listenable. Johnny Cash cried from the van's tinny speakers, barely audible above the endless drumming of the rain atop the metal roof. Trent smiled. To Hell with Eddie and the "Hour of Faith." He'd take Cash as his preacher any day.

He shifted uncomfortably in the driver's seat as the van bounced along Interstate 15. His right thigh ached—an old injury from the crash—the only physical wound that had lasted. The wet-slick road trashed the van's handling, making every steering adjustment a nerve-wracking event. He had always hated traveling. But after the crash, the hatred had become dread. He wondered again why he had let Susan talk him into coming back here.

He glanced at her, and then at himself in the rearview and used a free hand to adjust the angle of the gray cowboy hat. He didn't think the hat looked silly. She had said that to him a few months back, on his thirtieth birthday no less, when he'd insisted on wearing it out to meet friends at a bar. She had been teasing, he knew, but still...

"You look ridiculous," Susan had said. "Like you're trying to be that guy from Pale Rider."

"You mean Clint Eastwood?"

Susan frowned. "No, the character, not the actor."

"The Preacher?" Trent laughed. "You think I look like an old-west preacher? I'm more like the guy in High Plains Drifter."

Susan had smiled at him then, one of her smiles that made him feel weak and strong at the same time. She leaned in and kissed him on the forehead. "You're not that guy," she whispered. "That guy's pure evil. He only looks out for himself. And that's just not you, honey."

Trent smiled at the memory and turned his attention back to the road, fingers drumming on the steering wheel.

Johnny sang out from the radio, "Well, there's things that never will be right I know—" And then an intense, screeching burst of static, timed perfectly with a shuddering thump upon the roof of the van that set the entire vehicle to ringing. The noise dashed Trent's smile and he ground his teeth together in surprise.

Susan sat up, alert and confused. "Wha—?"

Trent gripped the steering wheel even tighter as another massive impact dented in the roof above him. The van skidded wildly on the road. He peered through the window, up at the sky, and saw white dots growing larger and larger until one of them resolved into a chunk of ice that slammed into the windshield right in front of him and exploded, sending icy shards in a radial spray across the glass.

Trent snapped back in his seat. His foot hit the brake. The cowboy hat flipped backwards off his head. The moving van squealed and fishtailed, the popping coming faster now, rapid-fire against the metal panels, a tumultuous barrage of softball-sized hail.

"Shit!"

He over-corrected and the vehicle swerved on the two-lane interstate and crossed over the middle before he managed to bring it back into its original lane. Balls of ice smashed against the road and the van. It was all he could do to keep the tires tight against the pavement. Out of the corner of his eye, he could see Susan, fully awake now, gripping the door handle in frozen panic, her lips moving. Trent couldn't hear anything except the pounding hail.

He turned his full attention forward again. Something in the road. A tire? A hubcap? No, green and rigid, like a piece of a highway sign. Trent threw the wheel to the left, desperate to avoid the debris, but too late. The broken sign jumped halfway up onto the hood, then screeched back down, gouging the paint, until it vanished beneath the tires.

The van screeched, swayed, and veered off into the left lane again. Then Trent heard the loud pop and felt the sickening sideways drift. The van careened out of control.

He jammed the brake to the floor and squeezed the wheel in a death-grip, gritting his teeth as the van pitched off the left shoulder and headed for dirt. He wrenched his right hand free of the wheel, threw his arm across Susan's chest, and felt her slam against it as the vehicle dove into the muddy desert and slid to an awkward stop.

Everything went quieter for a moment, save the hail, which continued its staccato rhythm in time to Cash singing, "Well I know I had it coming, I know I can't be free—"

"Susan, baby, you alright?" Trent leaned across the cab, arm still pinning his wife to her seat.

She looked up at him, eyes wide and mouth agape. She blinked, coughed, and then formed a weak smile. "Holy shit," she said.

Another massive ball of hail exploded against the windshield. They both jumped.

They looked at each other for a silent moment and then began to laugh, quietly at first, inaudible above the din, and then louder, until they were both cackling, foreheads pressed together. Trent kissed her and could feel her shaking with both laughter and adrenaline overload. He pulled back, looked at her with a crazed grin on his face, and shook his head.

"I think we blew a tire," he yelled, gesturing behind him with his thumb.

"Holy shit," she said again, still chuckling.

Trent looked around the cab for something—anything—that he might use as a shield against the falling hail. He thought about waiting the storm out, but it didn't look like it intended to let up soon. He needed to get the van moving, or they might end up stuck in the gathering mud. He couldn't see anything useful, just the old gray Stetson behind his seat—the hat the hospital staff had given him from the wreckage of the plane. They had thought it was his but he never had the heart to tell them it wasn't. He grabbed it and put it back on his head, covering up his short black hair. He shrugged and kicked open the driver-side door with his foot.

"Trent!?" shouted Susan.

He turned to look at her. "What?"

She gave him one of those you're-doing-something-stupid-again looks that both infuriated him and made him smile. Susan had an arsenal of those kinds of looks; it was part of what made him love her. And Trent had a history of doing stupid things since the crash. Maybe it was facing certain death and winning that had left him dull to the sense of threat. Or maybe the impact with the ground had just knocked a few screws loose. He wasn't quite sure.

"It's too dangerous!" she shouted. Another icy softball punctuated her statement by smashing against the windshield right in front of her. She winced.

"Gotta change the tire!" Trent replied. "Or we'll get stuck in this mud!"

She stared at him for a moment and then, with a determined look, she grabbed the hardcover novel in the passenger-side floorboard, lifted it above her head, and popped open her door.

"Wait—" said Trent, but she was already out, yelling at the top of her lungs, the book barely covering her head.

He stared for a moment, irritated but not surprised. Susan was like that. Farmer's daughter, never one to stand by while others worked. He shrugged and leapt out the driver's side and into the pounding hail, expecting that he could make it to the back of the truck without any major damage. After all, he was the luckiest man alive, right?

The first ball smacked against his arm, bringing up an immediate welt and intense, stinging pain. The second smacked against his denim-covered thigh as he dashed toward the back of the van. The third chunk of ice crashed down atop his head. The sudden shot of pain was like a hammer blow, blinding, and he reeled and barely caught himself on a handhold at the back of the U-Haul as the cowboy hat tumbled to the ground.

Susan was there and already had the back of the van open and had jumped inside. She was rummaging through the few pieces of furniture and boxes. Trent grabbed the fallen hat and then managed to climb gingerly in next to her. He slumped down in a beat-up old recliner they had taken from her apartment. Most of the stuff in the van had belonged to Susan. After the Gaming Control Board blacklisted him, they needed money. Trent's expensive items brought in more cash at the pawnshops. Pawnshops and the GCB—two more reasons he hated seeing that glowing city on the horizon again.

"Yes!" She held up an old whiteboard she had used while studying for her nursing exam. It was large enough for them both to hide under if they crowded close.

"That'll work," said Trent. He reached up to touch the sore spot on his head. His fingers came away with sticky blood. "Dammit."

"Oh, honey, are you okay?" Susan set the whiteboard down and rushed over to him.

He waved her off. "No, no, don't worry about it. It's fine." He jammed the Stetson back onto his head and grinned at her, but her expression still showed worry. "I've had a lot worse."

She gave him a plaintive look.

"Come on," he said and got up from the recliner. He walked over to the spare tire hanging on the inside wall of the van, next to a hand-crank jack. "Let's change a tire."

The off-road jaunt had sent the front driver's-side tire across a jagged chunk of rock, cutting its rubber flesh like a knife. No way would this roll any further. Trent brought the new tire over, trying his best to avoid the crashing hail as Susan struggled to keep them both beneath the whiteboard.

They worked as a team, Susan holding the flashlight and whiteboard as Trent worked to break the lug nuts on the ruined wheel. Every few minutes, he heard her yelp as a ball of ice crashed down on some part of her that had snuck out from beneath the rectangular shield. He wanted to tell her to quit—to get back inside the truck and let him handle this—

but he knew better. She wouldn't leave him here by himself, even if he told her to.

Trent forced his weight down on the tire iron, struggling to break the last nut. "Dammit!" he swore, as the hail battered the whiteboard over his head. He summoned as much strength as he could find and gave the tire iron a powerful shove. The lug nut broke with a pop, nearly sending Trent pitching forward to the ground as the tire iron started to spin. He dropped to his knee, removed the final nut, and pulled off the useless tire.

The hail stopped, as sudden as it had come.

Susan looked up at the sky and then down at Trent with a quizzical look on her face. He shrugged. The rain had not abated, but at least the pounding hail had quit. She hesitantly lowered the whiteboard. A sudden, sickening *thwack* startled them both. They looked at the top of the van as Susan shone the flashlight on it. A thin stream of—blood?—was running in a rivulet down the white side-panel.

Trent dropped the tire and stood up. "What the—?"

Another splat as something landed on the van's hood and they both jumped again. A fish? Another slammed down next to it, splattering Trent with blood. He grimaced and leapt back, away from the van.

Susan screamed as a sudden multitude of fish began to rain down. Panicked, she dropped the whiteboard and ran for the back of the truck, still shrieking, hands covering her head.

Trent watched her go, astounded. He had never seen her so terrified, not once in the years they had been together. She usually had a remarkable fortitude and a stern strength in the face of obstacles. But this... He looked up as dead fish began bouncing off the top of the van.

Fucking Eddie is right, he thought.

He grabbed the fallen whiteboard and sprinted for the back of the van. He reached it and found Susan curled up inside the truck, tears streaming down her face.

"You okay, baby?!" he shouted.

"Jesus Christ!" She looked at him with tears in her eyes. "What does it look like?"

Trent climbed in and put an arm around her. "It's just fish."

She sobbed. "It's not about the fish, Trent." Tears streamed down her face. "It's everything. Everything's gone wrong. We shouldn't have come back here. The job at the hospital and fucking James and you didn't want to be here anyway and your head. This place fucking hates us both—"

Trent grabbed her by the shoulders and kissed her on the lips. She kissed him back, hard.

After a moment, they pulled away and Trent looked her in the eyes and smiled. "Come on, babe," he said, gesturing toward the storm raging around them. "It's just fish. Happens sometimes. Bad storm, tornado picks up some garbage from a lake and throws it a few miles. It'll be over soon. Least it's not hail."

They stared at each other for a moment. Finally, Susan cracked a tentative smile.

Trent laughed. "You gotta find the humor in this, right?"

Susan nodded and took the whiteboard from him. "Okay," she said, smile widening. "Thanks."

After a minute, the rain of fish lightened, and they made their way to the front of the van, to the ruined tire. Susan lifted up the whiteboard, just in time to catch another bloody slap on top of it. Trent dove under the shield and grabbed the spare tire. Something about fish dropping from the sky encouraged him to work harder. Then the pace picked back up again, as another wave of slimy bodies splattered against the van and the pavement and the muddy shoulder, some still alive, flopping and writhing as they died.

"This is awful!" shouted Susan, struggling to be heard over the thumping sounds of flesh against the metal van.

"At least it doesn't hurt as much," Trent replied without looking up from his work. He had two of the lug nuts back on the new wheel; two to go.

Susan stumbled as a particularly hefty fish slammed down atop the whiteboard. Blood ran off the edges in glimmering red streams. "Hurry up!" she yelled.

"Okay, got it!" Trent torqued the final nut down and kicked the release on the jack. The van slumped back down, mud squelching from beneath the shiny new tire. "Let's go."

They dove into the cab and slammed the door shut. Susan scrambled across the center into the passenger seat. She dumped the whiteboard into the space behind them.

She looked at the windshield, now nearly opaque with fish guts and bloody smears. The periodic thumping against the roof seemed to have a predictable rhythm. "What the *fuck?!*" she exclaimed, laughing. "This is insane!"

Trent looked at her wryly. "You never been in a fish-storm before?"

She punched him in the shoulder.

He chuckled. "Well we better get this thing out of the mud. Hope it can still move. You need to be at work in the morning."

The statement made him feel worthless. He had no job. It had only taken a year of unbeatable pro gambling before they blacked him out. A lot of money gained and a lot of money lost; now he did odd jobs if he could find them, and those rarely lasted long. Bad things happened at job sites when Trent was around. After the crash, when the swelling had gone down and his spine turned out to be intact, the doctors called him the 'luckiest man alive,' but he didn't really feel it, not anymore at least. Except at the poker table, he felt just the opposite.

He glanced at Susan, who had pulled her blood-smeared rain slicker around her shoulders. The storm had brought an unusually cold chill with it. She grinned at him, still shaking her head. He smiled back. Well, *mostly* unlucky, he thought.

A trio of fish smacked wetly on the glass in front of him and then slid slowly down onto the hood. He flicked on the wipers, creating a transparent pink window amidst the blood, illuminated weirdly by the coruscating shafts of colorful light from Las Vegas in the distance.

He gunned the engine. The wheels spun in the mud, but eventually caught, and the van hauled itself back onto the road. The hail chunks had nearly all melted, but the dead fish were not going anywhere, making driving even worse than before. It felt like riding on grease.

Trent eased the vehicle back into the proper lane and gave it just enough gas to set it trundling down the Interstate, barely topping 10 MPH. Only twenty miles to go, but he figured it would be near-morning before they made it to the new apartment.

"Hey, hon?"

Trent glanced at Susan. "Yeah?"

"Thank you."

Trent nodded, then ran his hand through his hair, matted and wet with rainwater and blood. He winced when he touched the spot where the hail had struck.

"It's okay," he said.

But he wondered at the truth in that. It didn't seem like Vegas wanted him back any more than he wanted to be there. It definitely did not seem okay.

2

THE RAIN SLUICED DOWN OUT of a concrete sky onto concrete earth, cold needles pricking at the old man's skin. Neon of every conceivable color filled the firmament with a *gray*-brown sludge, like the puke-stained parking lot in front of a strip club. It was a place, he thought, where no one ever looked up. There is no night sky in Las Vegas; only a dull smear of a ceiling where the tallest building ends.

Salvatore Cortina shuffled wearily along the sidewalk, as he did night after night, his brain churning through the memories that always threatened to slip away and be lost forever.

Alzheimer's, the doctor had said years before. Salvatore remembered that the man had refused to make eye contact as he delivered the bad news. It was the tiny, sour memories like that that always remained. And the big, awful ones.

He walked past the Luxor hotel, tattered shoes slopping through puddles of ice-cold rain and sidewalk grease, in which swirled endless parades of naked women on soggy paper cards. The usual men who lined the sidewalks handing out the cards had retreated for the night to wherever they go when the weather turns foul. It was, thought Salvatore, a small blessing.

The weather could not stop the gamblers, though, who still filed in and out of the casino entrances like drowned rats. A soaked, over-endowed prostitute stood upon a street corner, no umbrella, rain soaking her bleach-blonde hair as her trembling hands fumbled to light a too-wet cigarette. This is the Hell that I have chosen, thought Salvatore, and not for the first time. This is my penance.

And one of those huge, terrible memories came rushing back.

He snarled and coughed and tried to force the images of fire and sounds of screaming from his mind. *There was nothing I could do*, he thought. *Nothing at all. God took them. It was His will, not mine.*

He cracked his knuckles and then pulled his threadbare long coat tighter around his shoulders in a futile attempt to stave off the waves of chilling rain that were coming down now at an angle, blown by sudden gusts of wind. The sheets of cold sent young women in skimpy dresses into laughing shrieks as they sprinted inexpertly from one casino entrance to the next, stilettos clip-clopping. One of the women, tall and thin, twisted her ankle as her high heel snapped in half; she went down with a huff and a childlike cry and laid there in a puddle, looking pathetic. Her friends stood under a casino awning, pointing and laughing. Salvatore shuffled past, and couldn't stop himself from mumbling, "whore" as he did so. The woman was too preoccupied to hear.

Past the jet-black Luxor pyramid and the Excalibur with its gaudy castle facade, past the New York-New York and then down an alley between it and the Monte Carlo. Salvatore had made this trip many times. He needed an ingredient, and with the tunnels flooded for a few hours, there wasn't much else he could do other than forage.

Salvatore Cortina lived in the drainage tunnels beneath Las Vegas. Built over a number of years, and stretching well beyond the city proper into the desert beyond, the tunnels were a means of channeling rain from torrential downpours—like the one ongoing—into the desert rather than into the streets and casino lobbies.

But Las Vegas was not a place where rain fell often, so the tunnels remained mostly dry. Squatters, bums, and junkies set up camp when they could, occasionally shooed out by the LVPD, only to return in a few days time to a different section of tunnel where the police would leave them alone.

Salvatore had a fairly permanent residence there, with an assortment of propane tanks, gas burners salvaged from turkey-frying kits, and odd pots and pans pulled from dumpsters behind hotel kitchens. It was another sort of penance, a Purgatory that he shared with those cast out by the surface-dwellers, the underclass of the weak and ruined and addicted. And Salvatore was their preacher.

His sermons came weekly, as they should, on Sundays in a large cross-connect between several tunnels. His was not the only 'church' in the tunnels, but he had a reasonable congregation; a dozen or so broken souls hoping for salvation in their lucid moments and hunting for their next fix anytime else. If Salvatore could lengthen the former and diminish the latter, he considered it God's work being done through his voice. If he could fill their bellies with something more than despair and alcohol, he knew that God was directing his hands.

He reached the back alley behind the Monte Carlo's first floor kitchen, now a swamped, gravel-strewn resting place for several green metal dumpsters and an assortment of loose beer bottles and the ever-present escort service flyers. Under an awning, a fat Hispanic man with a goatee, face tattoos, and white line cook's uniform was taking a smoke break. He looked up as Salvatore approached, smoke curling from his nostrils.

"Whatchu want, Sallie? I ain't got no more tonight. You already picked me clean, bro."

Salvatore did not recognize the younger man, but knew that he had allies in the kitchen here, once-members of his flock that had escaped the tunnels and found gainful employment, willing to part with kitchen scraps and mostly-empty jars of spices, tomato pastes, and olive oils. With the basics and some scavenged, uncooked pasta, Salvatore could work miracles.

"Seriously, man," said the cook, "I'm out. Whatchu looking at me like that for?"

It was the day-to-day memories that disappeared. The recognition of someone's face or name, the hourly sequence of events in his life, the things said or unsaid—those were the casualties of Salvatore's disease.

The doctor had proclaimed, matter-of-factly, that Salvatore wouldn't even know his own name in six months. That was eight years ago. He had beaten the odds. His mind still felt sharp and clear. He had no confusion, just holes where bits should be. Things forgotten. He could probe the empty spots with his mind, like fingers probing a bloody wound whose edges were well-defined, but the more he did, the more it brought on migraines. He had, instead, learned to accept the forgetting and forego the pain.

"I don't remember you," said Salvatore, his voice quiet and trembling from the cold. "Did we meet recently?"

The Hispanic looked shocked. "What the Hell, Sallie? You known me for two years. George Rodriguez. I helped with your church until I kicked the crank and got this job. You been getting food from here every week." He gestured at the kitchen door behind him and took a long puff from the cigarette with his other hand. "Come on, Sal, you never forgot me 'fore now."

Salvatore shook his head. "I'm sorry, I have a rare form of—"

"Yeah, yeah, you got the old timer's. My uncle got the same thing. I know that. But you forgetting *me* now? You must be getting worse, Sallie." He took another drag on the cigarette.

"I was here recently?"

George nodded and blew out a big cloud of smoke that was quickly torn apart by the falling rain. "Last night. You was looking for some stuff for an *arabiatta*." He shrugged. "Gave you all I had. I'm tapped out."

Salvatore felt his shoulders slump. Had he forgotten the sauce he had been making? He had left his ersatz kitchen ahead of the coming storm, knowing that the tunnels would likely flood. Had he secured his equipment to the tunnel ceiling to keep it out of the floodwaters? He couldn't remember, and the probing was threatening to bring on a new migraine. He pictured his favorite saucepot, boiling away above a propane burner as the tunnel waters rose up and carried it off. There would be no meal for the congregation this week. And had he really known George for two years? Maybe the forgetting *was* growing worse.

"So you have nothing," he tried, hoping to salvage what would be a disappointing Sunday with no food. "Nothing at all?"

George frowned and flicked the remains of his cigarette into a puddle. "Nothing, bro." He stood up. "Hell, I gave you more last night than I probably even shoulda. I get caught given stuff to bums and the owner'll have my ass." He made a shooing motion with one hand and then turned to open the kitchen door. The smells of high-end cooking spilled out into the night. "I can't help you no more. I could lose my job." Then he stepped into the kitchen and let the metal door slam shut behind him.

Salvatore's stomach rumbled in response to the kitchen smells. His head ached. Had he not been through this a dozen times or more already, he might have cried.

The next two visits went no better. At the rear of one restaurant, he knocked and had the door slammed in his face moments later. At the other, the speed-addicted line cook that talked with him gave him a single dinner roll and told him not to eat it all at once, laughing. It was the stop after that where Salvatore finally scored some provisions.

The giant black man that answered Salvatore's knocks looked him up and down and then said something inaudible back into the kitchen. A reply came, the black man nodded, and then turned and said, "hold on," in a gravelly voice. He shut the door.

Salvatore had almost given up and turned to leave when it creaked back open. The black man appeared with a plastic grocery bag full of jars and cans, topped by two half baguettes, obviously going a bit stale, but still good. "Here you go," said the man. "Don't tell nobody." Then he shut the door.

The old man's heart danced in his chest. Enough for at least a halfway decent Sunday meal. The congregation would get something, rather than nothing. He stared at the restaurant's kitchen door with its tiny, faded sign that read: Antonio's. Italian restaurant. Salvatore had no recollection of the place and that made him worry. How could he not remember an Italian restaurant? The wash of joy faded from him before the reality of his deepening memory loss.

He sighed, clutched his plastic bag tighter inside his coat, and left back down the alley by which he'd come. He was nearly to the street when the coked-out mugger stepped into his path.

The man was jerky and highly agitated and waved a trembling knife at Salvatore. "Empty your pockets, gimme the bag." Just for good measure, he made a mock thrust with the knife and added, "now!"

Salvatore stood frozen, his brain confused by the unexpected situation. What to do? He had no money. Would the thief stab him for being poor? At first, his arms clutched the bag tighter to his chest, as if it were the only thing left that mattered to him. But then, a quiet, defiant voice rose up in the back of his mind, deep beneath the years of memories, sliding through the mists of forgetting.

"No," he said, voice quivering.

The mugger let out a weird little shriek. "Dammitdammitdammitdammit just gimme the shit, man! Just gimme the shit!" He took another step forward and threatened a few more stabs with the blade.

Salvatore felt his bladder loosen and warmth trickled down his left leg. The defiant voice was drowned out by feelings of anguish and embarrassment. He was so old, too old for this sort of thing. He just wanted to go back to the tunnels, where he could be alone, where it was quiet and the smells of his junk kitchen were all that mattered.

"Please." He shook his head. "I don't have anything. I'm just homeless."

A look crossed the mugger's eyes, a look that suggested a moment of clarity, but it was quickly replaced by rage. He rushed forward, knife outstretched.

Salvatore fully evacuated his bladder then and his arms went weak and the plastic bag fell to the ground, spilling its contents into the grime. The loaves of bread went immediately soggy. Glass jars shattered and splashed their contents onto his feet. The provisions were lost. But no matter. Salvatore knew that he would be dead in minutes.

The knife was inches from Salvatore's throat when the mugger's eyes suddenly went wide, a grimace of pain struck his face, and he dropped the knife and leapt backwards. His feet went out from under him and he fell, landing ass-first in a puddle on the cement. Salvatore could see blood soaking through the pants over his right ankle. Beside the mugger's feet was a long, *gray* snake, fangs bared.

The mugger saw it too, let out a scream, and began crab-walking backwards, hands and feet scuffling against the soaked concrete as he desperately tried to put distance between himself and the creature.

A voice rang out in the alleyway. "Hey, fucknut. Mugging a bum? Really?" A short, scrawny man in a hooded sweatshirt stepped up beside Salvatore from behind. He gave the old man a glance and a wink. "Heya, Z."

Salvatore had no idea what that meant, and simply watched in awe as the snake, and three more like it that had appeared from behind piles of trash in the alley, began chasing the thief out of the alley. The man finally managed to stand, hopped a few times on his injured foot, and then ran sidelong, letting out a series of whooping shrieks, while never turning his gaze from the oncoming snakes.

Still shrieking, he reached the end of the alley and stumbled out into street. There was an ear-splitting screech. The smell of melting brakes. A delivery truck moving at high speed. One second there, standing frozen against the headlights. Next second, a stomach-churning thump and the mugger went from vertical to a tumbling pile of pink and *gray* under the tires. The driver fishtailed, stopped, and then laid on the horn.

The short man in the hooded sweatshirt looked at Salvatore with a surprised grin on his face, looked back at the mess in the street, let out a sharp, 'Ha!' and then whistled appreciatively. "Shit yeah!" he exclaimed. "Gotta love the timing."

"Y- you-," stammered Salvatore. "You killed him."

The short man shrugged. "Snakes were poisonous. Would've died anyway in a few minutes. Better than a crack addiction for the next ten years, if you ask me. I did him a solid."

Salvatore's mouth opened, but he couldn't find the words.

The short man gave him an ear-to-ear grin. "So how you doing, Z? Took me a bit to find you."

"My- my name is Sal—"

"Salvatore Cortina," interrupted the short man in the hood. "Sure, I know." He nodded. "Interesting choice by the way. Feeling poetic, are we? Fire and ice?" He walked a few feet down the alley so he could get a better view of the truck driver, now panicked, bending over the corpse-heap of the would-be mugger. The driver had a cellphone to his ear.

The man in the hood turned back around to face Salvatore. "Smart, really. Made it harder to find you, but it's gotta diminish you some." He walked back and poked Salvatore hard in the chest. "This guy really want you hanging around?"

Salvatore shook his head. He hadn't the slightest clue as to what the short man was talking about. Fire and ice? And it seemed like the man was talking to someone else. Salvatore turned to look briefly over his shoulder, hoping to see another person that could clear up the confusion.

"Huh," said the man. "You're really out to lunch right now, aren't you? Alzheimer's, right?"

Salvatore turned back and nodded.

The man laughed. "Right."

He reached under the hood and scratched at his head, then reached into his sweatshirt and removed a manila envelope. He thrust it toward Salvatore, the motion making the old man stumble back a step. "Here," he said. He shook the envelope as if to make the point. "Take it."

With a trembling hand, Salvatore reached out and took the envelope.

"I think you'll find it interesting. You've been looking for what's in there." He paused. "Well, 'you' is a relative term here. Just hold onto it for now." He turned to leave, watching the commotion in the street, which had now grown to several people. Sirens wailed in the distance. "Oh," he said, without turning back around. "And you should probably check up on your hidey-hole. Some pretty bad floods tonight."

Salavatore could only mumble, "ok" at first, as he watched the hooded man, hands in his pockets now, walking slowly down the alley toward the commotion-filled street. Finally, Salvatore regained enough composure to shout out his questions.

"Why are you doing this? Who are you?"

Without turning, the man in the hood replied, "Just a messenger." And then he rounded the corner beyond the alley and disappeared from Salvatore's view, leaving him standing in the rain in a dark alley, feet covered with ruined tomato sauce and bits of soggy bread, leg soaked in urine, clutching a manila envelope in both hands. Police sirens screamed in the distance, growing closer by the second. Salvatore stood there wondering just what the Hell was going on.

3

THOUGH SHE GASPED AND GASPED for breath, Celia found each tortured intake shorter and tighter than the last. She felt as though she were drowning, as though a thick fluid had infiltrated her lungs. The lack of oxygen made her head pound with pain. The headache flowed with each gasp of air and then ebbed again as she exhaled. Tears dribbled down her cheeks.

She felt stupid for crying. *Thirteen year-olds don't cry*, she thought. *I can get through this. It happens, like, every month.*

But it had not happened before, not like this. Celia had been hospitalized on several occasions for anaphylactic shock, brought on by severe allergies. Once it had happened outside, during the summer, while playing in the sprinkler with her younger sister, Haley. The doctors had decided a bee had stung her, though she had insisted otherwise. Then, one time, it had happened at school, after lunch, and some of the kids still shied away from her.

She now carried an epinephrine pen everywhere she went. She could feel it in her hand still, and she knew she must use it. She hated the thing, hated the idea of stabbing herself with a needle. She tried another breath, but her throat felt even tighter than before. Her eyes had already swollen shut. Her ears felt like they were filled with a thousand tiny insects, moving and tickling and making her flesh itch and burn. No, this was not like the other times. This was far worse.

She squeezed her eyes against the pain and the drowning sensation and the burning in her chest. She whimpered quietly between gasps, as the fingers of one hand gripped the upholstery, white-knuckled. With the other, she raised the epinephrine pen, and then jabbed it into her thigh.

She whimpered again with the new pain.

From the front seat of the car, her father kept repeating, "it's okay, honey, just relax. Just relax." But she had long since passed the point of relaxation. Panic had taken over. Her skin felt ice-cold. The tips of her fingers, buried in the car seat fabric, burned as if she pressed them against frozen metal. In the darkness behind her swollen eyelids, she thought she could almost *see* the fluid filling up her lungs, sloshing around, killing her from the inside.

"Please, Daddy, help," she moaned. "Please!"

"We're almost there. Just relax, okay?" The car tires squealed as her father cornered into the hospital parking lot. "Just hold on, Cee."

Celia opened her eyes to watch the glowing lights of the University Medical Center advancing on them. The lighted sign of the Children's Center wing was familiar to her, and a part of her wanted to protest that she was too old now to be in the Children's wing; her thirteenth birthday had passed a week ago.

Another wave of chest-tightening pain hit, buckling her spine and sending panic-induced nausea raging through her.

She closed her eyes and felt sweat beading on her forehead. The sweat was freezing cold and it stung and burned her skin.

"We're here, Cee, it's gonna be okay." Her father opened the car door and began to yell, "Help! Help!"

A multitude of voices rang out, punctuated by the sudden noise of heavy rainfall as the door next to her was pulled open. She felt hands grip her shoulders and legs and then they lifted her from the seat.

"Why is her forehead bloody?" A deep voice with a street accent.

Her father's voice answered, muffled by the sound of the rain. "She's anaphylactic. I don't know, maybe she hit her head in the car. She was sleeping and woke up like this. Call Doctor Marcus! She's seen him before for this—"

Celia felt the strong hands lay her out on a gurney and then some bumps as she started rolling across the pavement. She heard the hydraulic hiss of the emergency doors opening.

"Dammit, where is everyone?" asked her father.

She could hear their voices amidst the metallic rattle of the gurney and shoes slapping against the tile floor of the hospital hallway, and she focused on their conversation to keep herself from screaming in fear. Even with her eyes closed, she could feel the blazing glare of fluorescent lights zipping past her. Cold swept into every part of her body. Her stomach convulsed.

"Short-staffed," said the deep voice. Then, to someone else, "She's gonna vomit. Get ready to intubate if she needs it."

Someone nearby, a woman's voice, assented. Celia could barely hear anything now beyond the squeaking of the gurney wheels and a high-pitched ringing in her ears. She struggled to hear the deep-voiced man, to hold on to something mundane and comforting.

"Lot of turnover this week. Please, just get out of the way."

Celia could hear a crash cart roll up next to the bed with a jingle of metal and plastic.

"In here!" yelled the deep voice. "Give her the epinephrine and antihistamines."

Celia felt the bed swing around, stop, and then hands gripped her arm and several needles went in and then came back out.

A softer, woman's voice said, "BP is dropping."

Celia's back seized then, and a peristaltic shockwave ripped through her abdomen. She vomited. It felt like gallons of water were pouring from her stomach, but none of it relieved the pressure in her chest. Panic welled up even stronger than before and the voices around her dropped in pitch and became unintelligible. The ringing sound filled her mind. She was going to die. She tried to open her eyes but saw only blinding white.

"Throat's closing up. Let's intubate."

She felt hands grab her head and neck and mouth and suddenly there was something choking her, something sliding painfully down her throat. Her body convulsed again and she was dimly aware of fluid splashing onto her face and neck.

"Do the hydrocortisone. And get a line of dopamine to keep the BP up. She's gonna be fine..." The voice faded beneath the screaming in her ears. She vomited again. It felt even longer this time.

Before she blacked out, she heard someone close-by say, "Jesus Christ, how much water did she drink?"

4

SUSAN GROANED AT THE TINY alarm clock and its incessant buzzing. She rolled over, wondering why her back was hurting, and then her fingers touched the carpet and she understood.

They had arrived at the apartment complex at three in the morning and had promptly gone to bed, bringing in from the van only an old inflatable mattress, the irritating alarm clock, and their gym bags with some clothes. Trent would unload the rest in the morning. Susan needed sleep.

The first day of her new job at the hospital was tomorrow, working with Dr. James Marcus, an old friend from college who had constantly berated her about getting an education degree. James had insisted that she had the chops for medicine, but Susan had never shared his confidence. Now here she was in Las Vegas, nursing degree in hand, with an offer to work in the Children's Center at University Medical. James had offered her a better salary than usually given to green nurses, in part, she suspected, because he had always had a thing for her, feelings she did not share.

She looked over at Trent, sleeping soundly on his side of the air mattress. His side was still inflated. Hers was flush with the carpet. She rubbed at her aching back as she sat up. Of course, Trent's side had not changed. Living with the 'luckiest man alive,' she never expected less. She shook her head and sighed. She loved him for his idiosyncrasies, for his warm smile and the glint in his eye when he was determined. She adored him for his attempts to look tough when she knew he was as worried about something as her. But the 'lucky' thing? That sometimes got old.

Another thought lingered there, too; a thought she often tried to dismiss, but still it waited for her, festering. She felt angry at Trent, angry that he made her feel guilty for coming to Las Vegas, even though she knew he did not do it on purpose. She was angry at the world for the plane crash, and for Trent's crazy luck that had somehow soured her own achievement, her one big career moment. But most of all, she was angry for feeling angry, and the guilt chased its tail and reminded her constantly of the sore spot in their relationship, the thing that was always better left unsaid.

She stood and stretched, taking in a deep breath to clear her thoughts. Her long nightshirt felt cold against her skin; the apartment's heat had cut off overnight. Even with her increased pay, they had a small budget and the rent was cheap in the rougher parts of town.

She watched Trent sleeping and wondered what he dreamed about. She worried that his nights were filled with fire and wind, nightmares from the singular tragedy that defined their lives together: the plane crash Trent had only barely survived.

Going in and out of a coma dream for weeks, Trent had mumbled something about 'monsters' and 'his hat,' which the nursing staff at the hospital in Nebraska had eventually found amidst the wreckage. Susan had never seen the hat before. The crash had been well over a year past, but she remembered those weeks of grief and worry as though they had happened yesterday.

After recovering, Trent had promised to start looking for work, but fell into pro gambling instead. A year of unbeatable wins and the Board put a black mark on his name and all the money—the millions of dollars—went down the drain in an instant, burned away paying off furious casino owners and other, less reputable individuals, all of whom felt cheated.

Susan looked around at the empty apartment and out the balcony window toward some of the boarded-up apartment buildings a few blocks away—grimy, unwashed, uninhabited. *And now, here we are.*

She felt guilty. She knew Trent did not want to be back here. This place—the casinos, the porn-littered streets, everything—held a lot of bad memories for Trent. It made Susan's heart sink whenever he told her things were 'fine.'.

She padded to the small bathroom as she listened to Trent's quiet snoring. Sometimes she wished he could get up with her and have a real breakfast like those families on TV. But then, they had tried for a family without much success. She frowned and looked at herself in the smudged bathroom mirror, one hand on her lower stomach. She thought about the kids that she would get to work with in her new job. Kids that needed help. Kids that needed a lot of love.

"Ugh," she said out loud, still feeling groggy and dim and just a bit dizzy from the rough couple hours of sleep and the wave of thoughts that had assailed her upon waking. She always over-thought things when she was nervous.

She frowned and stumbled back into the bedroom and looked at the clock and wondered why she had thought it said 5:00 AM because now it said 6:30 AM and that meant she was—

"Oh, dammit!"

Trent snorted. "Wha—?"

"Back to sleep, hon," she whispered. "I'm just late." She leaned over and kissed him. He had morning breath but that didn't stop her. "I love you. I'll see you later, okay? Don't hurt yourself unloading."

Trent mumbled something unintelligible and rolled back over.

She pulled a pair of turquoise scrubs and a white nurse's blouse with a repeating sports pattern from her gym bag. She dressed quickly, threw on her shoes, and practically flew out of the apartment.

She had checked the schedule before going to sleep and knew that the bus came at 6:45 and if she was late, she would have to catch the next one thirty minutes later, fifteen minutes after her shift at the hospital started. By the time she had reached the bottom step of their apartment stairwell, she could already see the bus coming down the street toward the stop. She only gave a moment's thought to the unusual chill in the air and the light rain that felt cold against her skin. She wished she had grabbed a jacket, but the jacket box was buried somewhere in the van. No time to go back now. Sprinting, she reached the bus stop just in time.

The doors opened and she climbed in, frazzled and breathless. The driver gave her an expectant look and pointed at the fare canister on the dash.

She was confused at first, and then said, "Oh— Oh, shit. I'm sorry," she pleaded. "I forgot my purse. I'm gonna be late, please, just this once..."

The driver, an old black man with a thick white mustache, rolled his eyes and frowned, then jerked a thumb backwards.

She thanked him repeatedly and took the nearest seat. The bus rumbled away from the curb and headed southwest across the city.

5

TRENT PADDED AROUND THE EMPTY apartment, bleary-eyed and still exhausted from the night's events. Outside, a light morning rain fell on the mist-shrouded city. The cold front that had swept into the city overnight had forced Trent to turn on the apartment's heat, and while the heater clanked and hummed along, he opened the sliding door and stepped outside, a lit cigarette in his mouth.

He had spent a year living in Las Vegas after the airplane crash, after his long weeks of recovery, but he could not remember an autumn day this cold. Even in the dead of winter, Las Vegas barely dropped below the mid-40s. The weather outside now, in early November, felt more like Chicago—rainy, lower-40s, chilly breeze. It almost felt like winter coming.

After the cigarette had burned down to a stub, he flicked the remains over the balcony, then turned and went back inside the apartment, which was now heated and comfortable. He looked around for a place to sit and then realized that he had not yet brought in any of the furniture from the van. Trent sighed and thought about lighting up a second cigarette.

He had promised Susan that he would return to Las Vegas with her in order to support her career. But he had never promised to be totally happy about it. He hated it here. He hated what Las Vegas represented, what it claimed to be, and what it really was, deep below the surface, under the makeup and the colorful, backlit veneer. But, like it or not, here he was again, back after a year away, jobless and mostly broke. He knew that fixing the former could help with the latter. He had to get started on the job hunt. Now was as good a time as any.

But Trent had a problem. The Gaming Control Board had put his info in the black book, and that meant that not only was Trent barred from gambling in any of the casinos in the city, but he wasn't even allowed to *enter* them in the first place. So jobs in hotels and tourism were mostly out of the question, and that cut down his options in Las Vegas significantly. Construction jobs—another huge part of the local workforce—would probably be a tough sell, too. Much of the construction revolved around the casinos, and no one would hire a blacklisted gambler of Trent's visibility.

They made a TV special about me, for God's sake, he thought. *No one wants a cheater putting up the drywall in their new casino's basement and security rooms.*

He paced around the empty apartment, trying to come up with some other industry sector that might find him employment. High-tech? Half of it was computerized security, and they'd be more hostile to him than the construction companies. Bartending? Maybe at the seedier, off-the-Strip joints, and he wasn't much of a bartender, nor did he really like spending that much time with strangers. He shook his head. The ideas were not coming quickly. Who did he know that could help him out?

For the year that he had spent in Las Vegas, making money hand-over-fist, his social circle had been mostly in the world of gambling. He had been on a first-name basis with the big casino bosses, but none of them would talk to him now. The GCB had put on a stink on him that would never wash off. He knew a lot of more minor characters too, but still, all of them in the casinos. And then he thought of the one person that was different.

Charlie V.

Charlie was a diminutive Russian fellow—with an unpronounceable last name—who ran a successful pawnshop in the less-glamorous downtown area. It was the kind of place that never called attention to itself; the kind of place you might not even know about unless someone took you there. It was a sort of local secret, and the best place to pawn something in Las Vegas, bar none.

Trent and Susan had unloaded a lot of Trent's fancier stuff on Charlie V after the blacklist, even things other pawnshops might have refused to take. But not Charlie. He had taken it all in with a smile, and gave them top dollar to boot. Rumor had it that Charlie could resell anything, and always made a profit. The Russian's flexibility had kept Trent and Susan afloat during their transition from high-wealth to low-income.

Over the final few months before they'd left for Chicago, Trent and Charlie had become friends, of a sort. The thickly-accented, wry little man always made Trent smile, even when things had taken turns for the worst, even while Trent was handing over things he could hardly bear to part with. He had even sold Charlie his custom, black, Ducati motorcycle, albeit with more than a few tears in his eyes. If there was anyone in the city who would give Trent the low-down, and maybe a few clues on where to start his job search, it would be Charlie V.

With a smile at the thought of seeing the old Russian again, Trent grabbed his keys and gray Stetson hat off the kitchen counter, made his way to the front of the apartment, and headed out into the unusually cold morning. He was so flush with renewed purpose that he even forgot to grab his jacket.

Charlie's shop was called City Pawn, and it occupied the dead-end of a half street on the edge of downtown, near a mostly-abandoned industrial park. City Pawn's only neighbors were a barred-window liquor store, a miniscule storefront that had hosted a For Lease sign for as long as Trent could remember, and a sleazy convenience store on the corner that sold mostly cigarettes and pornography. Unlike The Strip, there were no street vendors to be found here; no men in lines on the sidewalks handing out advertisements for escort services; no Metro cops on bicycles chatting amidst the throngs of tourists. The dusty little half street reminded Trent of the old West, of the main street of a ghost town, now turned from wood and tumbleweeds to concrete and tumbling scraps of newspapers and plastic bags.

Trent parked the moving van in one of the three parking spaces in front of City Pawn, right next to a clean, polished black sedan with tinted windows. He got down from the van and stared at the other car for a moment. It looked entirely out-of-place in this part of the city. He shrugged and made his way to the shop entrance.

A small bell let out a tinny ding as he opened the iron-barred door and stepped into the pawnshop. He immediately searched the place for Charlie V, and saw him behind the counter at the far end of the store. Charlie looked to be engaged in a heated discussion with two blond men in sharp gray business suits. The men had identical, short haircuts and stood at the same height and build, and Trent wondered if they were twins. They even seemed to share similar postures, confident and straight through the back as they argued with the much smaller Russian behind the counter, who seemed to be shifting and nervous.

Charlie looked past the two blondes and caught Trent's eye. Trent thought he looked surprised at first, and then Charlie frowned and his expression became one of frustration and concern. "Good morning, sir," he said with his thick accent. "I will beink right with you, soon."

At first, Trent wanted to protest at the non-acknowledgment, but something in the older man's look gave him pause. *Why is he acting like he doesn't know me?*

Both of the blonds turned then to look at the newcomer, and Trent saw that they were, indeed, identical twins, save one strange feature: though both men had one blue eye and one green, their faces seemed to be mirrors of each other. Other than that, everything about them was the same, right down to the same quizzical expression they both held as they analyzed him.

"Hi," Trent said, and waved politely, before turning away from their gaze in order to pretend to browse the shop's wares. If Charlie didn't want him to know, then he would gladly play along. *Maybe these guys are GCB*, he thought. *Or worse. Could be casino folks looking to settle a score.* He had never met the two blonds, but then, he didn't know all of the big names in town, and some he knew *of* but had never met in person. And besides, the top of the ladder never came after you himself—he would send a messenger to break your legs, or worse. These looked like just the kind of freaks that some of the more eccentric bosses liked to employ for the more delicate 'errands.' Trent had pissed off some important people when the GCB declared him a serial cheater. Maybe a year away from the city had not been long enough.

He watched out of the corner of his eye as he idly browsed some of the shop goods. Charlie had a penchant for taking in the more unusual trades: strange art objects, bizarre and grotesque furniture, even prop pieces from casino shows, bankrupt wax museums and funhouses. He also did a solid trade in antique books, of which he maintained an entire wall, with shelves from floor to ceiling.

Trent randomly picked a small, green journal-sized book from one of the shelves and absently looked it over, while focusing on Charlie's conversation with the two men.

"...and anyhow, I am not findink that for you," he was saying. "I am a seller of goods and thinks, not a bounty huntink service."

"You cannot hide him," said one of the blonds. His voice, like his companion's, was calm and even, almost monotone.

"Protecting him will only further degrade your situation," said the other blond.

His companion added, "The rules must be followed."

"Damn you and your rules," replied Charlie, almost spitting out the words. "You are not welcome here. Get out of my store." Charlie pointed forcefully toward the door.

Trent turned away quickly, not wanting to be caught eavesdropping. He looked down at the flimsy book in his hands. Though it was bound in a green binding, it seemed to be composed of leather, apparently dyed that color. The pages were worn and frayed at the edges, and not a single inch of paper bore ink or markings of any sort. Trent turned it over in his hands, eyebrows furrowed. Even the cover bore no indication of the book's title or purpose. It was an empty journal, albeit antique, judging by the age of the paper.

He had never had an interest in writing before, and he never carried a notebook, but suddenly Trent found himself wanting this one. He liked the strange, embossed artwork on the cover that resembled interlocking snakes and flowers and a multitude of tiny circles connected by razor-thin lines. It had no price tag, and he wondered how much Charlie wanted for it.

The bell above the door jangled. Trent glanced sidelong at it and saw the two blonds walking out. The door shut behind them. After a moment, he saw Charlie hustle around from behind the counter. The little man went to the door, closed the deadbolt with a clunk, and then turned back to face Trent.

"Mister Trent," he said, angrily. "You are not supposed to beink here."

Trent, taken aback by the tone, returned the green journal to the shelf and faced his diminutive friend. "Who was that, Charlie? The Board? Somebody's thugs?"

Charlie shook his head. "You are forgettink about them now. Are very dangerous men, those two. You do not be wantink to know them. Not at all."

Trent had no patience for secrecy. He wanted real answers, not pacification. "They looking for me? Is that why you blew me off?"

Charlie stepped closer, and Trent could smell alcohol on the little man's breath. "Please, trust me. As a friend. Be leavink this one alone. You must go away from here."

Trent was astonished. "Are you kicking me out of your store? After all the stuff—"

"No, no," Charlie interrupted, holding up his palms in defense. "Not the shop. You must be leavink this city, Trent. Las Vegas. It is not a good time for you here."

Trent chuckled at the mangled English. "I haven't had a good time here in a while, Charlie. You know I didn't wanna come back. But I owe it to Susan. After all she's done for me, after all of the shit she put up with while I was here..." He shook his head. "She deserves this chance, even if it means I have to come back to this fucking place."

Charlie's frown deepened. He sighed. "No good will be comink of this."

"Who's after me? Is it that slimy shit, Mars?"

Charlie stepped away and began eyeballing the shop, as though worried that someone else might be lurking in the shadows of his store. "No," he said. "I have not heard from Jack Mars in a long while. But there are..." He paused, thinking. "There are *other* concerns here for you."

"The only thing I'm concerned about right now is finding a job," said Trent. He was tired of trying to talk down the obviously paranoid shopkeeper. "I came to you because I figured you might know of some work. Construction, service industry, hell, I'll bag groceries. I just need a paycheck."

"So you are not leavink, then?"

Trent rolled his eyes. "Jesus, Charlie!" he said. "No! No, I'm not leaving. But if there's heat on me from the casinos or something, well, I promise not to push any buttons. Just get me an ordinary job, I'll stay under the radar, ya know? It'll be fine. I haven't broken any laws."

The anger melted from Charlie's face. A faint smile appeared at one corner of his mouth. "How are you, Trent?" he asked quietly.

Exasperated, Trent replied, "Fine. I'm fine." He glanced toward the door, half-expecting the two blonds, or even the cops, to come barging in, guns drawn, based on the way Charlie had been acting. "I'd be better if this city wasn't giving me the third degree for coming back. Fucking fish fall out of the sky on me last night, nearly wreck the van, Susan ends up late for her first day, and now here you are, treating me like a leper. I'd be better if things would straighten the hell up."

Charlie's smile seemed sad, and he shook his head again. "You are lookink good. Strong. No more drinkink, yes?"

"Can't say I've quit entirely, but I don't drink much. Another promise to Susan, ya know?"

Charlie nodded.

"Still smoke like a chimney, though." Trent grinned.

"Is bad for your lunks."

"Jobs," said Trent, trying to redirect the conversation. "Heard of anything?"

Charlie sighed and walked away. After resuming his place behind the glass counter, he answered, "Don't know what to be tellink you right now, but there are always thinks to do. Maybe job on the internets? Work from home?"

"No computer skills, Charlie. All I am is lucky at poker and I've got most of a History degree. What can that buy me?"

"Not much." Charlie smiled. "You should try beink a dealer in a casino."

Trent gave him the middle finger.

Charlie winked. "Perhaps," he said, "I can be hearink about some construction jobs. Or grocery, yes? But I have nothink right now."

"Damn." Trent frowned. He looked around the small pawnshop, as though he might find a job hiding on one of the shelves, or behind a rack of once-worn Halloween costumes. "Nothing?" he asked.

The Russian waved his head from side to side, as if he had some idea that only motion could work out of his brain. "Eh," he said, with a shrug of his shoulders, "perhaps be checkink tomorrow? I might be havink something then. Must make some phone calls, ya?"

"Fine, fine." Trent retrieved another cigarette from the pack in his jeans pocket. He lit up, inhaled, and blew out a smoke ring while pondering his lack of any real options. "Tomorrow, then. I'll come back." He turned to leave the store and then stopped halfway to the door. "Hey, Charlie."

"Ya?" Charlie had already begun rearranging items in the display case at the counter. It consisted of a weird assortment of small metal figurines.

"You ever sell that bike I gave you?"

Charlie looked up and smiled. "No, Mister Trent. I am tellink you that it is always here for you when you want to buy it back. That motorcycle is for you—nobody else, ya?"

Trent laughed. "You could get a lot of money for that bike."

Charlie shrugged, still smiling.

A digital tone interrupted them. Trent fished his cellphone out of his pocket and looked at the tiny screen. Susan. He put the phone to his ear. "Hey, babe."

"Hi," she said. He could tell by her voice that she was stressed out. "What are you up to?"

"Just job hunting. You okay? You sound stressed."

He heard a long sigh on the other end of the line, and then, "Yeah, it's a zoo here. Marcus still hasn't shown up this morning and nobody can get hold of him. Half the staff quit last week because of the kids— they've only given me one case and I'm already overwhelmed."

"They quit because of kids? I thought it was the Children's Center? Aren't kids normal?"

"No, it's the kidnapped kids. The ones that've been turning up all over town a few days later?" She waited for a response from Trent. When she didn't get one, she explained, "Some freak has been taking kids, and then a day or so later they show up on a sidewalk or a street corner, alive but totally gone."

"Gone?"

"Vegetative state. Our wing has twelve of them. They just brought in the twelfth kid this morning. Poor little boy they found in the loading dock behind the Luxor."

"Jesus."

"Yeah, it's awful. The place is filled with parents. They're all a wreck. A lot of nurses just couldn't take it anymore and quit. Others have called in sick."

"Jesus, that's terrible. Anything I can do?"

"Yeah, actually. I left my purse at home. Don't have money for the bus home tonight."

"Oh, sure," said Trent. "I'll run by the apartment and get it. I can bring you a sandwich or something, too."

The relief in Susan's voice was almost palpable. "Oh, God, you're the best." She let out a long exhale. "Thank you. I don't know what I'd do without you here."

Trent chuckled. "Oh, you'd be fine. I'm the one that would be lost. See you in thirty minutes or so, okay?" He turned and caught Charlie's eye and gave him a short wave goodbye.

Charlie waved back.

"Okay," said Susan. "Love you."

"Love you too, babe."

6

SALVATORE'S EYES OPENED TO SLIVERS of light streaming in through the partly opened manhole cover eight feet above him. His back ached terribly and his clothes had been so drenched that they lay around him in a sopping wet fabric halo. A faint trickle of water still moved along his throbbing sides and under his legs. The concrete beneath him felt ice-cold, hard, dead.

He blinked a few times. The migraine had retreated, but he only had a vague sense of how long he had been out. Sometimes the migraines came like that—so intense that he would blackout for hours at a time. Sometimes he would even wake up somewhere other than where he went down. Some of the other squatters accused him of sleepwalking through the tunnels, muttering incomprehensibly and snapping at anyone that tried to help him.

After a few minutes of self-assessment, Salvatore finally built up the courage to move. With a pained groan, he lifted himself from the tunnel floor. The soaked clothes weighed him down, but he finally managed to struggle to his feet. Hunched over and shivering, he looked up and down the nearly pitch-black tunnel and thanked God that he had somehow survived.

Then he tried to walk. His first step nearly sent him back to the floor as his foot slid effortlessly out from under him. With a wrenching snap of his back, he threw his weight forward and managed to retain his balance. Gingerly, he squatted and touched the floor. Solid ice. He looked around, confused and squinting to try and make out some detail in the darkness.

Behind him, where he had been lying on the tunnel floor, he could dimly make out a man-shaped imprint in the ice, as though it had frozen into place around his supine body as he lay unconscious.

He wondered how he had even gotten here in the first place. His last memory had been in the alleyway, victim of a near-mugging and his meeting with the strange man in the hooded sweatshirt named Snake. And ice? In the Las Vegas tunnels after a summer rainstorm?

Nothing made sense anymore. The forgetting was growing worse and worse by the minute, it seemed.

He blinked a few more times and then took another tentative step forward, back toward his encampment farther down the tunnel, back toward the propane heaters that he hoped had been spared by the flood.

This time, when his foot touched down upon the ice, it plunged through a thinner spot. His foot splashed into freezing water that clawed its way up his ankle. He whimpered at the unwelcome surprise, but brought his other foot forward for another step. He had to make it back to his heaters.

Every footfall sent more lightning flashes of frozen pain into his legs, but he pushed on, desperately trying to reach the one place he knew where he might find warmth. He briefly considered turning back, trying the ladder to the surface, but he banished the notion. Coated with ice, the rungs would be almost impossible for him to climb. He knew he had only one option.

His shivering turned to violent trembling, and then seizure-like spasms, but still he pressed forward. His fingers, splayed with pain, clawed at the icy concrete walls of the tunnel, and he began to notice that as he moved farther away from the place where he had awoken, the ice grew thinner and wetter and soon vanished entirely. And then, up ahead, he saw the dim light that must be the lantern he had hung from the ceiling of his camp.

As he rounded the corner of where the tunnels joined, his momentary relief turned to frustration and intense disappointment. His encampment had been ruined. The lantern overhead still hung as it always had, but the pallets supporting his cooking equipment had been toppled by the floodwaters. The table was on its side, most of the shelves had collapsed, and bits of glass and empty plastic bags lay scattered about the place. The propane tanks had come loose from their moorings and now lay half-submerged against one side of the tunnel. Salvatore suspected that the tanks would still operate if he could get them dry and righted, but he needed a means of lighting them. With the shelves collapsed, his books of matches, painstakingly collected from each of the casinos, were nowhere to be seen, likely washed down the tunnels with the rest of the debris.

Trembling, he sloshed over to the biggest mass of refuse and began to sort through it, tossing aside plastic bits and waterlogged food packages and shreds of cardboard, desperately searching for even one book of matches that had somehow stayed dry.

He did find a few of the books, but they had been so thoroughly soaked that he knew they wouldn't light. He tried anyway, but with no success. Defeated, aching, freezing, he put his hands and forehead against the tunnel wall and began to wail quietly. He had survived a mugging, but was now going to die right here, in his own home, of exposure, surrounded by propane tanks and no matches. He thought it fitting, after the events of his life, that he might die desperately craving fire. He let out a series of curses in Italian.

And that's when he saw the envelope floating in a puddle amidst the trash.

His wailing ceased and his shaking fingers reached into the muck. It was a manila envelope with a metal clasp on the back, closed tight. He undid the clasp and, standing beneath the lantern, peered inside. The sense of relief was overwhelming. Inside the envelope was a document, a plastic card of some sort, and a book of matches, all miraculously dry.

With a hoarse cry, he thanked God and the Virgin Mary and Jesus and any religious figure he could think of. Hungrily, he pulled the matches out of the envelope, placed the remaining items on one of the few shelves that had not collapsed, and then set about lighting one of the propane heaters.

He finally got the tank setup on one of the wooden pallets again, and then fumbled open the matchbook, noticing

absently that it was from the Luxor, one of the few he had
never gotten around to collecting. A compulsive part of him
reveled in the inadvertent satisfaction of that, in the order that
his collecting represented, especially now, in the face of such
chaos.

With the tank lit and the hissing flame finally providing
Salvatore with much-needed warmth, he pulled an old plastic
drywall bucket over and flipped it upside-down to use as a
seat. He retrieved the strange envelope and sat down next to
the fire, beneath the flickering lamp, his feet propped up on
the edge of the pallet to keep them out of the cold filth.

He took out the plastic card first and turned it over in his
hands. It had the pyramidal logo of the Luxor Hotel on it and
he recognized it as the keycard for a room. But it had no
number or any other sort of indication as to what room it
might open. He shrugged and set it aside.

Then he retrieved the document, a single sheet of thin
paper, printed on both sides in black ink, with lots of boxes
and check marks and information, like a tax form. He squinted
at in the dim light and realized that it was not a tax form, but
a medical record from two months back. For a child. A
teenage girl named Celia Cagill. And in the upper corner, a
street address for her family home.

He wondered why in the world someone would give him a
child's medical record and a keycard for a room at the Luxor.
He shook his head. The night had only grown stranger since
his incident in the alleyway. But then a thought occurred to
him: maybe if he returned the medical form and the keycard,
the family would be grateful enough to give him a few dollars.

He could buy new supplies for Sunday's mass, maybe even some dry clothes at the second-hand store.

He sat awhile longer in the cold, dark tunnel, listening to the hiss of the propane tank and warming his arms and legs, until he slowly drifted off to sleep.

He awoke a few hours later with his head and chest aching. After he felt well enough to travel, he got up, shut off the tank, and headed up the tunnel toward one of the places where he knew it exited into a street-side wash. In his hand, his withered old fingers still gripped the manila envelope with the keycard and the medical record that would hopefully be his meal tickets.

1

WHEN JOHN CAGILL OPENED THE front door of his two-story suburban home, the last thing he expected to see was a small, white-haired old man wearing a threadbare, stained white sweater, faded khaki slacks, and a tattered long coat, soaked from head to toe in rainwater, squinting up at him like a man staring painfully into the sun. The Cagills lived in a nice community on the west side of the city, just off I-95. It was not the sort of place in which one expected to see bums wandering the street, let alone knocking upon your door.

"Can I help you?"

The old man, still squinting, said something very quietly that John could not quite make out.

"I'm sorry?"

From inside, his wife's voice called out, "Who is it, John?"

"I'm not sure," he replied. He looked back down at the old man. "Who are you?"

"Salvatore Cortina," the old man said quietly. "Please, I have something for you."

John's wife called out again. "John, whoever it is, tell them to come back tomorrow. You have to get Celia's stuff to the hospital, and I have to get Haley to school."

John nodded. "I'm sorry," he said to Salvatore, "but I think—"

The old man frowned and his wrinkled hand pulled something from inside his threadbare coat: a manila envelope. "I found this," he said, his voice wavering. "It's about your daughter. I was hoping—"

John grabbed the envelope from the man and opened it hurriedly, analyzed the contents. A medical record about Celia? He looked up again. "Where did you get this?"

The old man's eyes shifted and he looked at his feet as he talked. "Ah," he said, slowly, "it's a strange story. I was hoping for some food..." He trailed off.

John stared at the paper again. Sensitive stuff. Personal records. Their home address, Celia's social security number, a list of her prior admissions to the hospital. Absently, he waved the old man inside. "Yeah," he said, "sure. I can get you a bowl of cereal. I want to know where you found this?" He was concocting stories in his head of irresponsible hospital staff absently tossing out important records into the dumpster. He was thinking about the short-staffed Children's Center, his dissatisfaction with their inability to truly diagnose Celia's strange allergy. He was thinking lawsuits.

He stepped inside, eyes still glued to the paper. The old man in the dirty clothes followed close behind.

At the kitchen table, he spread out the remains of the manila envelope: several more papers like the first, documenting nearly everything about Celia and the family.

"And you said you *found* these?" He didn't look up for the old man's reply.

"Uhh," the old man stammered. "Yes."

"Where?"

"Well that is a bit strange."

John finally looked up, his impatience growing. "You said that already. These are very personal documents. Tell me where you got them."

From the other room, his wife questioned why he had gotten sidetracked from gathering Celia's things to take to the hospital.

"This man found some of Celia's medical records," he said.

The old man looked at John with a nervous smile and fidgeted with his hands. "The food..."

John's wife came into the kitchen then, a querulous look on her face. "I'm sorry, he found what?"

John grabbed a handful of the papers and thrust them towards her. "Celia's medical records," he growled. "I'm thinking the hospital has been throwing them out, probably to cover their asses. They know we're thinking of a lawsuit, I bet. Incompetent idiots. Can you believe this?" He looked at the old man again, who never ceased fidgeting. "Get him a bowl of cereal, will you? I want to hear this whole story."

He nodded at Salvatore and made a 'go on' gesture with his hand, as his wife poured a bowl of cereal behind him. "Again, you found them...?"

It was then that something strange passed over the old man's face. Salvatore blinked, three times, rapidly, almost as if he were having a minor stroke. His face muscles twitched. John could see his eyes defocusing, staring blankly.

"Mr. Cortina?" he prompted. He held up a page and shook it. "The papers..."

And then one last convulsing twitch of his eyebrows, a narrowing of the wrinkled old mouth, and Salvatore Cortina came back. His pupils widened and his eyes grew dark. His focus seemed suddenly greater than before. His lip curled into a lopsided grin.

"Mr. John Cagill," he said, his voice smooth now, lacking any sort of trepidation, though still quiet. "What do you know about your daughter's unusual illness? Specifics."

"I'm sorry?" John felt confused. One second ago, an old, broken bum had sat before him. Now, this dirty-clothed man seemed to have complete control of his faculties. He seemed possessed of a stronger backbone, a serious edge that had not been there moments before.

Salvatore Cortina frowned. "The illness, Mr. Cagill. What do you know of it? What have the doctors determined?"

And then it dawned on John Cagill who, exactly, sat before him. This was no dirty old bum, half-mad and hungry. It was all an act. This was a private detective of the foulest kind—the kind that walks the streets, digging through trashcans, looking for lawsuits. Not wealthy or successful, but tenacious. Here was a man that knew exactly what he had found and wanted to get in on the lawsuit action against the hospital.

John nodded, as his wife placed the cereal bowl down in front of Salvatore. The old man pushed it to the side, uninterested. "I get it," said John. "I see what's going on here. How much do you want?"

Salvatore arched an eyebrow. "Money?" He laughed. "Oh, I'm not here for money. Just information. Now let's get to the point, shall we?"

John shook his head. He wasn't getting out of this easily, he realized. "Look, those are our personal records. I appreciate you bringing them here, but we're not yet ready to take action—"

There was a screech of chair leg against floor and the old man was across the table, withered hands gripping the front of John's shirt. Papers scattered. John's wife gasped and dropped the glass milk bottle into the sink, where it shattered.

"The allergy," roared Salvatore, his lips turned up in a foul sneer. His face was inches from John's, and he could smell the old man's rank breath. It smelled somehow of burning coals. "How does it manifest?"

That's when John noticed the change in the old man's eyes. The pupils had vanished entirely and the eyeballs had become solid black. All the fight went out of him then. This was not natural. He heard his youngest daughter, Haley, calling his name from the other room.

"Stay in there, honey," he said, his voice wavering. Out of the corner of his eye, he saw his wife reaching for the large chef's knife on the counter, next to the sink. "Baby, no, just be still—"

From deep in Salvatore's throat came a growl. His black eyes flicked to one side. John watched in horror as a tendril of milk leapt up from the sink, looped itself around his wife's wrist, and pulled her hand away from the knife. With a sudden, violent tug, the tendril yanked her clawed hand down into the sink and jammed it into the garbage disposal.

"The allergies, Mr. Cagill. You should be telling me about them, now."

John shook his head, flabbergasted by the situation and panicked, all at once. "I- I don't—"

Salvatore twitched one of the fingers gripping John's collar and a second tentacle of milk leapt from the sink and bumped a switch into the 'on' position. There was the familiar grinding sound of the disposal and the sudden, bloodcurdling shriek as his wife's hand became ground meat. Blood sprayed from the sink. The tentacle flipped the switch back 'off.'

The words came tumbling out of John's mouth, even as his wife wailed like an injured animal. "They- they say she has aquageni— an allergy to water. Rare. It only happens sometimes—"

The switch flipped again. Another horrible grinding sound. Another shriek. More blood. Switch off.

"When did it start?" asked Salvatore, his voice calmer now that the information was flowing. "As a child, or at puberty?"

"Puberty," John replied. "Near her twelfth birthday."

There was crying, then, and Haley came running into the kitchen.

John cried out, "No, honey, please go—"

Salvatore threw John back into his chair and stood, his spine elongating and allowing him stand to his full height, not the hunched form of an old man any longer. "No," he said, grinning. "She should stay. We still have some things to discuss." He turned and settled his gaze on the child, who stood frozen, eyes wide. "Perhaps she can contribute."

"Wha- what do you want from us?"

Salvatore turned back to meet John's frightened look. "Just information," he said. "And the chance to thank you, personally."

"For what?" asked John, weakly.

The old man's grin deepened. "For taking such good care of my child," he replied. "Many of the others died. This one lived. Because of you. Wonderful parents."

John's wife whimpered, hand still bloodied and wound into the disposal up nearly to her elbow.

"But," said Salvatore, finally, as he craned his long neck to stare out the nearby window into the small suburban backyard. He seemed to be looking for something. "All good things must come to an end." He considered that for a moment. His attention snapped back to John. "Or, perhaps, things are coming to a beginning. The pieces are moving. Snakes in the grass." He chuckled. "And my time with you is growing short."

Haley dropped to her knees on the kitchen floor and began to sob.

Salvatore ignored her. "Don't worry," he said, his voice a terrifying mix of calm assurance and insidious threat. "I only have a few more questions about Celia's upbringing."

John worked up the courage to squeak out, "And then what?"

Salvatore arched an eyebrow again. "Oh," he said, "and then I suppose you'll be free to go see your God." He laughed again. "Though I don't believe he's speaking with your kind anymore."

And with that, he flicked a finger and the garbage disposal burst to life again. The air filled with the sounds of grinding meat, screams, and blood. John began vomiting up answers and bile in equal measure, as Salvatore took his seat and dug into his bowl of cereal.

8

IN THE BLACKNESS BEYOND THIS realm, a creature stirred. In its world, it would have seemed a sudden awakening, but to our realm, it would have been a slow and inexorable motion, a thousand or more years of patient, quiet rousing, triggered by only the briefest of contacts. Where there was light, there was shadow, and mortal man stood in between, and for a singular moment, a shard of a broken creature had touched one of its counterparts.

The Render awoke.

Through the dust-black, windswept plains it lurched, seeking a weak point, a place where it might cross over. It was both an independent thing and a fragment, a microcosm of the macroscape that was its environ, a fractal within a fractal. It sensed now. It hunted.

Across an indeterminate distance and time, it could smell its quarry. It had a vaguely arachnoid shape, but was also amorphous and indistinct at times, and it felt the motions of our world, the lines and strings of fate that bound up the machinery of reality. It followed the patterns, traced the steps, and made its way to a point of entry.

It crossed over and, for the first time in its very long existence, encountered true light, the light that poured down upon the mortal shores. It recoiled, feeling its very first pangs of pain. It moved through this light, but with every sweeping beam or errant glow, its insubstantial form weakened a little. Its motions lacked strength. Only in the darkest, most pure of shadow did it retain its power.

With its limited understanding and emotion, the creature began to abhor the light. Every dim pool, every cutting strand of brightness caused it pain. Every slanting beam that sliced across the thing's lines and form was a blade across insubstantial flesh, and it picked its paths carefully. It longed for night, for the coming black, and every second until then seemed an eternity.

The ends of its black appendages could touch down only in pools of shadow, forcing it to writhe and convolute its shape to avoid the light. To an onlooker in our world, it might have looked like the impossible shadow of some monstrous, invisible spider, or an irregular splash of black with a thousand legs dancing spasmodically upon the alley wall; a protean silhouette, independent of matter, moving of its own accord, sliding across surface and ground and object. It sensed its prey—the man—amidst the steel and concrete.

It moved with singular purpose.

9

TRENT PARKED THE MOVING VAN in a spot near the side door of the Children's Center, near where he saw a couple of nurses smoking, backs against the outer wall of the building. He got out and walked over, Susan's purse dangling from his left hand. The nurses—a man and woman—eyed him curiously.

Trent gestured at the cigarette in the man's mouth. "Mind if I...?"

The male nurse hesitated at first, then shrugged and offered the pack. Trent took a cigarette. "Light?" he mumbled.

The woman flipped open a Zippo and Trent leaned down, cupping the cigarette's tip to protect it from the rain-soaked wind.

"Goddamn it's cold out here," he mumbled. "Windy, too. Wish I had brought my jacket."

"Yeah," said the other man. "Supposed to pass by tomorrow though."

Trent nodded and blew smoke out through his nostrils. After a few long drags, he took the cigarette from his mouth, looked at the glowing end for a second, and dropped it to the asphalt, where he ground it out with his cowboy boot.

He nodded and tipped his hat at them both. "Thanks," he said, and headed for the side door.

"Wait," said the woman. "You're supposed to go through the front—"

Trent pointed up the side of the building. "Wife started today. Gotta delivery for her." He held up the purse.

"Oh," said the woman. And before she could say anything more, Trent had gone. The metal door clanged shut behind him.

She and her male cohort looked out over the parking lot and shuffled back and forth on the concrete sidewalk, shivering as they smoked. They watched a short, old man in a grimy white sweater moving toward them, his feet splashing through oily puddles on the asphalt.

Trent opened the door that led from the dingy, chemical-scented stairwell into the well-lit hall of the Children's Center. He was immediately assailed by the sounds of crying, machines beeping quietly, doctors and patients and their parents chatting.

He hated hospitals; he had spent far too long in this very one after the crash, and the experience had left him with an irrational distaste for the white walls and the smiling, but haggard, staff. He had already made up his mind that he would not stay long; just give Susan the purse and the sandwich and then he would take off. Besides, he had a moving van to unpack, especially if the weather was going to get worse.

He wandered down the hall, purse dangling from his arm, listening for Susan's voice. He finally heard it, coming from the room at the far end of the hallway.

"Yeah," he heard her say. "But we'll figure out what it is. Lots of stuff they haven't tried, I'm sure."

Trent walked around the corner of the doorframe and stopped at the foot of the bed. Susan was sitting in a chair at the bedside, talking with a thin, pale, blond girl wearing a hospital gown that looked way too baggy for her tiny frame. Susan looked up, saw Trent and then the purse he was carrying. She smiled.

"You're the best." She stood from her chair and walked over to give him a big hug. "You didn't have to do that."

He shrugged. "No problem. Gets me out of the house, right? There's a convenience store sandwich in there. All I could afford."

Susan pulled away from him and then gestured toward the girl in the bed. "This is Celia."

The blond girl waved and forced a tired smile.

"Celia, this is my husband, Trent."

"Hey," he said and tipped his hat.

"What's with the cowboy hat?" asked Celia, smirking.

Susan grinned.

"Won it in a poker game, I think—"

"Wait a sec!" Celia's eyes widened. "I know you!"

Oh, here it comes, thought Trent. *Thanks a lot, History Channel.*

He nodded. "Yeah."

Celia smiled, genuine this time. "I totally watched this show on you last time I was in here. 'Luckiest Man Alive.' That's what it was called. You, like, survived—"

"Flight 2778. I know. Only survivor. I don't really like to talk about it."

Celia's smile disappeared. "Oh, sorry."

Trent shrugged. "It's alright." He felt bad for dampening the girl's enthusiasm. "I just get a lot of questions about it."

"Probably, like, the same ones all the time, huh?"

"Exactly."

"Sorry," she said again. "My mom was, like, glued to the TV that day. You know, with the plane crash and all."

Trent nodded. Desperate to change the subject, he asked, "So what're ya in for?"

Celia rolled her eyes. "They can't figure it out. I'm allergic to something, I guess. I couldn't breathe last night, so Dad brought me in. I was crying and puking and stuff. It was really embarrassing."

"This happen a lot?"

Susan looked at the chart hanging from the end of Celia's bed. "Wow."

"Yeah," said Celia. "Like, once a month or something. I practically live here."

Susan got up from her chair and said, "Celia, I need to talk to my husband outside for a moment, okay?"

Celia shrugged and grabbed the remote for her tiny, wall-mounted television.

Trent followed his wife out of the room and into the hallway. Once they were out of sight of Celia, she turned and gave him another big hug and kiss.

"Thank you so much, honey." Trent could sense that she was on the verge of tears. "You don't know how much this means."

"It's just a sandwich." Trent chuckled.

She looked at him, smiling but shaking her head.

"Anyway, I should probably get back to work, but I should be home..." She trailed off as she watched a small, rain-soaked man with white hair plastered to his pink scalp walk past them and straight into Celia's room. She pulled away from Trent's embrace.

"Excuse me," she said, approaching the old man. "Can I help—"

But instead of acknowledging her, the old man mumbled something about being 'Salvatore Cortina,' stepped into the hospital room and, without turning around, pushed the door shut behind him, nearly smacking Susan in the face.

"What the...?" Susan stood frozen for a moment, gob smacked. "Who the hell is that?"

Trent ventured a guess. "Looks like grandpa. She expecting visitors?"

Susan stared through the small window at Celia and the old man. He had taken a seat next to her bed. Celia looked confused and slightly revolted at his soaked, disheveled appearance. "Her parents were supposed to be here an hour ago with some of her things."

Without hesitation, Trent walked over next to Susan and turned the doorknob. It turned, and he pushed open the door.

"Hey," he said. "You supposed to be here?"

Celia looked up at him with a strange, horrified expression on her face, as though the old man had just said something terrible to her. But the man in the white sweater did not turn around.

Trent walked in and put a hand on the old man's shoulder. "Hey, I'm talking to you, grandpa. I think you've got the wrong room—"

With the slightest of gestures, Salvatore reached back and touched his fingers to Trent's chest. He did not bother to turn around and look.

Trent gasped, but was unable to suck in any air. It felt suddenly as though his lungs had filled with fluid, and he clawed at his throat as he stumbled backwards, away from the man and the young girl.

"Trent?" said Susan, at first questioning of his strange behavior. Then, as she saw him struggling with his neck, she raised her voice. "Trent!"

But Trent could only look at her with panic in his eyes. He staggered and then fell back and collided with a wheeled cart. It fell over with a clattering of metal trays and medical equipment.

"Oh, shit!" exclaimed Susan. Then she yelled, "Security!"

Salvatore snarled and turned to face them. Trent, still gasping unsuccessfully for air, saw that his eyes were solid black, all the way to the core, and the sight brought up a measure of panic deep in his being—an ancient feeling, like being alone in the woods on a dark night. His hands grabbed at the white ceramic-tiled walls and a nearby countertop as he slid further down to the floor. His flailing arm swept a plastic box of syringes off the counter and they clattered to the ground.

Salvatore stood then, still gazing at Trent and Susan, and reached back to grab Celia's arm. Where the old man touched her wrist, steam poured forth, heralded by a sizzling sound, like bacon on a pan. The smell of burned flesh filled the room. The old man gritted his teeth and growled as he fought with the girl. Celia kicked at him and thrashed her arms, but he kept pulling, trying to get her out of the bed.

Susan screamed her husband's name again and entered the room to try and help him, crossing directly in front of Salvatore's path. With a quick motion of his arm, he brought it against her sternum and shoved her aside as he pulled Celia out of the bed. Susan tripped and fell and smacked her face against the countertop, drawing blood from her nose.

Trent, still floundering like a fish out of water, watched the retreating old man, who was dragging the teenage girl along the ground like a child throwing a tantrum. Then he caught a glimpse of his fallen wife, who was touching a blood-smeared hand to her face and looking at him in astonishment and confusion.

Anger burned its way up Trent's spine. And as the rage rose, the sense of fluid in his lungs seemed to dissipate. He sneered and focused on his fury. He kicked the fallen cart out of his way and pulled himself up and strode after the old man. "Nobody hits my wife," he coughed, still trying to draw in full breaths of air. With one hand he grabbed Celia's free wrist, and with the other he grabbed Salvatore's shoulder. The old man turned to look at him and raised his palm again to touch Trent's chest, but this time Trent was ready.

His right arm came around in a sweeping arc, bringing a roundhouse punch to bear on Salvatore's face. His fist connected solidly, pounding flesh and bone against the old man's cartilage. He could feel the beaklike old nose shatter.

Salvatore dropped hold of Celia's wrist and staggered back a few steps, into the hallway, blood dribbling down his lips and chin.

The sounds of the confrontation had alerted others in the Children's Center, and Susan's cries for security had raised the expected alarm. Voices were yelling out, patients and parents were talking in hushed tones, and the sounds of footsteps could be heard in the distance, ascending the metal stairwell.

Salvatore stopped in the hallway and looked down at the blood on the floor—his blood. Then he looked up at Trent. To Trent's surprise, the old man had a look of utter astonishment and betrayal on his face. He also noticed that the old man's eyes looked normal, not black but a pale, cloudy blue. He looked around him frantically, confused and scared and suddenly a very small, very frightened old man.

As quickly as the moment of quiet had come, it went again. Salvatore dropped to the floor, screaming wildly, palms against his eyes and forehead. When he looked up a moment later, his eyes were black once more, and a sneer formed on his lips. His gaze settled on Celia, who had run out of the hospital room and was half-hiding behind Trent.

"My child," the old man growled. "My daughter. Give her back to me."

It dawned on Trent then that maybe he was facing down the serial kidnapper, the man that had put Las Vegas into a state of paranoid panic, the man responsible for so many of the broken children in the rooms around him.

"It was you," he hissed.

"They're mine," Salvatore replied. "All of them, of my blood, my lineage. Mine!"

"Not yours," came Susan's voice from behind him. In a flash, before Salvatore could turn, she had struck him in the back of the neck with an epinephrine syringe, plunging the needle in as far as she could send it.

Salvatore spun like a dervish, howling, suddenly now more like a scared little man again. His eyebrows arched and his eyes blinked as he yelled and flailed wildly to get at the needle jutting from his neck. He took a few steps backward, away from his attackers and back into the hospital room, and Trent could see fear and anger in the man's eyes, both fighting for control. He was a man at war with himself.

Trent looked at Susan and nodded his head at Celia. "Take her!" he yelled. "Go!"

Susan needed no more encouragement. Still hobbled from the pain of her fall, she stumbled into the hallway and grabbed Celia's arm. "Come on," she said, and the two of them half-walked, half-ran toward the far end of the hall.

Trent watched Salvatore spinning and howling. *The kidnapper*, he thought. *This old guy has been doing all of this?* He could scarcely believe it, but then, it did make sense. He had come back to the hospital, where all the children he'd ruined went; a thief returning to the scene of the crime. Trent made up his mind. This would end now.

He took off at a sprint and then dove at the old man. He slammed into him in the hospital room doorway and his shoulder caught the man's ribs. His arms wrapped tight in a football tackle. They tumbled backwards together and crashed against the bed, then careened into the counter, spilling a plastic bin full of pamphlets onto the floor. They fought and grappled and rolled away from the counter and then together slammed into the wall with a sickening thud. The drywall cracked and dented with the impact.

Trent looked up from his tangle with the old man, saw people looking into the room, and yelled at them. "Get security in here, now!"

Salvatore regained a measure of strength and pulled free of Trent's grasp for a moment, then came back in, fingers extended like claws for Trent's neck. They struggled, arms cracking against arms, fingers pressed into each other's faces, fists balled, until finally the man had secured a grip on Trent's throat. In an instant, Trent felt the tight constriction in his chest again, the rising of fluid, the sense of drowning from the inside out. He ripped free of the old man and pitched backwards, pawing at his aching chest.

The old man straightened himself and made a motion as if trying to smooth his rumpled, moth-eaten sweater. He sneered down at Trent. His mouth twisted up into a malicious smile. Trent noticed that the needle still remained embedded in the back of the old man's neck. Salvatore raised a quivering hand.

Another involuntary gurgle erupted from Trent's throat and he slumped to the floor. *This is the end*, he thought. *I can't breathe. I'm going to die.*

The old man walked over to him and raised his arms, palms facing the ceiling. "You are nothing here, in this place," he hissed, "and my glory shall not suffer these indignations." He brought his arms down. "Goodbye."

The ceiling erupted, showering the room with water and flakes of overhead tile and dust as sprinkler heads burst from their moorings like saw-shaped bullets propelled by fluid thrust. Down they came, whirling and speeding fast toward the fallen man. Trent looked up.

This can't be possible. This can't happen.

He raised a hand, fingers splayed, gritted his teeth and squeezed his eyes shut in anticipation of the end. The shadow-world behind his eyelids screamed with raucous shrieks and his mind's eye saw black-on-black images of swirling dust, flashes of darkness against the darkness, the motion of projectiles bearing down upon him and a strange figure standing above, an inhuman, winged thing overlaid upon a human shape in the smoky gloom. And Trent could see a thousand possibilities of how this moment might go, like layers of translucent onion skin burning with imagery, and he hoped—believed—that the truth would come to his aid.

I can't die, he thought. *I've lived through worse than this.*

With a rush, a memory of the plane crash slammed into his thoughts. Fire, human screams, the plane pitching toward the ground, screeching, children's terrified wails, and a tall, dark-skinned Mexican in a cowboy hat, with a craggy, heavily lined face, standing in silhouette, facing down a nightmare creature with blades for teeth and roiling, smoke-like skin. Trent screamed out as the projectiles hit home with a series of dopplered screeches and blasts and a splash of cold water.

But no pain.

He opened his eyes, shocked to be alive. The sprinkler heads had embedded themselves in the floor all around him and every one had missed. Water poured from holes in the ruined ceiling, framing the old man who stood above him, clearly puzzled.

"Who are you?" Salvatore demanded.

But Trent had no interest in further conversation. This was no normal fight; it was something otherworldly, something beyond his understanding, something he could not win. He answered with a leg sweep that caught Salvatore by surprise and sent him sprawling to the floor with a groan. Trent scrabbled backwards to his feet and used the momentary diversion to escape the small hospital room, slamming the door shut behind him in a desperate attempt to delay the strange old man, if only for a moment.

In the hallway, he found himself amidst a sea of chaos. The sprinkler system was on full blast, soaking the Children's wing with a torrential cold downpour. Doctors and nurses frantically pushed gurneys in every direction, shuttled sick children toward the elevators, desperately tried to protect suddenly-soaked medical equipment and expensive electronics, grabbed mushy paperwork, and stumbled over those who had slipped and fallen, all the time yelling, cursing, shouting orders. Trent shoved aside a nearby gurney and then looked up to see a trio of hospital security heading his way.

"Run!" he yelled at them. "Get out of here!"

He glanced around for Celia and Susan and saw them fighting their way through the chaos to the stairwell at the far end of the hall. He looked again at the guards and saw them still coming down the hallway.

"Dammit!" he yelled, "Get—"

Before he could finish, the doorway behind him exploded, sending a shower of drywall and wood splinters across the hallway. Metal pipes tore down the walls and out, writhing like tentacles, reaching for him as he ran. He ducked and barreled forward, barely escaping the pipes that dove into the opposite wall, shattered a glass observation window and entangled themselves in the plastic blinds on the other side. Trent headed for Susan and Celia and the exit.

He could hear the old man behind him, bellowing curses in some language Trent could not understand. Ahead, the security guards went wide-eyed, frozen at the sight of the impossible violence at the end of the hall. Trent plowed on toward them, pushing past frantic hospital staff.

Suddenly, the air went cold, bitter cold, and there was a wild drop in pressure, enough to make Trent's ears hurt. The sprays of water from the overhead sprinklers arced in an instant, twisting about themselves, forming shimmering cables of braided water that danced like downed power lines and whipped at the panicked people. Each cable that hit its mark wrapped around a neck, dragging nurses and doctors and orderlies toward the ceiling, choking and gasping. Even sick children were ripped from their beds and slammed headfirst into the ceiling and then released, a hellish rain of lifeless bodies that splashed into the puddles at Trent's feet.

"Run!" he screamed as he fought his way through the insanity. "Goddammit run!"

The trio of guards didn't need any more convincing. They turned to flee, but were each caught by the whipping cables of fluid.

Trent hurtled frantically past the choking, kicking bodies above and caught up with his wife and Celia at the end of the hall. Without slowing, he ran between them and slammed his shoulder into the closed fire door that led to the back stairwell. The three of them dove through and Trent gave the door a mule kick to slam it closed behind them as Salvatore bellowed and splashed closer through the paper-and-corpse swamp that had once been the Children's Center.

Through the glass in the door, Trent saw Salvatore raise his hand again to point at him. The old man snarled, baring nasty, yellowed teeth.

Instinct took over and Trent ducked, a split-second before a flailing mass of metal pipes crashed through the tiny glass window in the fire door, grasping at him with futile stabs, hampered by the heavy metal door.

"Go go go!" he shouted, and they half-ran, half-fell down the clanging stairwell as the old man struggled to open the door behind them. By the time they'd reached the bottom floor, they heard the fire door above slam open. Salvatore's voice rang out in the metal stairwell.

"You can't hide from me!" he screamed.

But I can sure as hell try, Trent thought, as he followed Susan and Celia across the parking lot to the van.

10

"I WANNA GO HOME," SAID Celia, crying. "Please..." Her entire frame shuddered as the tears fell. She was sandwiched between Trent and Susan in the narrow confines of the van's cab. "Please," she said, "please take me home. I want Mom and Dad."

Susan tried to comfort the teenager by telling her that things would be okay, but it didn't seem to help. Instead, it only made Celia more frantic and she called out over and over for her parents.

"We're taking you home, kiddo," said Trent, trying to calm the situation. "I promise we'll get you home."

Celia put her head between her knees and bawled and soon her lurching sobs became retching, which made her cry even harder.

"Oh, God," said Susan, as she held back the girl's white-blond hair. "Trent, what are we gonna do?"

"We're taking her home," he said, and turned the van down a side street. "We'll get her to her parents and then deal with things from there."

"How can they protect her from— from *that?*" she gestured behind them, in the direction of the hospital.

Trent shook his head. "I don't know, but she's better off with her own family than with us. They can get out of the city, maybe, until this blows over."

"What *was* that? How did he—?"

Trent turned on her then, yelling. "I don't know, okay?" The outburst drew a hurt look from his wife. He felt ashamed for yelling at her and lowered his voice. "I don't know what's going on. I've never seen anything like that. I'm sorry."

And yet, even as he said it, Trent felt a weird sense of déjà vu. He *had* seen something like it, something unnatural and powerful and frightening, though he couldn't quite place the memory and could not dredge up the images; just a lingering sense of fear and a memory of smoke of fire and his airplane hurtling toward the ground. Anxiety about the lost memories buzzed around him like biting flies.

Celia's cries reached a pitiful wail that reminded Trent of police sirens. "Kiddo, it's gonna be—" he started, but then he realized, with a sinking feeling, that he *did* hear sirens. He looked in the rearview just in time to see a police car squeal out of a side street and pull in behind them, red-and-blues flashing as it caught up with their van. The headlights flashed and the siren let out a short whoop.

Trent did not want to stop. All he could imagine, after the chaos in the hospital, was that no cop could possibly protect them from a force like the old man and his powers. He wanted to get Celia home, to reunite her with her parents, and then maybe he could deal with the cops. Then, he and Susan would get the hell out of Las Vegas. Coming back had been the worst decision of their lives; he was sure of that now.

The officer flashed the headlights a second time, punctuated by another whoop from the siren.

"Shit!" Trent yelled and banged a fist against the steering wheel. The loud noise caused Celia to look up in alarm.

Susan had already turned in her seat and was watching the cop behind them. "We've gotta pull over, baby. Just tell them the truth. We're taking her home."

Trent, frustrated, shook his head and eased the van into the parking lot of a convenience store. The van came to a stop in a parking space and he shut off the engine.

The squad car pulled in behind them, pinning the van between the cop car and the curb that bordered the street. Trent looked in his rearview and saw two officers now—a bald, clean-shaven man and a diminutive woman in the passenger seat with spiky black hair. The man put a megaphone to his lips.

"Out of the car, now! Hands over your heads! Leave the child inside!"

Oh shit, thought Trent. *They think we've kidnapped her!*

Trent kicked open the driver's side door and stepped out, hands in the air. Susan did the same. Trent turned to face the cop car and yelled, "It wasn't us! We—"

"Shut up and lie down, hands behind your back!"

"But we're not—"

"Down!" the cop yelled. "Now!"

"Fuck," Trent mumbled beneath his breath. He looked over at Susan, who had already dropped to her knees. He shook his head and did the same.

The two Metro officers got out of their car. Trent looked up at them. They both had guns drawn, aimed at him and

Susan. The man matched Trent's gaze for a moment and then yelled again for him to get down. Trent dropped flat on his stomach and felt the ice-cold, oily puddles soaking into his white, button-up dress shirt. He idly wished that he had remembered his jacket.

"Face down!" yelled the cop.

Trent could hear their footsteps as they came nearer.

"Get the kid," said the male cop to his partner.

Her feet splashed through a puddle as she jogged to the van.

Trent lifted his head to look at the male cop again. "Have you seen what happened at the hospital?" he asked. "You really think we—"

"Shut up!" the cop replied, and used a booted foot to grind Trent's face back down into the asphalt. He started to rattle off the Miranda. "You have the right to remain silent anything you say may be used against you in a..." There was a strange moment of silence and Trent wondered why the officer had stopped talking. And then he said, quietly, "What the hell is that?"

Immediately, Trent imagined Salvatore striding across the street toward them. His heart raced with fear as he pictured the Children's Center massacre, the bodies writhing in midair, choked by tentacles of water, blood everywhere, screaming, crying, and for a split-second he flashed back again to the airplane crash and had to fight back the waves of panic that rolled through him.

"What the *fuck*?" said the cop.

Trent could see the officer's feet as he turned to run. He looked up. The cop was sprinting away from the van, toward the squad car. Trent looked over his shoulder in alarm and saw the *thing* coming on.

It was something dark and oddly shaped and at moments looked something like a spider and at other moments like an indistinct mass of roiling, smoky shadow. Its protean form culminated in a series of long, shadowy appendages, whose number seemed to change with every movement. The appendages appeared as pointed legs that came to perfect, sharp tips where they touched solid surface, and each appendage touched down upon a pool of shadow as it advanced.

It flitted suddenly into the shadow cast by a nearby telephone pole. Then it jumped to the shadow of the van. Its shape collapsed as it disappeared into the darkness and it looked for a moment as though the black thing had vanished entirely. But then it reappeared again; a sudden, lurching movement that carried it out of the darkened recess. It expanded in a split-second until it was bigger than a man, and soared through the air toward Trent, who lay astonished on the asphalt.

"Trent!" yelled Susan.

Her shout broke his bewildered fascination with the creature and he rolled quickly to his right as its shadow-legs stabbed into the ground next to his face. It seemed insubstantial, ever shifting, and yet it had a strange solidity. Its legs splashed into the greasy puddles on the pavement, throwing up sprays of rainwater. Radial cracks appeared in the asphalt, as though the thing had a weight and a force that the ground could hardly withstand.

Trent leapt to his feet and ran towards Susan. When he reached her, he grabbed her arm and hoisted her off the ground. The creature sprung into motion again, jumping from shadow to shadow as it chased them, its body emitting now a strange, humming sound, a vibration that buzzed into Trent's skin and rattled his bones and skull and sinuses and made his eyes water as he worked his way, with Susan on his arm, toward the van. They ran hard, legs pumping, toward where Celia and the female cop stood side-by-side, mouths agape, watching the impossible.

Trent knew without a doubt that this creature had come for the girl. He figured it was something that the old man had brought into being, some aspect of his horrible powers made manifest. Holding Susan's wrist, he ran to Celia and the cop. The creature's humming sound grew louder. He could feel the vibration traveling the length of his body, all the way to the bones in his feet. He shoved Celia down and pushed Susan behind him and turned to face the thing.

It reared up out of a shadow cast across the parking lot by a street sign, its two foremost appendages raised, the deepest black emanating from them like an anti-glow, dripping smoke-like coils of black nothingness that dissipated as they fell. Trent could feel intense cold as the thing lurched forward at him.

He felt a painful thump in his chest then, like someone taking a hammer to his lungs, and he blinked with pain and, for a second, saw that other world, that black place that came when his fate stood on the edge. It was the odd thing that had happened from time to time on the poker circuit. It was his impossible ace-in-the-hole, whose mechanism he had never understood, and only partially believed. He imagined a million possibilities for this moment, and desperately wished for one where he could get through alive. He hoped that his luck might hold out again.

"Duck!" he screamed, knowing even as he did that they stood no chance, that the thing would descend and slice through them in an instant.

A bright flash of light burst from the nearby squad car, a spotlight beam from the top of the car, accidentally engaged as the male cop fumbled in the driver's seat, desperately trying to start the vehicle. The beam illuminated the spider in an instant and the creature's deep hum became an ear-splitting screech. The dark tips pulled back like a child touching a hot stove. It dropped from its mid-air leap and tumbled into a nearby puddle of black, legs writing as it vanished, like a black widow spider under a child's magnifying lens on a hot day.

Trent turned to the others cowering behind him, terrified and hunched over. "Run!" he screamed, and they did.

Susan grabbed Celia and they splashed across the parking lot toward the van.

The female cop sprinted for the squad car. With every step, her throat let out a panicked, incoherent shriek. She had lost all of a cop's composure, her arms waving wild, frantic, her legs churning across the pavement. She sprinted up to the police car, but as she reached out for the passenger door, the thing reappeared, its black, ever-changing shape looming out of the shadow cast by the vehicle. She shrieked and fell backwards onto the pavement and drew her gun. She raised it and pulled the trigger as rapidly as she could.

The spider shuddered and twisted as the bullets tore through it, pop pop pop, throwing off swirling puffs of smoke that vanished into the air. The gun ran dry and, as Trent watched in horrified awe, the creature dove down at her, leaping from the car's shadow into hers, front legs hungrily devouring all of the light around them as it disappeared beneath her. For a few seconds, the woman scuttled around on the pavement, eyes wide, screaming wildly as she threw her head from side to side, trying to see where the thing had gone.

"Help!" she screamed, looking first at Trent, then at her partner in the car, whose attention was focused purely on putting the vehicle into reverse.

"Helpmeomigodhelpme!" She sat upon the wet pavement on her knees, legs folded, fists balled, and screamed in abject terror.

The spider burst out of her shadow then and the woman convulsed as the roiling blackness traced her edges. Then it leapt away from her and onto a dark line cast atop the squad car. Her scream shifted and became almost inhuman, an animal noise, a horrid squall. She turned to look up at the rain-filled sky and brought her fingers to her face. She screeched and clawed at her eyes. Blood ran down her cheeks in glistening streams.

Trent, frozen with revulsion, realized suddenly what had happened. The woman no longer had a shadow. She knelt upon the ground as if she bore no real connection to the world any longer, her flesh and clothes touching pavement that seemed unaware of her presence, not darkened by her interposing before the light. His breath caught for a moment, his own sanity briefly questioned. He forced himself to inhale and focus. A sudden, loud honking recaptured his attention.

He turned to see Susan pounding on the van's horn, Celia squeezed tight against her, face blank and horrified. He needed no further encouragement. His cowboy boots clattered against the asphalt as he sprinted for the van. He jumped into the passenger seat next to the teenager and slammed the van door shut as Susan gunned the engine.

She dropped her foot on the gas. The tires squealed against the wet pavement. Suddenly, the van caught traction and lurched forward and Susan sent it hurtling through the convenience store lot, past the squad car and the flailing man inside who was still desperately trying to get the vehicle started. With every motion, the spider sent a darkened leg piercing through the roof of the car, ripping it open like a flimsy soda can. Finally, it opened a hole in the top and then leapt inside and disappeared. The cop screamed and banged on the windows, staring desperately at Trent and Susan and Celia as they sped past in the moving van.

Celia dropped her head and began to vomit again. Trent averted his gaze. As the van bounced over the curb and onto the street, he could hear the howling behind them as the creature severed the cop from his shadow.

"What the *fuck* was that?" said Susan, yelling now as tears ran down her face. She nearly clipped another car as she maneuvered the van through traffic. Her voice lowered. "What the goddamn fu—" She looked in the rearview and her eyes went wide and the tears came faster. "Oh God, no. *No!*" She screamed and pounded the wheel, causing the horn to honk several times in rapid succession.

Trent glanced into the side mirror and saw the black monstrosity. It had turned its attention on the escaping van. It leapt over the ruined squad car and hit the ground on the other side in a shadow cast by a tree, then burst from that and came after them, pouring itself into the shadows of the vehicles moving through the busy midday traffic.

Susan had the gas pedal smashed against the floor, but Trent knew the creature could move faster. He looked forward, seeking options, and saw an alleyway approaching on the right.

"There!" he shouted, pointing.

Knuckles white, Susan threw the wheel to the side and the van careened into the alley, knocking aside piles of trash and trash barrels and old plastic paint buckets. The rain drummed noisily on the van's metal roof. Trent looked in the mirror again. The creature had slid into the shadow of an unlit streetlamp and then reemerged and shot into the alley, hopping through the shadows cast by the tumbling debris in the wake of the van.

"Faster!"

"I can't!"

Celia shrieked, head still between her knees, her voice cracking with the bloodcurdling volume.

The van rumbled out the other side of the alley, crashed through a flimsy chain link fence, and burst into a busy street. A taxi hit its brakes and swerved sideways as the van passed. A delivery truck squealed, smoke erupting from its axles. The van dodged both obstacles, and just barely cut in front of a bulky SUV with its horn blaring.

In the rearview, Trent saw the creature bound into the street, leaping through the shadows of the cars. It soared over the taxi and came down amidst the shadow of a building cast atop the roof of the SUV. The SUV's top buckled and the driver hit the brakes. The shadow-creature's momentum carried it off the vehicle as the SUV tipped and rolled and crashed into the pavement with an explosion of glass and chrome.

The van's tires cried out as Susan sent it down another alley. It dove between a liquor store and an old diner, and at the far end, Trent could see Interstate 15, wide and free of trees and buildings, open to the sky, and he knew that this was their chance to lose the creature, there in the open, rain-gray light, free of the complex shadows of the inner city.

He pointed and yelled at Susan, "Get to the Interstate!"

She downshifted and floored the gas again and the engine revved to a high-pitched whine. The moving van barreled toward the stack of cardboard liquor boxes at the end of the alley.

Celia had her hands over her ears now, still shrieking, still looking at the floor between her feet, and she had leaned into Trent. Susan's hands gripped the steering wheel tight. Her eyes were wide. Trent gritted his teeth as they shot toward the opening. He squeezed the teenager tight to protect her.

The creature jumped then and soared into a shadow of a window overhang and then rocketed down at the top of the van. Trent could feel its humming vibrations and could hear the screech as its front legs cut through the metal roof.

The first shadowy point to puncture the cabin came down fast at the passenger seat. Celia was still hunched over in

Trent's arms, and with the new hole in the roof, the rain poured in on her. But instead of washing over her and Trent, instead of the creature's point piercing into either one of them, Celia let out a high-pitched wail and the rain solidified in an instant. The arcing streaks turned to ice, forming a hemispherical, glittering shield above them. The black spike slammed down onto it and the shield vaporized in a burst of steam. But the creature's leg whipped back as if it had been burned. Trent blinked, unable to comprehend what he had just seen. All he could think was that it wouldn't happen twice; the creature was regrouping for another strike and they needed to get it off the van before it killed them all.

The hammer to his chest came on fast. He blinked, saw darkness for an instant, and then squinted as his eyes adjusted to the bright light beyond the alley. A billboard truck barreled past, heading up the on-ramp to the Interstate, its flat panel side advertising a casino magic show with a bright silver logo and hundreds of glittering mirrors. The mirrors caught the overcast light from the gray-white sky and glared for a split-second at the van. Trent could hear the spider's screech and felt the van rock as the thing tumbled off the top and dropped back into the shadows in the alley behind them.

Susan maneuvered the van across the road, onto the ramp and swerved into place with the southbound I-15 traffic. In the mirror, Trent watched as the thing made tentative, writhing advances into the street for a moment, and then leapt back into the alley shadows and disappeared.

11

THE SCREAMING IN SALVATORE'S HEAD died away and his headache burned off like cold morning mist, but his flesh still trembled from the dropping temperature outside and his neck ached and he felt a burning sensation at the base of his skull. He sat up in the dingy alleyway between what appeared to be a run-down strip club and an abandoned commercial pad that had once been a convenience store. A chilly wind whipped through the concrete canyon, blowing with it tumbleweeds of plastic bags and escort service flyers and fast-food wrappers.

He tried to stand, but his throbbing legs gave out and his knees buckled. He staggered backwards a few steps and collapsed into a heap of black plastic trash bags. His thighs and calves screamed with pain. He felt as though he had run a marathon. He put a hand to the back of his neck, felt the sudden twinge of searing pain as his fingers touched, and grimaced. He brought his arm back around and saw that his fingers were sticky with blood and his arms were similarly streaked. The blood on his arms, though, was dry, crusted, older than the glistening fluid on his fingertips.

What have I done?

He looked down at his other arm and saw that it too was coated. His hands glistened in the gray, midday light. A part of him wanted to insist that it was not the obvious, that the red streaks were pasta sauce, or cayenne pepper soaked into his skin from a dry rub on a filet. Or maybe it was the blood from a juicy cut of steak. But he knew otherwise. He had done something horrible.

He ran his fingers through his wispy hair and tugged with grief at his scalp.

In God's name, what have I done?

His mind raced as he fought with his aching legs, forcing them to carry him along the sidewalk. He hugged close to the closed-up storefronts and avoided the glass-filled facades, averting his face as he passed, so that onlookers might not spot him. He had little notion of what had transpired in the past few hours since he had survived the flood in the tunnels, but he knew better than to let himself be conspicuous. He was pious and simple, but not stupid. He had blood on his hands.

He fought hard to dredge up anything from the black pit in his mind beyond the flood. A dim memory trickled back. A remembrance of his making the cross-town trek to the suburbs, to the residence of a girl whose medical papers he had been given by a strange man in an alley.

The girl? Who was the girl? Why did I go to see her family?

Suddenly frantic, he stopped on the sidewalk and turned his back to the glass window of a 24-hour buffet as he dug in his pants pockets.

There was a paper, a medical record. What did it say?

But nothing came forth. He had dropped it somewhere, maybe? Left it with the girl or her family? Had he been returning the lost record?

He dug in his other pocket, hoping to find some shred of evidence, some clue to help him drag the hiding memories back into light. He could sense them there, in the back of his mind, lurking in the shadows. His fingers in his left pocket came upon something sharp, plastic. He pulled out a keycard, dark blue plastic emblazoned with the image of black pyramid and a brilliant white beam of light emanating from its point. The Luxor.

The memory from the tunnel flooded back. He remembered setting up the heater, opening the envelope given to him by the hooded man. The medical record, the Luxor matchbook, the keycard. He had taken the record to the child's home, to return it. He was no murderer!

He looked around, nervous that someone might see, and then looked again at the card in his palm. His fingers shone red. Blood on his hands.

Salvatore needed answers. Something had gone terribly wrong. His migraines frequently caused him lost time, but never had he awoken in such shape as this. Never with blood on his hands.

Blood.

He quickly pocketed the card, looked around again, and then hunched himself involuntarily, making his small stature even smaller, terrified that someone might see him before he could learn the truth of things. He was a good man, a holy man. This was a challenge from the Almighty. He was not a murderer. He hoped the Luxor might have the answers he needed.

12

"WHAT WAS THAT THING?" SUSAN asked quietly. Then she gestured at Celia. "And how did she do that?"

Trent could barely hear her over the noise of the rumbling van and Celia's choking sobs. "I don't know," he said. "A monster, right? You saw it too? Black, like a spider almost?"

Susan nodded.

"That Salvatore guy must have sent it." Trent shook his head. "As for her," he said, quieter than before, "I'm not even sure what I saw."

"Monsters? Baby, I'm scared. What the Hell is happening?"

"I know. Just hold tight. We'll get through this."

Susan nodded at the teenager, who still had her head down and was shaking, crying. Susan whispered, "How can her parents protect her from this?"

Trent shook his head. "We gotta convince them to get out of the city."

"They'll never believe us."

Trent sighed. He had no better answers. He just hoped the Cagills had seen the news; hoped that with their insistence, they would flee Las Vegas and the supernatural forces that had, for some reason, descended upon their teenage daughter.

Susan turned her attention back to the road. The van slid a little as she changed lanes. "It's getting icy."

Trent peered out the window and saw that thin sleet had begun to fall on the city. "Yeah," he said. "Just be careful."

"Where am I going?"

"To her house."

Susan gave him a frustrated look.

"Oh."

He tapped the back of Celia's head. "Hey, kiddo."

She looked up at him. Her face was puffy and red, and the crying had left strange, shimmering lines down her cheeks. Trent instinctively reached over to brush them off and realized the lines were frozen to her skin. Celia winced as his fingers brushed the ice away.

What the hell is going on with this girl?

"Celia," he said, shaking away the questions swirling through his thoughts. "Can you give us directions?"

The teenager sniffled and ran the back of her hand beneath her nose. Her lips trembled as she explained, tersely, where her family lived.

Trent nodded and tried a forced smile that did not seem to make Celia any happier. His heart was breaking to watch the girl go through this. The world was an awful place; he'd decided that long ago. *But for a child*, he thought, *it should never be this bad.*

Luckily, the Cagills' neighborhood wasn't far—only a few miles south and they were already heading in the right direction. Trent hoped that they could convince the family to escape the city. He didn't believe for a second that either the monster or the old man would stop hunting for the girl anytime soon.

They found the neighborhood with relative ease, and as they moved along the quiet streets, they marveled at the sudden change in weather. Where there had been icy rain before, now snow had begun to fall. It was a light snow, interspersed here and there with sleet, but it was definitely snow.

"It never snows here," said Trent. "This is crazy." But his sense of wonderment was subdued. He had seen crazier things already today.

He looked at Susan, expecting her to be awed by the strange sight. Instead, he saw a look a grim determination on her face. Her hands gripped the steering wheel like a vise, and she seemed almost oblivious of the weather. He felt awful for her. This was not the day she had been looking forward to for the past three months, ever since she got the offer letter from James. This day had turned from a dream to a nightmare, and Trent felt that somehow it was all his fault.

"I hate this fucking place," he said, watching the suburban neighborhood react to the new weather.

Front doors opened and children, newly home from a cancelled school day due to the ice, poured onto their lawns, grinning widely as they twirled, faces upturned, watching the sky as the white fell. Even Celia's tears had dried up for a moment. Kids who grew up in Las Vegas only ever saw snow on television, or in photos; almost never in real life.

Trent smiled then, for real this time, glad that the teenager had been distracted, if even for moment, from the terrifying events of the morning. But his smile faded fast as they reached the Cagill home.

Something was wrong. He could just feel it. The shades were all drawn. The cars were still there. A small child's backpack lay unattended on the front porch. One of the front windows was broken, the shade billowing behind the irregular hole.

They parked their car and got out. Celia began to cry again and made a beeline for the front door. She tried the doorknob.

"It's locked," she said, her voice frantic. She tried the knob again, squeezing harder this time as she slammed her shoulder against the door.

Trent and Susan walked up behind her. Trent looked first at his wife, who had a hand over her mouth and tears running from her eyes. Susan knew too, somehow. Trent was afraid of what they were going to find.

He reached out to put a calming hand on the teenager's shoulder. "Celia, there's a broken window over there. I'll go in and—"

"Don't touch me!" she shrieked.

Trent felt the temperature around them drop in an instant and a chill shot up his spine. Icy tendrils stretched out from where the girl's hand touched the doorknob. Celia let out a scream of anguish and wrenched the knob and there came a loud, metallic snap from inside the door. The knob turned and the door creaked open and Celia stood in the doorway, sobbing, the metal knob dangling from the skin of her palm as though it had been glued there.

Trent's jaw dropped open as he looked inside. Susan gasped, let out a clipped shriek and averted her gaze. She buried her face in her husband's side.

A huge mass of sticky red had matted down the carpet in the center of the living room. A second red splash stained the wall next to the stairs. At the base of the stain rested a pile of broken picture frames, also spattered with blood. A path of crimson led to the kitchen.

"No!" shrieked Celia. "No!" She stood on the threshold, neck arched forward and screamed at the stain on the floor. "NO!"

Trent tried again to comfort her, but she pulled away and dashed into the house and up the stairs, still shrieking. A second later, they heard a door slam upstairs and her ghostly wails grew quieter. Trent and Susan stepped inside and gingerly shut the front door behind them.

Susan was crying too, her face still buried in Trent's side. "What are we gonna do?" she moaned. "Goddammit, Trent. What are we gonna do?"

Trent had no answer. He looked down at the floor, half-expecting to find a solution there. Their plans for reuniting Celia with her family had been dashed.

Trent and Susan listened to the muffled cries of the teenager through the ceiling as they sat across from each other at the red-stained kitchen table. Susan's tears had stopped, but her look of hopelessness remained. The pit in Trent's stomach felt endless, cavernous in its dimensions, a source of growing nausea. He wondered idly where the bodies had gone, leaving behind all this blood.

"I don't know," he said and shrugged. "I just don't know. There's no options left. We're stuck."

Trent switched on the small, blood-spattered television on the kitchen counter. The news was filled with photos of Trent and Susan and Celia. The media had identified them as the kidnappers—judge and jury be damned. There was no mention of Salvatore, or the shadow-spider; just a famous ex-gambler gone evil and his crazy wife. They'd even dug up their old obstetrician in Chicago, who admitted that Trent and Susan had had 'reproductive difficulties' that might be 'contributing factors' in their crime.

Trent swore and punched the off button so hard that it knocked the small set off the counter and onto the floor, where its glass face shattered.

"We have to turn ourselves in," said Susan, quietly.

"They're gonna execute us," Trent replied. "We're cop-killers and serial kidnappers. They're already juicing up the chair."

Susan glared at him. "Stop it, Trent! Just! Stop!" Her angry expression melted, making way for tears, and she put her head down on the table with a thump and sobbed.

Trent took off his cowboy hat and dropped it on the kitchen counter. Then he got up and began to pace the large, luxury kitchen, hands gripping his scalp through his sweat-stringy black hair.

A distant scream caught his attention in mid-stride. The scream had come from outside, beyond the back porch. Trent grabbed his hat, jammed it on his head, and sprinted to the double French doors that opened from kitchen out in the backyard. He stepped out into a thin coating of snow.

Another scream echoed out across the suburban landscape. "Fuck," he said, and turned to go back inside. Susan was looking up at him in alarm as he strode past her.

"What—?"

"Go get Celia," he interrupted. "Then start locking doors."

Susan shook her head. "I don't—"

"That thing, that black thing is coming. We have to hold out until the cops arrive. Maybe they have enough firepower to take it down."

"But the van—?"

He whirled on Susan. "We'd never get out of the suburbs before it caught us. Too many turns and short streets. This is our only chance, baby."

Susan nodded.

Trent headed for the living room, but stopped in the hallway and looked back at his wife. An idea drifted through his racing thoughts. "Turn on all the lights," he said. "All of them!"

"What are we doing?" yelled Susan, as she raced behind Trent into the living room.

"The thing doesn't like light. So turn on all the lights. Fast as you can." Trent ran to the front door and slammed it shut. He stared at the broken window for a moment. Nothing he could do about that. He flipped on the living room lights and dragged an upright torchiere lamp over by the window, as far as its cord would stretch. He hoped it was enough to deter the creature from coming too close. He looked at Susan and pointed up the stairs. "Get Celia, put her in the bathroom with all the lights on and shut the door. I don't think it can move through walls."

He hit another switch and the downstairs hallway came to life. Then a switch by the front door that lit up the cheap, faux-luxury Home Depot chandelier over the stairs. He could hear police sirens in the far distance, but they were still too far away. Trent wondered how long they could hold out against the spider.

A heavy thump sounded on the roof of the two-story house. Susan came running down the stairs.

"I put her in the—" She stopped midsentence when she reached the bottom of the stairwell and saw Trent staring at the ceiling. She looked up, too.

Another thump, louder this time.

"It's trying to find a way in," said Trent, quietly.

A series of crunching slams and then an even louder crash.

"The attic!" Trent yelled, and took off up the stairs. He reached the second-floor just in time to see the ceiling erupt, showering the hallway carpet with a column of white dust and drywall and plaster chunks. An undulating black shape dropped down through the debris and planted itself on the far end of the hallway from Trent.

It moved slowly, as though confused by the wash of light in the hall and from the open bedroom doors. The long, black appendages touched expanses of lit wall and pulled back sharply, as if in pain. But then one of the appendages found a long, thin shadow cast by a doorknob. Its leg made contact and the creature poured itself into a narrow line and it slipped into the black and vanished, like water down a drain.

Susan reached the top of the stairs and Trent could sense her approaching him from behind.

"Where is it?" she said.

"It's here," Trent whispered. "It's hid—"

The black shape leapt from a shadow at the corner of ceiling and wall and dove down at Trent, front legs roiling with shadow-stuff. Instinct took over and Trent's hand balled into a fist and came swinging forward, timed precisely with a painful thump in his chest.

He saw black, windswept plains and smelled ash and dust and his hand felt numb, deadened, and he opened his eyes wide as his fingers dug into the ethereal flesh of the spider. Its front legs waved awkwardly. It tumbled backwards into a pool of light beneath a hall chandelier. Its incessant humming became a wild screech. It slid up the side of the wall, became two-dimensional, and then fell clumsily to the floor and slipped back into the shadows cast by the debris from the ceiling collapse.

The house was silent again, the humming gone, but Trent knew that the creature had not left. "Get Celia," he said, quietly. "Take her downstairs. Turn off the bathroom lights." He moved forward as he said it, advancing on the pile of rubble.

Susan ran past him and then opened the bathroom door. After a moment, she emerged with Celia, still crying. She flipped the bathroom light switch, bathing the tiny chamber in darkness.

In an instant, the creature leapt from its hiding place and rushed down the hallway, screeching as it passed through the light. Susan and Celia ran for the stairs. Trent stood firm beside the dark bathroom, fists shaking. The creature came at him fast, and at the very last moment his chest hurt again and he ducked and the thing's smoking spike swung over his head and crunched into the wall.

Trent stood quickly and reached out both hands to grab the spider. The smell of ash ripped through his senses again, and the deadening sensation nearly crippled his hands, but he held firm. With a growl, he shoved the creature into the bathroom, where it slammed against the ceramic tub.

In the darkness, Trent watched for a moment as the thing reformed, its shape and size growing larger and more definite. It stood up in the tub, like a real spider in stature and pose, its glowing claws clacking against the ceramic. It leaned backwards and then lunged at him. Trent spun on his booted heels and flipped on the light switch.

The series of bright white globe lights above the mirror burst to life. Another mirror on the opposite wall from the sink reflected the lights back, catching the leaping spider in an illuminated crossfire. Trent turned, fist raised, and sent a powerful blow to the thing's midsection. The spider crumpled back into the tub again, screeching and flailing wildly against the enameled surface, its body growing more and more transparent by the second. In its shrieks, Trent thought for a moment that he could hear voices, people's screams, and he had to fight off a sudden memory of the plane crash and the panicked faces, mouths all set in the same open scream, like a frozen tableau that he was dream-walking through he worked his way to the sucking hole in the side of the cabin...

He stepped out of the bathroom and back into the hall and slammed the door shut, and with it, the terrible memory.

He gripped the doorknob with both hands and braced his boot against the jam to keep the door tight as the creature inside struggled and crashed against the walls. He could hear its blade-like legs clattering across the ceramic tub and the sink and the wall tiles and its never-ending screeches. And then, suddenly, it stopped.

Had he killed it? He let go of the knob and waited, listening. No sounds issued from the bathroom; no screeching, no clawing, nothing. He reached out and turned the knob and pushed the door open, ever so gently. Nothing came lurching out. He peered inside and did not see the spider anywhere.

"Trent and Susan Hawkins!" came a booming voice from the front lawn. "Come out now, hands in the air!"

A series of thuds sounded from the roof, staccato, rhythmic, and Trent's heart raced for a moment before he realized it was SWAT, not the monster. They had the house surrounded. Trent slammed the bathroom door shut, leaving the lights on just in case, and went down the stairs.

Susan and Celia were waiting in the living room, the teenager wrapped up in his wife's arms, her tears dry, eyes wide and bloodshot. The young girl looked devastated, her expression dead and trance-like.

The voice from outside bellowed orders again, demanding that they surrender.

Trent stopped with his back to the smashed pile of picture frames and the bloodstain on the wall. He peered through the waving blinds of the broken window. Cop cars were everywhere, with officers crouched behind the doors, guns drawn. The neighborhood was deathly silent, save the sound of wintry winds moaning all around.

Susan looked at Trent with sadness plastered across her face. "It's gonna be okay, honey," she said. "We're gonna be okay."

Trent met her gaze and forced a smile. "I love you."

"I love you too."

Trent turned away and faced forward again. He reached out and opened the front door and let it swing inward, his hands raised above his head, a man defeated.

Susan watched him take his first step toward the door as tears ran down her cheeks. She could hardly believe it had come to this. And then she noticed the strange movement behind him, amidst the pile of broken frames.

Among the ruined photos there lay a framed mirror, cracked into irregular shards, some scattered in pieces on the floor. A blackness was seeping out of them, like a climber pulling himself from a pit. First came the long, pointed legs, then chunks of body that fused as the mass grew larger, until the black spider had formed fully. It looked weak, mostly translucent, but it stood, legs wavering. Susan let go of Celia and opened her mouth to scream, even as the creature shifted its weight in order to propel itself forward, toward Trent's retreating back.

"*No!*" she screamed, and took off across the living room, as fast as her legs could carry her.

Trent, confused by the sudden scream, whirled around and saw the spider in mid-leap, lunging for him. His brain reeled.

He'd killed it! Goddamn it, it was supposed to dead! He stumbled backwards a step and blinked. His chest ached with such an intense and sudden pain that he thought that maybe one of the cops had shot him. Susan came charging out of his periphery and all three of them—Trent, Susan and spider— collapsed together into a heap on the home's front steps. Trent watched in horror as the black shape diminished and formed into a smoky black stream and then slipped down into the shadows between them.

He could feel its presence, so close to him, seeking him, and knew in that moment that it had never come for Celia. It had been hunting him. He was filled with dread. He looked into Susan's panicked face and stared deep into her sky-blue eyes.

"God, I'm so sorry, baby," he said. He could feel the spider clawing in their combined shadow, could feel it like a web anchored to his skin, pulling, pinching, and aching with every infinitesimal tug. He pleaded with her, "Please tell them it wasn't me. I didn't—"

He stopped and watched as Susan's eyes filled with black. She blinked several times in rapid succession. She looked dazed.

"What?" For a moment, Trent was confused, and then he realized what had happened. "*No!*" He grabbed Susan and pulled her close. "Not her! No! God, please no! You want me dammit!"

But the spider *had* taken her. It had made a mistake; had found the wrong shadow at the last moment and now it reared up out of the black.

"*Open fire!*" yelled the cop with the megaphone.

For Trent, everything suddenly seemed to move in slow motion. A series of metallic clicks as triggers were pulled, followed by flashes and pops and the sounds of bullets whizzing past him. He smelled gunpowder and ash on the cold wind. He looked up at the cops in astonishment.

It wasn't us, he thought. *It wasn't us.*

But still they kept firing, and with every muzzle flash the creature before him shrieked. Trent watched in a sort of confused paralysis as bullets zipped through the creature's flesh, tearing off coils of black smoke. And then a bullet thwacked through the mostly limp body in his arms, sending out a spray of blood. Susan shuddered then, her back tensing within Trent's grip. Her mouth dropped open. Another bullet passed through her shoulder, splattering Trent's neck with warmth.

With each fraction of a second that passed, Trent felt that same pounding against his chest, that hammering against something deeper than his lungs, something way down, some deep part of his core. The aching slams felt like a creature trying to punch its way out of him, and each was punctuated by a bullet that screamed past, barely missing Trent's flesh. He let go of Susan's limp form and stood, staring down the assaulting police.

"He's not going down!" screamed one of the officers, but to Trent's ears it sounded like a record at half-speed.

The shadow-spider dropped to the ground, writhing with flashes of light from the guns and bullets that tore through its impossible corpus. Then, in a bid to protect itself, the thing gathered its remaining strength and hurled itself forward, toward the police. Some of the men screamed as it came on and descended amidst their jumble of cars and equipment and the falling snow. Guns stopped firing. The bullets passing Trent ceased.

Trent watched for a moment as the thing shredded through the police, as men began dropping to the ground, faces upturned, horrible, inhuman screams escaping their lips. Blood took to the air, staining the white snow on the sidewalk and lawn.

Another bloodcurdling shriek came from inside the house and Trent struggled to order the scene in his mind, to recount the players.

Celia's scream.

He looked down at his wife's unmoving form, shocked, unable to believe what had just happened. Susan's pale blue eyes were still open, glittering with her final tears. He grimaced and let out a roar of agony and knew what he had to do.

He turned his back to the cops and the spider's massacre and walked into the house. He looked at Celia, who had balled herself in the corner of the living room, fetal and rocking. No cops could help her now. The cops could not help anyone. If the shadow creature was Salvatore's minion, if the old man had the power to summon such a thing, there was no way the police could protect Celia. Trent shook his head. Turning himself in now would be her death sentence, and his own.

He walked over to her and grabbed her hand and lifted her to her feet. She looked up at him with bloodshot eyes. "We've gotta go," he said, grimly. "Out the back."

They raced across the backyard, eager to put as much space between them and the shadow-thing as possible. The

Cagills' backyard was bordered on one side by a wooden privacy fence, but on the other by a lower, chain link hurricane fence. They reached it and climbed over awkwardly, then got to their feet again and ran.

As they sprinted through the suburban Las Vegas jungle of yellowed grass and unkempt dirt lots, Trent looked around desperately for a better means of transport. Cars lined the streets and filled the driveways, but Trent had no idea how to hotwire. And his concentration kept faltering. With every juddering step, thoughts of Susan tried to reassert themselves in his mind.

Why did she have to die? Why not me? I left her there, dead on the sidewalk.

The guilt threatened to send him to his knees, but then Celia's tightening grip on his hand gave him strength. This was his task now, his sole mission to hold tight to, or Susan's death would have no meaning at all.

He looked across the street as they passed through a backyard full of children's toys and a jungle gym. He saw a man standing in the driveway, keys in hand, perplexed at the sight of Trent and Celia tearing through his neighbor's backyard. Trent pulled up short and caught his foot against a tricycle's wheel. He pitched over, fell and cracked his head against the tricycle's handlebars, but finally managed to kick the thing away and scrambled back to his feet. He yanked on Celia's arm and yelled "This way!" and headed for the man watching them.

It seemed to take a moment for the guy to realize that the two fugitives were bearing down on him. When he did, his perplexed look turned to panic. He dropped his keys in the driveway and yelled and ran for the front door of his house. Trent and Celia reached the car, gasping for breath.

The teenager ran up to the driver's side door and jammed her fingers against the handle. To Trent's amazement, her fingers passed straight through, shattering the metal and causing a terrible screech from the car frame. Celia freaked out at the noise and yanked her hand back, leaving a ragged, ice-encrusted hole in the steel door where the lock should have been. The door creaked open on its own.

Trent grabbed the keys from the ground, shoved Celia in through the open door, and then threw himself inside. He turned the key and fired up the vehicle—a silver luxury sedan—and backed it out of the driveway. Seconds later, they were flying down the suburban streets toward a nearby avenue, desperate to escape the madness they had left behind.

Celia's despondent moans were all that kept Trent from turning the car around and heading back to the house, back to Susan's body, back to the police massacre and the creature that had just taken his whole life from him. But a part of him, the rational part, knew that he needed to be as far away from Las Vegas as possible. For her. For Celia.

He guided the sedan onto Sunset Road and headed at full speed for the Expressway, the car sliding in the ice with every sharp turn. For the most part, his brain felt as though it were filled with a dense fog and he had no idea of where they might go or for how long they would have to run to escape the monsters behind them. And then, in a moment of clarity, he glanced down at the dashboard and his heart sank.

The needle was nearly on 'E.'

13

THE LUXOR LOOMED BEFORE HIM, a black monolith set against a gray sky, fronted by a replica of Egypt's Sphinx. The drifting snow and gusts of wind stung Salvatore's face as he stared up at the faux-ancient geometry, dark and unpleasant when juxtaposed against the foul weather, the guardian beast staring ahead, seemingly blind to the atrocities walking endlessly before it.

Salvatore wondered briefly what his wife might have thought upon seeing him here. Could she have ever believed her Sal standing before this artifice in the world's capital of sin and greed? Would she have dared imagine the blood that now stained his hands, despite his every effort to wipe them clean?

He closed his eyes, rubbed his temples. A headache still lingered. His moment of quiet was startled suddenly by the wail of police sirens and he spun to watch three cars barrel in a line down The Strip past him, lights flashing, sirens squealing. The snow, the chaos, the blood. Salvatore hunched over involuntarily and stared at his hands again.

Something is very wrong.

The interior of the place in many ways did not mimic the exterior. While the building sought to convey an air of awe, even mystery, the interior left nothing to the imagination. It was blatantly clear what transpired here: unending collection of unknown debts, a reaping of souls, all pushed from the cliff into the great abyss below, where they lingered happily, joyously, damning themselves over and over and over.

Salvatore's stomach turned at the sight of it, at the *unholiness* on permanent display. One of the bums in the tunnels had once joked with Salvatore that "gambling is just a tax on people who can't do math." But the old man saw it in much harsher terms. This was one of the Devil's feast halls, and neither the servers nor the food paid heed to the sole diner, who hid in everything and nothing at once, slowly consuming them all. It was a secret abattoir, drenched in blood and sin, just like Salvatore's fingers.

"Mr. Cortina!" The voice caused Salvatore to snap his head up in alarm, quickly shoving his stained hands into his coat pockets. He saw a skinny young man in a black suit and black tie approaching him. He could not have been much beyond his early-twenties, but had a confident swagger and wore his suit well. "Mr. Cortina," he repeated as he came near. "Welcome back to the Luxor."

Salvatore looked away, shaking his head. "No," he said. "No, I have not been here before."

The man's disingenuous smile vanished quickly, becoming instead a frown. "Are you sure, Mr. Cortina?"

"Stop using my name!" Salvatore snapped. "Why do you know me?"

The young man stopped in his tracks and then, after a moment, took a step backwards as if sizing up the situation. "Umm..." he muttered, his normally rapid-fire greeting sequence suddenly broken. "Umm, hold on." He turned his side to Salvatore and placed a finger to his ear with his head bowed slightly. "Yes," he said. "Mr. Cortina is here but he doesn't—" He looked up at Salvatore, but only held the gaze for a split second before turning away again. "Yes. No, he doesn't know— Of course, I—" There was a long pause as the man listened to the earpiece. Finally, he said, "Okay, I will." Then he turned back to Salvatore, the fake smile glowing once more.

"Certainly, sir. There must be some sort of mistake. A manager will be here shortly to answer any questions you might have."

No sooner had the young man finished the sentence when one of the nearby elevators slid open, revealing two nearly-identical men in gray suits. They both were tall, thin, with blond hair and mismatched blue/green eyes. They moved through the casino crowd like fish through water, never deviating far from their path, but shifting imperceptibly to avoid collisions with gamblers and pit bosses and scantily clad servers. It was as if the crowd itself flowed around them and Salvatore watched them, mesmerized, frozen in place by their piercing gaze that never left his, even as they reached out with subtle, gentle gestures to move human obstacles from their careful approach.

"Good day, Mr. Cortina," said one of the blond men as he approached.

His companion followed up with, "I'm sure you have many questions. And we can surely answer them." He glanced at his fellow.

"Please, sir," he said, gesturing toward the elevators with a careful bow. "If you would accompany us, we will be happy to show you the truth of things."

Salvatore stood mute, both in sound and motion. He did not know what to make of these two men. They fascinated him, even attracted him in some strange way, and he wanted desperately to follow them wherever they might lead. But a part of him rebelled at the notion. *What would my wife have thought of this... this, den of iniquity? This place is not safe, not holy.* He felt like a man on enemy turf and he momentarily revisited the terrified emotions that had stirred in him as a child when, during the War, his family had hid their anti-Hitler leanings from the Italian authorities; a stranger on his own soil, an enemy in his own world.

But then, he had come here for answers. He took a deep breath and let the cool sensation wash through him. He imagined the red stains on his fingers and his mind toyed with a collection of memories buried deep in the darkness, a mass that pulsed and snarled in the black, refusing access, pushing his thoughts away from their hiding place. He needed these answers, even if these men were about to turn him in for whatever crimes he had committed. He had to know. He had to face his punishment before the Almighty, whatever that might be.

Salvatore nodded, and followed.

The two blond men led Salvatore down a long corridor, somewhere near the top of the thirty-story pyramid. They stopped at a heavy wooden door, ornately carved with a gold handle. One of the men swiped a black plastic card through a reader next to the doorframe, and the light blinked green. They pushed the door open into the darkened space of the penthouse suite.

A soft glow came to life as the door swung open. Can lights embedded in the ceiling shone careful, dim spotlights down upon ornate furniture and Egypt-themed books and art objects. The carpeted entryway to the suite and the mottled-paint walls all radiated a deep, comforting, rich brown and tan. As Salvatore and the two men stepped inside, more lights came to life ahead of them: table lamps, more cans in the ceiling, and point spotlights that brought paintings to life on the walls. None of the paintings were of things that Salvatore found pleasant or calming. One in particular caught his eye: an ash-black horse against a fiery backdrop, rearing up on its hind legs, nostrils flared. It reminded Salvatore of stories from the darker parts of the Bible and he immediately looked away. His gaze then fell on something far worse.

As the three of them stepped into the main living area of the suite, Salvatore leading, he spotted an incongruous table amidst the fancy furniture. Stainless steel, like a hospital gurney, but with special railings bearing black leather straps, the table gleamed in the dull light from the cans above. Next to it, on one of the ornate wooden end tables, sat a plastic tray covered in surgical tools. And upon the table, strapped down, was a boy, lying still, eyes and mouth and nose and ears all stitched shut, his hair matted in a thin pool of blood beneath his head.

Salvatore recoiled instantly at the sight. "No!" he shouted. "What is this? Why have you taken me here?" He turned to run but was caught instantly by one of the blond men, who gripped Salvatore with surprising strength.

"No?" asked the blond man. "You run from your own work?"

Salvatore shook his head, but a glimmer of doubt slid into his bones as the suite lighting played across his red-stained fingers. "No," he repeated. "I do not remember this!"

"This is you," said the other blond, stepping close. "This is your legacy, Zamagiel-horse."

"Your fingers sewed the mouth," said the blond holding him.

"And the nose—"

"And the eyes—"

"And cut out the tongue." The other blond stepped up and placed his hands on Salvatore's shoulders as he struggled. "This is your work, your greatest work. This is redemption for that which rides you."

The other blond removed one of his strong hands from Salvatore's arm and pointed at the painting that had upset the old man. "You are the horse to the Loa, Mr. Cortina. After Kalfu it styles itself, but it was one of our kind once."

Salvatore quit his struggling and stared up at the two men, frozen now with fear. "What— what are you?"

The men smiled. "Angels, Mr. Cortina. Angels."

The blond on the right added, "In the flesh."

There was a long moment of silence, and then Salvatore lost himself in terror. He yelled out for help and struggled even harder than before, managing to dislodge himself from the angel's grip. He threw himself to the floor next to the metal table. When he looked up and saw the child's sewn-up face moving, twisting slowly in his direction, he scrambled to his face and darted across the penthouse suite.

"No!" he screamed as he ran. "No! I don't believe any of this! Please, God, please help me!"

And then the migraine came on, and Salvatore fell to the floor, hands gripping his skull as he mewled pitifully for God's forgiveness.

One of the angels walked near and squatted down next to the old man's writhing form. "The thing inside you," he said, quietly, "it will not stop. It will not rest, nor coddle, nor come to peace. Not until it has been redeemed. Not until the Garden is returned."

"And that can only happen," intoned the other angel as he joined his companion next to Salvatore, "once you have captured that child—"

"That girl."

"She hides your Loa's power." The blond gestured toward the sewed-up child on the table. "You have gone to great lengths and incurred many debts to gain the thing that now rests inside this child. It will help you regain your power, and then your winter shall ruin this den of iniquity."

"And in its place, the Garden will be reborn, meadows amidst the sand—"

"Heaven on Earth."

"No," pleaded Salvatore, his voice cracking and broken from the pain in his mind. "Please, Lord..."

"Let the creature Zamagiel come forth, old mortal. Let it ride you one last time."

"Zamagiel can find the girl. Zamagiel can *feel* her, somewhere out there." The angel pointed at one of the drape-ensconced floor-to-ceiling windows.

"Let Zamagiel finish this task."

"Let it clean this stain."

Salvatore screamed with pain, worse than any he had ever felt before, and the familiar sense of nothingness overtook him and his mouth filled with the taste of ash and blood.

Before he passed out completely, Salvatore heard the angel say, quietly, "Go, Zamagiel. Find your only daughter."

14

WITHOUT A CAR, TRENT KNEW that they had no shot of getting safely out of Las Vegas. They could hit Interstate 15 going northeast and run out of gas before they had even crossed the city line. 515 southeast would take them into Henderson; they could maybe make it to the town's southern border. No help there—the Henderson PD would be waiting as soon as they crossed the county line. And cutting all the way across the city to catch Highway 95 northwest would leave them out of gas somewhere around The Strip, Trent figured. He didn't have a wallet with him, or any cash; both were in the van back at the Cagills' house. There was no way they could buy gas, and a fuel-and-run would just give the cops a better lead on them. They had to stay in the city, at least until they found better transportation. And then Trent thought of Charlie V.

The motorcycle! His mind raced with the possibility. *Charlie's still got that thing. If there's any time he'd give it to me—* Trent looked around at the falling snow and the swaying street signs buffeted by icy winds that had begun to pick up in tempo. Even the sidewalks had begun to clear. *If there's a time for help, this is it.*

The only question left was how to proceed on foot without being seen—or caught by the monstrosities still chasing them. That answer came quickly: the tunnels. Las Vegas had hundreds of miles of tunnels beneath it, built as storm drains to protect the desert city's streets during the rare heavy thunderstorms. Most people did not know about the tunnels, but Trent did. He had once used the tunnels after narrowly escaping the 'discussion room' in the dingy basement of one of the off-Strip casinos. Through the parking garage and into a storm grate and he had practically been home free. Even the casino's thugs had been wary of the tunnels, and had only followed Trent a short distance into the darkness before turning back.

He exited I-515, pulled a U-turn and got back on heading the other direction, north back into Las Vegas—into the fray.

"We're going back," he said, mostly for his own benefit.

Celia did not respond. She had her head down, quiet tears dribbling onto the floorboard.

Trent grimaced and tried not to think of his own loss. Part of him found it easy. He simply could not believe what had happened. It just had not registered yet. Susan wasn't—

He shook his head to clear away the train of thought. No need to go there. Not now. He focused on the road, and his current task, and the sad little girl beside him that he needed to keep safe.

By the time they had reached Tropicana heading west, the sedan had begun to sputter. The 'refuel' light blinked on and then off and then on again, and stayed. They were coasting on fumes. Trent floored the gas to try to get up some extra speed, weaving in and out of the traffic on the avenue as he passed

UNLV on the right and then McCarran Airport on the left. A plane soared over them, its engine noise rattling the ground and the car. *Judging by the weather*, Trent thought. *That'll be the last flight in tonight*.

To keep his mind away from thoughts of Susan, Trent focused on his fragmented memories from the crash. He remembered the lobby at McCarran. He remembered buying trinkets for Susan from the old Asian guy that ran a kiosk in the airport. He blinked back tears, wishing he could see her smile again as he opened his eyes in the hospital bed, her hand in his. He frowned and pulled the cowboy hat down tighter on his head, afraid that someone might see him crying. He cursed himself and then Las Vegas. Everything bad that had ever happened to him had started here, and now it looked like it would end here too.

The sedan's engine let out a final loud clunk and then the car began to slow. Trent pumped the gas pedal a few more times, hoping to squeeze whatever was left out of the gas tank, but to no avail. The car sputtered to a stop and he rolled it off onto the shoulder. They were between the MGM Grand and the Tropicana, only a few hundred feet from the intersection of Tropicana and The Strip. To his right, the palm trees swayed rigidly in the blustery winds, their green now covered with silvery ice. In the distance, he could see the roller coaster at the New York New York, stopped on its track, abandoned; no more fun today.

Trent looked at the ditch off to the side of he road. He knew the tunnel entrance was nearby. It would have to do.

"Come on," he said and tapped Celia on the shoulder. "We've gotta walk."

She looked up at him, eyes bloodshot and tired. "Walk?"

"Outta gas. I told you way back—" He saw the deadened expression on her face and knew that it didn't much matter what he said to her now. The teenager's world had turned upside-down, much like his, and at the moment, that was all they shared: a deep, gut-wrenching sense of loss and a depression that refused to cease its hammering away at their faith in the world.

He simply gestured with his head, opened his own door, and got out of the sedan. After a moment, Celia did too, and Trent's depression deepened. It had somehow escaped his notice until now that she still wore the hospital gown from the Children's Center. She began to shiver almost immediately as she looked around at the palm trees and the buildings and the few improperly-dressed tourists moving stiffly along the sidewalk in front of the Grand.

Trent wished he had brought a jacket to give her. He heard the familiar chirp of police sirens nearby; they were only a few blocks over. *No time to waste*, he thought. *We'll just have to risk the cold.*

"Come on," he pleaded, holding out his hand. "I have a friend, a little ways north of here. We just have to make it there."

Celia looked at him, a mask of betrayal on her face. She moved around the front of the car and took his outstretched hand.

A few cars zoomed by on the avenue, heading for the Interstate past The Strip. When the coast was clear, Trent guided the teenager across the street. They ran past the oncoming traffic, hopped over the divider, and took off west, the chilling winds whipping the power lines overhead and fluttering Celia's turquoise gown. Trent had to keep one hand on the top of his head to hold the hat down.

An opening to the tunnels wasn't far, just inside the parking garage at the nearby Excalibur. As they passed under the concrete structure, Trent noted that the puddles of water from last night's rain had now all turned to ice. In some places, tiny nubs of icicles had begun to form as water dripped down the outside of the slightly warmer garage. They made their way to the back of the garage and approached the tunnel opening.

The hotel had put an iron grate across the opening, not so much to keep people from going in, but to keep the tunnel-dwelling vagrants from coming out, and into the Excalibur garage. But the lock had long ago been broken open, and no one ever bothered to replace it.

Trent pulled on the gate, his tired arms straining to make a space large enough for the two of them to squeeze through.

Before they slipped into the dark, Trent surveyed the garage and the road beyond. He saw the lights of a police car as it turned into the far end of the garage, moving slowly. He grabbed Celia's arm and slipped inside the tunnel and pulled the iron gate shut behind them.

The storm drain tunnels were not a sewer, though the heavy rains from the night before had filled them partially with ankle-deep, waste-topped water, now freezing cold. Some of it still ran freely, while in other places it had frozen into puddles of partially solidified slush. The thin, wet coating on the tunnel walls had already frozen hard, and Trent found quickly that touching the ice-cold walls caused considerable pain. He noted with alarm that the same could not be said of Celia.

As she walked, bare feet sloshing through the freezing water, she seemed almost unaware of the cold now, and her fingers traced along the ice on the walls as if she were analyzing it by touch.

"Celia?" he said. "You okay?"

"Of course," she replied, her voice quiet and low, almost sounding as though she were hypnotized. "I like the cold."

"But the water—"

"I'm fine," she said.

And that's all they said to one another for nearly an hour's walk. Trent slogged through the filth and the muck behind her, trying desperately to keep his feet moving, trying hard to see in the scant light. He could barely feel his feet after the first twenty minutes. His vision started swimming after forty. And still the diminutive teenager marched on ahead of him, apparently oblivious now to the dangerous weather.

Trent tried to hold his grip on reality by analyzing his surroundings. The tunnels were mostly pitch-black, even during the day, but every so often they would pass beneath an inlet or sewer grate that would afford them a lit view of their surroundings. Those lit places with access to the surface were filled with cigarette butts, broken syringes and bent spoons, interstitial zones of rest and refuel for the unseen masses that lurked in the depths of the City of Sin, forgotten by those above. Other lit areas had been filled with graffiti, some racist propaganda, some beautiful and haunting. At the juncture of two tunnels, a warning had been crudely spray-painted on the pillar between:

IN CASE OF FLOOD SWIM FOR YOUR FUCKING LIFE.

The tunnel they were in headed north, almost directly beneath The Strip. In places, waste pipes jutted from the cement walls, pouring steaming fluid into the muck at their feet, effluent from the casinos above; and though the stuff reeked, Trent found himself longing for those spots where the slush thawed and the water turned warm, if only for a few steps.

As they walked, he began to have serious doubts about this plan. His legs had begun to falter, and his breathing had grown shallow. Though Celia seemed unaffected, he knew that he could not go much further. The temperature seemed to drop with every passing minute. Parts of the tunnel floor had turned from icy water with some slush to pure, freezing slime, and the curved ceiling threatened them with icicles like crystalline stalactites; more than once, Trent snapped an icicle off with his hat.

"Celia," he said, gasping for air as they passed beneath a dim beam of light from a vent above.

She turned to look at him, her face impassive, eyebrow raised. She said nothing.

"Celia," he said again, "I don't think— I can't—"

"There's warmth up ahead," she said, matter-of-factly.

"How do you know?"

"I can feel it." With that, she turned away and continued down the tunnel, one hand sliding lazily along the ice-encrusted cement wall.

Sure enough, around the next bend, Trent watched with relief as orange firelight broke the pitch-black. He hobbled after Celia.

The fire burned away inside an old metal barrel that someone had managed to drag down into the tunnels and left here, in a relatively dry, raised portion of the tunnel floor. Trent knew that a community of several hundred people was rumored to live down here. As he squinted at the suddenly bright fire, he noticed one of them lying next to the barrel.

The man was old, sickly thin and pale, and his scraggly white hair hung down to his shoulders. He had a full beard and moustache, also white, and his eyes remained shut as they approached. As soon as they were closer, Trent saw why. In the old man's limp hand was a syringe and next to him sat a crushed aluminum can, the top scorched and brown with heroin residue.

Trent stumbled over next to the old man and sat down, his feet outstretched toward the barrel. He could barely feel the heat coming in through his cowboy boots and worried that he had already suffered frostbite. He looked over to see how Celia was faring.

She had already taken a seat nearby and sat cross-legged on the tunnel floor, amidst the cigarette butts and drug debris. Her face remained impassive. The crying had stopped long ago. Trent wasn't sure if she had gone into some sort of shock or denial, or if she had snapped under the pressure. He worried about her more with every passing minute.

"Celia?" he said, but got no response. He tried again, louder this time, "Celia!"

"Belongs to me," interrupted a booming voice from the darkness further down the tunnel.

Trent stood quickly.

After a moment, the form of Salvatore revealed itself like a dream, wavering in the dim light from the fire barrel. It grew more solid as the old man approached. He had a smile on his face, even as his long black coat swished through the water on the tunnel floor.

"Leave us alone," Trent growled. "You've killed enough people today."

Salvatore's wicked grin shifted suddenly to a look of contrition that surprised Trent. "I'm sorry," he said. It sounded genuine. "I did not want to hurt them, but I had to. I had to end all of this."

"What?"

Trent watched as the old man's face struggled with itself. Alternating expressions of anger, sadness, malice, and fear wrestled for dominance. Finally, his head cocked to one side and a smile took the place of tears and grief. He spoke.

"This is my destiny, *gibborim*. This is my chosen path. I must undo what has been done. The child must be found, must be drained of her unnatural gift. It upsets the Lord. His will must be done."

Behind him, Trent could hear Celia moaning softly with confusion and terror.

A look of fury crossed Salvatore's face for the briefest of moments, before making way for a wry smile. "But I don't suppose you believe in God, do you? None of your kind really does anymore." He sighed. "I don't blame you. He's not talked to any of us in quite some time."

"Not my problem," replied Trent.

"So with no God to protect you, the police on your trail, what do you have left, then? What is there that is so important to you that you must continue to get in my way? Give me back my child and this will all be over."

"You're insane."

Salvatore raised an eyebrow. "Both godless and foolish? A terrible combination, *gibborim*."

But his words had raised doubt in Trent's mind. He was risking his life, risking the lives of the police and the hospital workers, all for this little girl he barely even knew. He had even lost Susan, all to arrive here, half-frozen in the dank tunnels beneath Las Vegas. And for what?

Salvatore chuckled.

"You're cracking, mortal. I can see it on your face. You want so badly to be the hero. But this is not about heroics. You are just a lucky child playing with fire, and soon you *will* be burned." A sudden look of anguish drifted across his face. "I should know." The sad look disappeared as fast as it had come and Salvatore began moving toward Trent and Celia, his steps splashing in the icy muck.

Trent raised a hand and pointed. "Stay back," he said. "Just stop right there."

"Or what?" Salvatore raised an eyebrow. "This is over, child. Your little game is done. The girl belongs to me, now. I will take her back with me, relieve her of the power she has accidentally inherited, and then leave her for the police to find. You can turn around now and walk away, turn yourself in if you wish. You will be exonerated as soon as my task is done and the child is found."

"He's lying," Celia hissed. "He's going to cover the city in snow."

Salvatore whirled on her, his lips twisted into an angry sneer. "How do you know that?"

"I know what you want," Celia shot back. "I can *feel* it. You killed my parents and now you're going to kill me and the blizzard will come and kill everyone."

Salvatore's sneer became a grin. "Come with me, or I will end him." He pointed at Trent.

"No," Celia replied without hesitation.

The old man's expression shifted again, a drastic change. Sadness once more filled his eyes. "Please," he said, "don't despise me. This is for the best. For the greater good. For the glory of God. Please, daughter..." He held out a hand.

Celia spit at him, a sound that echoed weirdly in the concrete tunnel.

Trent used the distraction. He charged. His fist came forward quickly, a right hook aimed squarely for the old man's nose. He had caught him off-guard before; maybe he could do it again.

But instead of connecting with flesh, Trent's fist passed through empty air as Salvatore moved. It was as if the old man had *poured* himself out of the way, appearing in the same position and stance, only one foot to the right. He roared and pushed both palms forward and water sprung up from the tunnel floor around his feet. The wave hit Trent hard and knocked him off his feet and he slammed back first onto the concrete. Salvatore, a few feet away from them both, stared down at the fallen man and the trembling teenager.

"You will not win this fight. My powers are stronger now than they have been in ten thousand years. God gave us all such wonderful gifts. But like many of my kind, I was stupid. I gave them away."

He gestured at Celia.

"And then I was nothing for so long. But when my children began coming back to me, I felt it again—the power, the gifts that God had bestowed. I've learned much over the years, and I intend now to retake what is mine. It is time for all of this to change, Mr. Hawkins. For the Glory of God. To save this world from a far worse fate."

"What are you?" Trent moaned, the pain in his back burning like he had fallen into the fire barrel.

"I was a Watcher, once. Sent by God to help *you*. We gave your kind *everything*." Salvatore's face twisted into a pained grimace. "And how did you repay us?" he screamed. "Your women spurned us! Your men hunted us, like beasts! Even our children—*your* children—became pigs for the slaughter!"

He looked at Celia. "Do you think, if your kind knew what she was—truly *knew*—that they would protect her?" He lifted one eyebrow and looked at Trent again with a questioning glare. "Or do you think they would hunt her down, lock her away, hide her powers and her secrets? Do you think that she would be treated like a *human*?"

He sighed in mock exasperation.

"You have the opportunity to end this. Turn her over to me. She is *my* child. Let me deal with her, as it should be under the eyes of God. Go back to your lovely wife, before she is lost in all of this. Leave the city and start a life anew somewhere else. Before all of this—" He raised his arms, as if to indicate the entire city. "Before all is destroyed and reborn."

Trent's entire body trembled, but not with fear. He had transcended fear at Susan's mention. Now he trembled with rage.

"No," he said, shaking his head. "My wife is already dead." Slowly, he climbed to his feet and stood amidst the freezing muck, facing down the old main in the black coat. "This ends now."

Salvatore growled and thrust out his right hand, palm-forward. Trent staggered back a step and clutched as his throat. He felt like he had back at the hospital, as if the old man were somehow drowning him from within. It felt like his lungs and chest were filling with ice-cold water and he began to tremble violently. He steeled himself and tried a deep breath. He found that the breath came easier than he had expected. He closed his eyes and focused.

When he opened his eyes again, the drowning sensation had subsided and he knew that Salvatore could no longer try that trick on him. He shook his head from side to side and glowered at the old man.

"Whose child are you, *gibborim*? Baraqel? Maybe Azaziel? How have you inherited such a wealth of power?"

"No powers," said Trent. "I'm just lucky." He shouted then and sprinted past Celia, coming on fast as he closed with Salvatore.

The old man sneered and gestured with his free hand and a curtain of icy fluid lifted from the floor of the tunnel.

Gleaming in the firelight, the fluid tensed and seemed ready for Trent's oncoming charge.

He barreled into the spray and lost his footing as tendrils of water slipped around his ankles and slid beneath his feet. The curtain of spray had more solidity than he expected. He pulled up short, not quite reaching Salvatore.

The old man winked and flicked a single finger forward. The wave rushed away from him, carrying Trent with it. He tumbled through the air, slipped and slid on the wet concrete floor, and finally lost his balance, tumbling head over heels into the muck at the bend in the tunnel. He crashed into a pile of debris there: chunks of broken concrete, spray-painted pieces of wood, sticky mats of soaked paper and plastic. For a second, his face went beneath the shallow water and he could taste filth as it poured into his lungs. He splashed back up, gasping for air.

The rage he had felt upon hearing Susan's name had grown. He now felt an almost alien fury, a wrath that bordered on insanity. He coughed and sputtered and thrashed around for something to use as a weapon. His hand came up from the freezing water holding a lump of concrete. He stood and reared back and threw it, as hard as he could muster.

And as the piece sailed across the room, Trent blinked, saw the black world, and then opened his eyes again, chest aching with a sudden battery of juddering pains.

Salvatore stood next to Celia and the fire barrel, arms hanging limp at his sides, waiting patiently as the projectile rushed toward him. His face was impassive and he seemed unconcerned. That impassive look changed to one of shock when the jagged chunk cracked against his forehead, drawing blood.

The old man screamed in pain and surprise and brought a hand to his face. He stumbled around for a moment, as the blood ran down over his fingers. Finally, he reset his gaze upon Trent.

"Lucky indeed," he growled. "No more games." Salvatore slammed a foot down into the running water and disappeared.

But Trent knew that the old man had gone nowhere. He watched the shimmering ripples in the water as they moved against the flow, advancing on him. He waited, waited, and then timed his attack perfectly.

Salvatore's form shot up out of the water, but his eyes went wide as he saw Trent's open hand coming on fast. Trent grabbed the old man's shirt collar, pulled him momentarily off his feet, and then slugged him in the face with his free hand. He could feel cartilage snapping as his fist shattered Salvatore's nose. The man soared backward and splashed into the muck, a trail of blood shimmering in the air for a moment as a crimson arc.

Trent stomped through the water to the fallen figure and began to rain down blow after blow, each hit sending up an echoing thwack and clipped shrieks as Salvatore tried in vain to twist away from the punishment.

"This is all your fault!" Trent screamed. "My wife is dead, goddamn you! *Dead!*"

As the punches crashed against his face, Salvatore reached out beside him with a trembling arm and placed his fingers in the icy water. The old man closed his eyes.

Trent paused when the rumbling began. The walls of the dank tunnel started to shake and groan, and the water's flow was broken by sudden disturbances. Trent pulled back a little further, fist still cocked. He looked around and saw cracks forming on the walls, ragged vertical lines stretching from floor to ice-encrusted ceiling.

"What the—?"

The concrete exploded as metal pipes burst through, writhing and shrieking with metal stress. They lunged at him from every direction, from every wall, and Trent dove backwards, away from Salvatore, desperate to escape the seeking, waving, thrashing metal tentacles. But he was too slow.

The metal pipes struck him and knocked him down and, like living things, curled around his limbs, creaking and groaning with every change of shape. In an instant, the pipes had him off the ground, spread-eagled, struggling wildly. He barely had time to yell before the pipes sent him hurtling backwards across the tunnel. He hit the cement wall back first. He felt his ribs crack. The pipes pulled him off the wall again, and then sent him hurtling back. He twisted desperately to keep his head from striking first. Each time he hit the wall, he felt another part of his body go numb. The pipes continued their assault upon him, unrelenting.

"*No!*" Celia shrieked. "Stop it!"

But the pipes would not listen. They had squeezed Trent so tight that he could barely breathe. He stopped struggling, sure that this was the end. He watched Celia, helpless against the assault.

The teenager had leapt to her feet and her eyes held a strange intensity that Trent had not seen before. Her lips moved and from her throat came a strange language, spoken in a creepy monotone, as though she had descended into some manner of trance. With each spoken word, her voice grew lower and louder and a discordant buzzing began to issue from behind her dulcet tones.

Black smoke burst suddenly from the tunnel floor at her feet and coiled into the air in front of Celia's chest. The smoke became solid then, resolving itself as an array of gray-green limbs, arms anchored impossibly to the smoke itself; arms that flailed at her, clawed fingers grasping, sinewy muscles tensing and relaxing as they reached for the girl.

"Oh God!" she screamed, and the strange, trancelike look dropped from her visage. "That not what I—!"

A hand shot out of the swirling gray and grabbed her throat and cut off her voice. She tried to back away, but was anchored in place by the grasping arms that had managed to get claws around her neck and wrists and into her shirt. The arms began to pull, drawing the teen closer and closer to the roiling smoke, her face now only inches from its mass.

Trent heard a splash and looked to where Salvatore had fallen. He had gotten to his feet and stood looking at Trent and then Celia and then back at Trent again. He let out a frustrated growl and waved a hand dismissively. The pipes went limp and fell, broken, into a pile on the floor. Trent fell with them.

In a wet, bloodied heap amidst the shattered metal, Trent watched as the old man strode over to the girl. Without hesitation, he reached out and grabbed at the arms, trying to pry them away from his prize.

"She's mine!" he shouted. "You cannot have her! Not until I'm done!"

Salvatore trembled as he fought with the arms, and Trent could see that the struggle was wearing him down. He already had blood coursing down over his face, his nose and cheeks broken, hands bruised and soaked in red. For every arm he managed to break free of the girl, another shot out of the smoke and grabbed her again.

Trent knew that he had to do something. This was his only chance. He grabbed a piece of broken metal pipe. It felt freezing cold in his hand. With pained, lurching steps, he moved behind Salvatore and raised the pipe, his arms weak and shaking. The motion made Trent's vision spin and he could hear a tinny whine in his ears that was growing louder by the second; shock coming on. He knew he would pass out soon.

He gritted his teeth and gathered his remaining strength, and then brought the pipe down on the back of Salvatore's head. The impact rang out in the tunnel, audible above the old man's yelling and Celia's screams as she struggled with the arms. Salvatore's fingers seized and he stumbled backward into Trent, slid off to one side and fell to his hands and knees on the floor.

Trent kicked him in the side to roll him over and then dropped onto the old man like a wild animal, pipe swinging, clanging against Salvatore's flesh. With every strike, Trent felt his own world spinning further out of control. His vision had begun to dim, and his hearing had gone quiet, almost silent. Not much time left...

"Please," gasped Salvatore, raising his hands in defense. Several of his fingers were bloody and broken. "Oh God, please stop!" he cried. "The Lord Almighty, please help me!"

Trent looked into the old man's eyes and saw real pain, real panic and turmoil, and he felt suddenly guilty. He faltered, pipe raised for a final killing blow. The tunnel seemed to be spinning, and every glance in the direction of the firelight made Trent's eyes ache.

He looked at Celia, still fighting against the tearing hands, though on her knees now. She had blood on her face, her neck, and her chest. The gray-green arms were straining, but succeeding. Part of her nose and much of her hair had already passed into the smoke, as though it were a doorway to someplace else. Blood dripped from her wide-open eyes onto the tunnel floor as she screamed and fought.

Trent looked back down at Salvatore, who cringed and averted his face. Tears streamed down his cheeks. Trent took a deep breath and tried to calm the spinning sensation one last time. Then he got to his feet, turned his back on the fallen Salvatore, and charged Celia and the arms, throwing all of his strength and all of his weight into the effort.

He collided with her and with the gray-green appendages that threatened her. He felt the claws digging into his flesh and then just as quickly recoiling, as if they had realized that he was not what they wanted. He brought the metal pipe down over and over on the gray-green limbs. Each strike brought to his muffled hearing the sounds of screaming, a cacophony of human voices buried deep inside the alien shrieks coming from within the smoke. He recognized the sounds as similar to those from the shadow-spider before, at the Cagill house. And then he heard Susan's scream. He knew it immediately; it could not be anyone else. Somehow, she was there, inside that mass of tortured voices, inside that swirling cloud of ash. Her pained voice gave Trent a boost of strength.

With a gut-wrenching, tremendous force, he yanked one last time and pulled Celia from the arms' grasp. He tumbled and landed flat on his back, his head only inches from the hot fire barrel. He watched as the gray-green appendages snapped back into the smoke and then, after a moment, the entire cloud dissipated into nothing.

Celia sat upon the concrete floor, her own hands gripping her hair now, face blotchy and red. She was crying, but alive. She looked at Trent and their eyes met.

He breathed a sigh of relief, forced a pained smile, and then passed out. The orange glow from the firelight mingled with the warmth radiating from the barrel, and Trent slid into the dream world smelling smoke and tasting ash.

15

WITH A HEART-POUNDING SNAP, Trent opened his eyes to survey the scene around him. Fire climbed the walls of the cabin and the lights were on emergency mode. Passengers' mouths hung open in silent screams while others mouthed "no" over and over and over again. Trent could only hear pleasant, classical music and the hiss of noise-canceling electronics in his headphones. He reached up, tore the headphones from his ears, and was assailed by the chaotic sounds of panic and despair. His gaze landed on a woman desperately clutching a small boy, screaming louder than the rest, eyes clenched shut as the child slipped further from her grasp toward the sucking, howling maw of a massive hole in the airplane's flesh.

Something had blown a hole in the cabin, and directly between Trent and it stood an old Mexican man with a gray cowboy hat, silhouetted against the blinking red lights, apparently indifferent to the plight of fellow passengers who were rapidly disappearing into the mad vortex of smoke and escaping cabin air. The old man faced the back of the plane with one hand pinned to the top of his hat in an attempt to keep it from being sucked off his head by the frantic winds.

Trent looked at the screaming mother and the boy again and then sprung into action.

He clawed his way back over his own seat and tumbled into the lap of an old man who lay dead. The little girl next to him, a granddaughter maybe, sat frozen in shock, silent and wide-eyed. The plane pitched suddenly, throwing Trent's body against the dead man's seatback tray, which ripped off the hinges. Then a pitch in the opposite direction and Trent landed at the shocked little girl's feet. He looked up and couldn't resist the urge to comfort her.

"It's gonna be okay, " he shouted, while gasping for air. "It's gonna be okay." He felt awful for the lie.

He contorted his body and landed with a thump in the aisle and then propelled himself forward, fighting against the rapidly shifting angle of the earthbound vessel. The Mexican stood firm against the cacophony, still holding onto his hat with one hand. Trent rushed past him, flailing to reach the child, whose grip on his mother's hand had diminished to only one slipping finger. The hull breach swirled and snorted like a living thing and then there came a ferocious, ear-splitting howl that made the vortex seem momentarily inconsequential. Trent faltered for a moment, tore his eyes away from the child and looked up.

The metal frame of the plunging jet rang out, either from the force of the howl or the metal stress, and then began to tear itself further apart. Sheets of metal ripped free, bolts shot out like bullets, and the plane trembled—a beast in its last throes. A rectangular sheet of hull whipped violently from its moorings and in a split-second the child vanished with it into the night maelstrom, mother still shrieking, still grasping, still clawing at nothing.

Trent stood there, transfixed by the horror and the despair all around him and his gaze began to wander indiscriminately, until it fell upon the progenitor of all of this madness. Something impossible. Inhuman.

A thing of black, with glistening reptilian hide and a coiling, smoke-like tail and maybe it had eyes and a mouth and maybe it didn't, and Trent wondered if the creature had followed him from one of the many nightmares he'd had since he was a child. The screaming cacophony of human fear and anguish seemed to amplify around the creature's form, and as it moved, Trent saw color and shape warping from the nearby passengers, connecting like translucent strands of aberrant light to the thing's shadowy nothingness and it settled its gaze on him then and let out another monstrous roar. Jet-black teeth gleamed with shadowy, dripping ichor. Trent felt his heart stop. The reptilian beast was coming for him.

It seemed to lose all interest in the Mexican as it barreled over a nearby passenger's seat, trampling the screaming man's face. It planted its legs against the far window and hurled itself forward, toward Trent, claws outstretched and jaw extending impossibly wide, wider even than the creature's body, wide enough to engulf any man in a single motion and tear him to shreds and Trent stared down the razor-filled maw and terror hit him like a freight train.

Panic threw him shoulder-first into the Mexican, catching the old man by surprise, and the momentum carried both of them toward the gaping hole in the plane. Trent tried to scream, but the air rushed out of his lungs even as his body rushed out of the plane. A painful scrape against the jagged metal wound in the hull slowed Trent's ejection just enough for him to grope wildly for the Mexican. He caught the edge of the old man's coat, pulling him fully off-balance.

At the last second, before both tumbled out into the void, the Mexican let go of his cowboy hat, freeing up his other hand. The gray hat whipped out into the cold blackness of night, but the wrinkled old hands shot forward, back into the plane's tortured cabin and the old man grabbed the screeching beast by the insides of its mouth. It bit down hard and scrabbled with knife-like claws against his flesh, still fighting to get at Trent, fighting to scramble over the Mexican's shoulder, like a massive, horrifying cat struggling to get free of its owner's grasp. The old man took the pain with a snarl and then, with unimaginable strength, wrenched the creature from its perch in the aisle and all three of them—Trent, old man, and monster—exited the plane at thirty thousand feet.

They fell, their bodies twisting and turning in the buffeting winds, one clawing at the other in a vain attempt to climb upwards, toward some heavenly sanctuary that couldn't be reached. But after a moment, a sudden and strange calm came over the old man. With the ground getting closer by the second, he smiled, leaned back, threw open his arms, and closed his eyes.

Trent watched from above as the old man descended, creating a weird sort of vertigo as a cornfield rushed up to meet the swan-posed figure. He saw the man shudder on impact and then the cornstalks blasted toward him and there came the sound of shattering, crunching bone and Trent slammed into the supine body with the force of a two-hundred pound bullet.

16

TRENT BLINKED AND GASPED FOR a breath of air. He felt like he had been hit in the chest with a sledgehammer. His breathing finally regulated after a few seconds and the pain behind his eyes subsided and he recognized reality and pushed the damage-birthed nightmare back into the recesses of his mind. His head was pounding, his body ached, and he could barely hear. He looked around.

Water still spurted from some of the exposed pipes. Icicles hung from the ceiling above him, like silver daggers aimed at his eyes. He could hear Celia crying softly nearby.

He rolled over and managed to climb to his knees. Looking at the fire sent memories racing through his mind, memories he had suppressed for nearly two years, memories just now coming back to him. He blinked and shook his head, trying to clear the headache and the remnants of the flashback.

"You look like shit," said a nearby, gravelly voice.

Trent looked frantically around, remembering Salvatore, though the voice did not quite match. Salvatore was gone. Where he had lain, a thick puddle of blood was left, some of it seeping down into the glittering water. To the edge of the fire barrel glow, Trent could see a series of bloody handprints and smears continuing along the tunnel walls, back in the direction he and Celia had come.

Salvatore had survived. *Not a lot of blood left*, he thought. *Not at the rate he's bleeding out.* Even with magic powers, Trent guessed the old man would not make it very far; and Trent had no interest in following. He just wanted to get Celia to Charlie's shop, get his bike, and leave this godforsaken place and all of its madness once and for all.

He struggled wearily to his feet.

The voice called out again, hoarse and tired-sounding, "Loan me a smoke?"

"What?" Trent looked around, and finally saw the source. The old, drugged-out bum had woken up. He was staring up at Trent from behind the barrel, blue eyes questioning.

"Smoke?" said the bum again, pantomiming the act of smoking a cigarette.

"Oh." Trent reached into his left jeans pocket, which sent a wave of pain up his arm. He finally managed to fumble a crumpled-up pack of Marlboros onto the tunnel floor. He bent down, slowly, and picked out the last remaining cigarette from the pack, and tossed it to the bum.

"Thanks."

Trent nodded, took a deep breath, and turned to approach Celia. She had curled up into a fetal position and was rocking gently, back and forth, eyes wide and fixed squarely on the opposite wall of the tunnel. She looked catatonic.

"Celia? Kiddo? You okay?"

No answer.

"Come on," he said. "You can't go nuts on me now, kid. We gotta get out of here."

"It was my fault," she said, quietly.

"What?"

"I cast the wrong spell." She turned away from him and stared at the fire dancing above the old, rusted barrel. "I made a mistake. The words, the voices, they came rushing into my head, and I picked the wrong ones."

Trent thought about the cloud of smoke and they gray arms trying to drag Celia inside. He could scarcely imagine something like that could even exist, let alone that it had been conjured by a scared teenage girl. "I don't think that was you, kiddo—"

"Don't call me that." She picked up a handful of ice and made a pitiful effort of throwing it at Trent.

"Fine!" he shot back and shook his head in frustration. He didn't know how to handle the situation, and he was not about to try and drag her from the tunnel by force. He was even a little afraid to touch her, after what he had seen.

He waited for a moment, unsure what to do next, until suddenly Celia shot him a pained look and stood up. Then she turned her back to Trent and the bum and the fire barrel, and began marching away, into the darkness of the receding tunnel. "Let's go," she said. "I need time to think about the words in my head. I need to figure this out." Her voice had a *lowness*, an unsettling quality that made Trent shiver involuntarily.

He surveyed the area one last time, looking for the gray Stetson that had flown off his head during the fight. He found it and brushed off a few shards of concrete and bits of trash, then sighed, jammed the hat on his head, and left, jogging painfully to catch up with Celia's retreating form as she disappeared into the dark maze beneath The Strip.

If the previous journey through the muck had been painful, the next two hours for Trent seemed like Hell itself. The teenager never faltered, and he found himself barely able to keep up with her. He stumbled like a movie zombie through the garbage-laden tunnels.

Finally, after two hours of trudging through the freezing cold, he stopped beside a ladder inset into the wall. "Celia," he said, barely able to find the energy to yell.

She turned and looked down the tunnel at him. He gestured to the ladder with a blood-encrusted hand. "Back here."

He looked up at the metal door atop the ladder and wondered what he would find beyond. The temperature had grown impossibly cold, colder than he had ever felt in Las Vegas, and colder than even the worst winter days in Chicago. And from somewhere above, he could hear the wind now, more intense than before, blowing in powerful, screaming and whistling gusts.

Celia walked back over to stand next to him, but would not meet his gaze.

Trent pointed up the ladder. "We should be a block from Charlie's shop here." He put his hands on his knees and gasped for air. "I think."

Without saying a word, the teenager reached out, grabbed a metal rung and started to climb.

Dusk had dropped on the city of Las Vegas like a veil. Where there had been torrential downpours the night before, there was heavy snow now, and Trent knew now that Salvatore had something to do with it. He had hoped that if the old man died, the storm would let up, but it did not look that way yet.

He and Celia stood on the side of the road, watching the panicked drivers as they smashed into one another. Others loped around in the streets, crying and terrified to be caught out in the storm, some stumbling through the snow as if caught in a sort of somnambulatory trance, unable to comprehend, lost in the blinding white. Evening traffic—in truth, Las Vegas itself—had all but shut down.

Trent looked around and tried to get his bearings. A glimmer of hope surfaced in him. They had come up in the right place. City Pawn was even closer than he had thought.

They trudged through the ankle- and sometimes knee-deep snow along the sidewalk, passing by run-down liquor stores and 'adult novelty' shops. They walked past a bum, lying fetal against the side of an abandoned storefront. Trent suspected he was dead. Up ahead, he could make out the faint, snow-obscured outline of City Pawn.

They shuffled through the snow and reached the front door. City Pawn was always open—24 hours a day, every day, including holidays. Trent had often wondered when Charlie slept; he seemed to be the only employee. He knocked on the iron-barred door.

After a moment's silence, the door cracked open slightly. "Da?"

"It's Trent, Charlie. We need some help."

"Who?"

"Trent," he said and then added, "Hawkins. I was in here this morning."

There was a pause and then the door swung open.

"Mister Trent. Of course. I've been expectink your return." But Charlie's wide smile turned to a frown as he looked at the two of them. "You are lookink terrible, both of you. Come in, come in." He gestured for them to enter, brushing back a few wisps of white hairs that clung to his liver-spotted scalp as they followed him inside.

Charlie shut the door behind them and they basked in the warmth of the spacious store. After the long trek through the underground, Trent's eyes hurt to look at the array of fluorescent lights, but the sudden feeling of relief, of temporary sanctuary, was overwhelming. He fell into a heap in a nearby metal folding chair. Celia eyed them both warily and wandered over to the far end of the shop where the women's clothes were on display.

"Trent, what is happenink to you?" Charlie placed a strangely comforting hand on Trent's cheek. "You are very hurt."

Trent looked up at him, working hard to fight back tears. "It's a long story," he said. "Not even sure you'd believe me."

Charlie smiled. "I believink more than you know. Monsters, yes? Dark thinks in dark places?"

Trent blinked, astounded at the sudden turn in the conversation. "Uhh—" he stammered. "Yeah. Exactly."

The little man nodded and turned away. He moved across the shop to a small office space in the corner and brought back a ceramic mug of coffee for Trent. "Drink," he said. "It gettink cold out there."

"Susan's dead, Charlie. I lost her." He looked up, unashamed of the tears that he felt pulling at the corners of his eyes.

Charlie clucked quietly and shushed him. "No time for that now, please. You will see her again."

"What? How?" Trent threw the coffee cup at the floor. It shattered, spilling ceramic bits and brown fluid across the linoleum. Celia looked up in alarm from over by the jackets display.

"How will I fucking see her again? She's *dead*, Charlie!" He moved to stand, but Charlie pushed him back down into the chair.

"Calm, Mister Trent." He smiled warmly. "You just trust old Charlie on this one. She is strong woman. She is beink in dark place now, but you will see her again."

Trent shook his head, reeling with the sudden emotional pain that had enveloped him after the physical pain began to subside. "What do you know of 'dark places?' Who are you?"

Charlie pulled over a second metal chair and sat. "Who do you think I am?"

"Who is Salvatore? What the *fuck* is going on? Tell me, dammit!"

Charlie smiled sadly. "We are related, Zamagiel and I. And there are others, too. Others you have known. We all are choosink our paths through this world. I have chosen one, Zamagiel has chosen another." He leaned forward, placed a hand on Trent's shoulder and looked deep into his eyes. "What path is yours, Mister Trent?"

"Goddammit, *who* is Zamagiel?"

Charlie shook his head. "Zamagiel has taken poor Salvatore's life from him. Has made him do horrible thinks. Has sent him down a dangerous path." Charlie stared deep into Trent's eyes. Again, he asked, "What path is yours?"

Trent pulled back, uncomfortable with Charlie's intense stare. He noticed that the old Russian had very slightly mismatched eyes, like the two blond men he had seen in the shop earlier, only less obvious. He wondered why he had never noticed Charlie's strange eyes before. He thought about the old man's question.

"My path?" He looked over at Celia, who had put on one of the black leather women's jackets from the clothing rack. The green book that Trent had been interested in before now jutted from her jacket pocket. The sight of it made his spine tingle, though he had no idea why. A strange sort of envy rose up in him, but he fought it down and looked back at Charlie. He shook his head, resigned to the only plan he had come up with. "I just have to get her out of here, out of Las Vegas. If you can give me my bike back, my path leads out—anywhere but this fucking place."

Charlie looked saddened by his answer. He leaned back in his chair and ran a hand across the top of his bald head. "That is not a path, just an action. In Russia, they have sayink, 'You are fallink down if you sit between two chairs.' I think you should be findink your chairs first, Mister Trent, before you try to sit."

Trent frowned, frustrated by Charlie's cryptic ramblings. He just wanted to get out, to find some way to keep Celia safe, to grieve in peace, without shadow creatures and psychotic old men harassing him at every turn. "Look, can you just help us, Charlie? It's not safe here for her, or me. We have to get out."

Charlie scooted the chair back and stood up. He sighed. "I will help you. You can have your bike, though it will be hard to ride in this weather."

Trent thought about the bike. He hated the idea of driving through what seemed like a blizzard in the open, but it seemed the only option.

"It'll have to do." He glanced at Celia, who was looking at herself in a mirror. She had put on semi-torn blue jeans and a white, long-sleeve shirt beneath the leather jacket. "Can she keep the clothes? And can I get a gun, just in case?"

Charlie nodded. "What kind of gun are you needink?"

"Handgun." He knew that Charlie collected firearms, and had more than a few assault weapons in the locked back closet. "But something big, powerful."

Charlie opened the glass case behind the counter and withdrew an Israeli-made Desert Eagle, black with a brushed nickel grip. "Dot fifty," he said. "Very loud, very strong." He pulled out a couple of cartridges in cardboard boxes and stacked them on the counter next to the gun. "I am givink you all this because we are friends, Mister Trent. No other reason." He retrieved the motorcycle key from his pocket and tossed it onto the counter next to the ammo.

"Sure."

"Will you be promisink me one thing?"

"What?"

"Remember there are others in this place who are hurtink. Maybe you can be helpink them, too, if you find right chairs to sit in."

Trent shrugged. "Sure, I'll keep it in mind." He had no clue what Charlie meant. His purpose was singular: get the Hell out of Las Vegas. "Come on," he said to Celia. "Let's get going."

He gathered up the supplies, grabbed a long black coat off a rack for himself, and walked to the front door of the shop. "Thanks, Charlie," he said, as he pushed open the door.

They stepped out into the cold. The storm had grown in strength, now more of a precursor to a blizzard than merely a heavy snow. The streets, the sidewalks, the buildings, everything covered with a thick blanket of white that shone dully beneath the orange sodium streetlamps.

"Fuck," Trent exclaimed.

After a minute, Charlie came around the corner of the building, pushing a jet-black Ducati motorcycle, souped-up and flawless. "Here it is," he said. "Please be takink good care of her."

Trent wasn't sure if he meant Celia or the bike.

A sound came from his pocket, the voice of Johnny Cash singing through a tinny cellphone speaker. He fished the phone out and looked at the small screen. Unlisted number. He frowned, pushed 'answer' and placed the phone to his ear. Celia stood next to him, looking at him with a confused expression on her face. Trent noticed that her hand was gently caressing the green book jutting from her pocket.

"Hello?"

"Nice, Trent." The caller's tone dripped with sarcasm. "You answered your cellphone with the cops on your ass."

"Wait," he ventured, "is this—?"

The caller cut him off. "Shut up. Don't say my name, idiot. We need to talk. Come to my place. You know where, right?"

"Yeah, but—" Trent realized his voice was shaking. "We're— I'm leaving— I mean, I can't come there."

"You're not going anywhere. They've closed the Interstates and highways. You're stuck here like the rest of us. Don't you think it's funny the bad weather is only over Vegas?"

"Uhh—"

"I have answers for you. Get over here." And then the caller hung up.

As his sense of surprise wore off, it occurred to him that the caller had been right: he was stupid to still have the cellphone. He dropped it to the ground and then stepped down hard, crunching it to pieces beneath his boot. He stood, staring into the night, watching the falling snow.

"Who was that?" asked Celia, her voice muffled by the wind.

Trent took a long moment to mull over the never-forgotten name in his head. "Jack Mars," he answered, finally. "He owns a casino. Last time I saw him, he tried to kill me."

17

THE LAST PLACE TRENT WANTED to go was back to The Strip. Camera-heavy, well lit, a crowd-packed nightmare, exactly the worst place for an alleged kidnapper and his kid to be caught.

The snow was coming down fast now and the arctic cold had settled in with a vengeance. The wind came in heavy gusts, blowing over loose signs and knocking down the few tourists left trying to traverse the sidewalks. Trent marveled as he watched some of the people on the streets—the serial gamblers—locals who plodded on just the same, half of them probably trashed on drugs or booze, none of them wearing proper attire or even so much as caring about the impossible weather. They tromped along through the piles of snow and turned into their chosen casinos, houses of vice and ringing, cacophonous solace that never, ever closed down.

Trent turned the bike onto The Strip and headed south toward Sands Avenue. Jack had a small casino—The Inferno— near the corner of Sands and Paradise, a quieter, off-Strip location surrounded by ordinary businesses and low-rent apartments.

As the bike wheeled slow through the weather-stalled traffic, Trent gawked at the chaos. A few casino employees on break in front of the MGM Grand were pelting each other with snowballs, using the bridge that arced over the boulevard as an ersatz fort. The police had a group of looters up against the side of the neon-encrusted Walgreens, guns pointed at them while bags of merchandise and piles of broken glass sat quietly on the sidewalk in front of the closed store. The Bellagio fountains had already frozen over, and the big pool looked like an ice skating rink. The insipid Sirens show at Treasure Island had closed (thank God, Trent thought, with a grin) and the pirate ship rested silently in its frozen basin below the faux bombed-out Spanish building. The two neon N's on The Wynn had been knocked out, and now the sign simply asked, in fancy cursive neon, 'Wy.' Street preachers in front of The Venetian bore signs that read 'Jesus is coming!' and 'The End is Near.' Trent thought about how he used to believe the street preachers were crazy. Now he wasn't so sure.

He steered the Ducati down Sands Avenue, then into an alley a few blocks down that ran behind a number of the off-Strip casinos and thinly veiled brothels masquerading as nightclubs. He stopped next to a steel back door on a raised loading dock. It was normally used for loading casino profits into armored cars, but Trent knew that Jack also encouraged his more secretive clientele to come in through the back. Trent had been through that same door many times.

He and Celia walked up the platform steps and were met at the door by a pair of large guards, both wearing handguns.

"Who are you?" one of the guys asked.

"Trent Hawkins." He added, "To see Jack."

The bigger of the two, who hadn't yet spoken, cocked his head slightly and pressed a finger to a black ear bud.

"Okay, Jack is cool," he intoned in a rumbling bass.

The smaller guard reached back and opened the door without ever taking his eyes off Trent and Celia. "In."

They did as commanded, but before they could make their way inside, the smaller guard reached out and blocked Trent's passage with an arm.

"Armed?"

Trent remembered the Desert Eagle in the back of his waistband. He frowned, drew the weapon and handed it to the guard. The big man smiled and then let him pass.

The back entrance led first into a small hallway that bordered a kitchen on one side and a conference room on the other. The kind of conferences held there were usually of the breaking-bones variety. Trent had had one conference there. It was the last time he had seen Jack Mars.

He put a hand on Celia's shoulder as he led her down the hallway, past the conference room. The guard followed close. It made Trent feel a tiny bit better to note that Celia had tucked The Book discreetly into her new jacket.

The less time she spent staring at the thing, the better, he thought. *I'll have to take it away from her next time I get a chance.*

They walked into the kitchen. It was pretty standard as kitchens go and had a special card table set up in the back. Jack Mars had come from the city's seedy underworld and made it his business to cater to the same. Though the bulk of the Inferno casino was on the up-and-up, this back-kitchen table was reserved for one thing and one thing only: high-stakes poker between people who had a lot of money that they were not supposed to have.

Jack sat on the table, his feet dangling over the edge. He waited alone, sitting casually on the edge of the felt. The kitchen was otherwise empty.

"Well, look who's here?" Jack had a shit-eating grin on his face. "Come back for more, Trent?"

Jack was middle-aged, only a few years older than Trent. His hair, though, had gone white at an early age and was pretty thin in the front. He had a slight paunch, but was otherwise impeccably dressed in an open-collar blue dress shirt, black pinstripe sport jacket and black slacks. A pair of small round glasses perched precariously atop his nose, as though they had climbed up there of their own accord and then refused to leave.

Trent pushed Celia in front of him. He wanted to make sure Jack could see her. He wagered that Celia would be enough shield for the both of them.

"No trouble, Jack. Not in front of the kid."

"Abandoned your wife for someone younger, huh? That's not so legal, but I don't judge."

Trent seethed at Susan's mention, but held back his fury. He lied, "She's my niece. Celia."

"Nice to meet you, kid." Jack nodded and smiled disingenuously.

"So tell me, Trent. Why would you and your *niece* come willingly to a man like me? Didn't I say I'd kill you if I ever saw you again?"

"You called me, Jack." Trent shrugged. "Do you have some answers or what? How can we get out of here?" Trent glared at him.

Jack laughed. "I hear you're in some sort of trouble with the law. What did you do, Trent? Exactly who are you running from, besides the cops? Not me, apparently."

"I'm betting you already know."

Jack wagged a finger in caution. "No, no! No more betting between you and I." He grinned. "Besides, this is a legitimate business. I can't just have kidnappers and perverts hanging around. At least not the ones who've gotten on the wrong side of Johnny Law. Metro don't like me and I don't like them."

He winked at Celia.

"If you just called me here to harass me, I've got far worse things I can go deal with out there." Trent gestured toward the door.

Jack pretended to think and stared again at the ceiling, though Trent could tell that his mind was already decided. Instead of answering, he pulled a phone from his suit pocket and put it to his ear.

"Seems I have Mr. Trent Hawkins here." He shot Trent a wink. "Would you finally like to meet him at the table?" A few seconds of quiet, and then Jack hung up.

"Looks like you have a choice to make, Trent. You can play a friendly game of poker, and maybe learn a few things." He patted the table he was sitting on. "Or you can hit the streets and hope the cops don't find you and your lovely *niece*. Don't worry, I probably wouldn't tell them I saw you, at least not right away."

It had been years since Trent had played a poker game. He had sworn off gambling after the Gaming Control Board trashed him. The Inferno had been the last place to kick him to the curb, and he had left owing Jack Mars a large sum of money, though not because of any losses. Trent had never lost, and that was exactly the problem.

But, on the other hand, he decided, if Jack had some unique info—which he tended to have—then Trent wanted to know. Anything to find a solution to his current troubles. Something told him that Jack Mars wore more faces than the fake one he was fond of winking with. Trent reached for his wallet and then realized with dismay that he had left it at the apartment early that morning.

"Don't have any cash. I couldn't even make the first blind," he said.

The guard reached past Trent and Celia and handed the Desert Eagle to Jack. Jack eyed it with an admiring smile.

"My, this trouble you're in is serious, isn't it? I thought you used to say that you didn't need a gun for protection? How did you put it? 'I'm too lucky for guns.' Something like that, right?"

"Something like that," Trent mumbled.

It embarrassed him that he'd been so cocky. The statement had been true back then. A couple of nasty run-ins during his casino days where he *should* have been shot, but wasn't. His luck had saved his life on more than one occasion. But things had apparently changed.

Jack twirled the handgun by the trigger guard. "Maybe the gun's worth something, then. At least enough to get you into the first hand. With your *luck*—" Jack spit the word out like it tasted bad. "—I don't imagine you'll need much more starting cash than that."

Trent weighed his options. He could agree to the game and get at least a few hours of security for Celia and himself, or he could turn it down and head back out into the streets.

"Jack," he said finally. "No one gets in here without you knowing, right? You promise we'll be safe tonight if I play in your game?"

Jack nodded. "I suppose I should warn you, though." His grin turned devious. "You'll be playing against some very *interesting* opponents." He chuckled and added, "I'll treat you right. Bygones and all. On account of my *good nature*." He grinned at Celia lasciviously. "You don't even have to win tonight. As long as you play a good game, I promise no harm will come to you. Just give our honored guests your best game."

"Fine."

Trent had grown wary of Jack's sudden accommodating attitude, but they had no better offer.

One of the bouncers crept up and tapped Jack on the shoulder. He whispered something in Jack's ear and then gestured a meaty thumb toward the front of the casino. Trent could have sworn he heard the bouncer say the word 'blond,' but kept his mouth shut.

Jack frowned. "I have a pair of irritations to deal with," he said. "Game starts in one hour, when the others get here. Help yourself to anything in the kitchen." He made a sweeping gesture, then hopped off the table and headed for the front of the casino.

Trent watched him go and scowled. Celia saw it and spoke up for the first time since they had arrived.

"I don't like him." Her voice quivered.

Trent sighed. "Neither do I," he replied. "You'll just have to trust me here. Come on, let's get you some food."

They wandered around the kitchen for a few minutes, looking for anything edible. Jack had known there wasn't much here and knew they wouldn't dare venture out into the main part of the casino. There were often cops hanging around, undercover.

The Inferno had been connected to dozens of crimes, big and small, though none of those tenuous connections ever panned out. The cops liked to keep a presence near the casino at all times, just in case. Trent just hoped that Jack would keep his word and not sell them out.

In a small freezer they found an unopened plastic bag full of frozen, pre-cooked shrimp. He hauled it out, brushed off some of the ice, and stared at it in dismay. Celia grabbed it out of his hand and tore the bag open. Trent had not realized how hungry she was.

"Don't you want those heated up or something?"

"I've never had shrimp before," she mumbled, stuffing two in her mouth. "They're good cold."

"You've never had shrimp?"

"No," Celia replied, in between handfuls of the pink crustaceans. "Doctors were worried about my allergies. Just in case."

Trent's mind drifted to thoughts of Susan. He remembered holding her slim hand in the hospital, remembered finding out for the first time that they couldn't have children due to the experimental allergy drugs, remembered her smile when she awoke from the hospital painkillers, remembered her trembling body as she came down from the adrenaline shots. The memories flooded in and Trent forced himself to fight back tears.

"What are you allergic to?" he asked, trying hard to force his mind away from Susan.

Celia had already eaten three handfuls of shrimp and said, with mouth full, "Just the water thing. Something about cell counts."

"Water?"

"Yeah, makes my skin itch and my throat close up," she explained. "Sometimes worse, like last night." She frowned.

Trent nodded. So many strange things had happened in one day, but already certain ones were starting to add up in his mind. Salvatore's powers. Celia's allergy. Snow in Las Vegas. All of it water.

Celia finished gorging herself on shrimp and set the bag aside.

Trent marveled at how many she had already eaten. "You really tore through that bag."

"Sorry."

"No, it's fine. You're hungry. Eat all you want."

"Why does that guy Jack want to kill you?"

Trent sighed, "Long story."

Celia gave him a we've-got-all-night look.

"Yeah, so you know about my luck right?"

"I saw one of the TV specials about you. It was called— umm— the Undying Gambler. I think that's right..."

Trent had expected that, but still frowned. He remembered the nickname as the title of a made-for-TV special about him. It was one of the more famous ones, more for its ridiculousness than for its adherence to fact. For weeks after the plane crash, he had been a news headline—the only survivor of Flight 2778. For months after, a piece of nostalgia. He had even made it into mass-market trivia games.

"Yeah, that was me, I guess."

"You guess?"

"Well yeah, that show was based on me, but it was really stupid."

Celia shrugged. "My Mom watched everything about you. That crash really sucked. But then you were famous, so that was cool, right?"

Trent shook his head. "I just wanted everyone to leave me alone."

"Yeah?" Celia frowned. "I think being famous would be cool. So why does Jack want to kill you?"

"Oh, well I'm sure the show highlighted my gambling career, right?"

"Right."

"Jack was my last stop. Last game. Lots of big stakes international players. He wanted me to throw the game, turn my back and let this one asshole win. Man, I hated that guy..."

"So you won it anyway, just to piss him off?"

"Actually, I tried to throw it. I knew what Jack would do to me if I didn't. I had a terrible hand, so I bet a bunch of money on first street, then tried to fold before the flop. The big asshole got all pissed, wanted me to stay in. I could tell

Jack wanted me to stay in, too. Guy didn't want to win on a fold. He wanted to beat me with his hand."

"What hand did you have?"

"You know Texas Hold 'Em?"

"I go to public school in Las Vegas."

Trent chuckled. "Okay, I had a seven-three off-suit."

Celia wrinkled up her face in disgust. It was the cutest expression Trent had seen her make all day. "That *is* a bad hand."

"Yeah, so to make everybody happy I had to go all-in. Something like twenty million."

"Whoa!"

"Yeah. High stakes."

Trent paused and looked at the ceiling for a second, as if waiting for Heaven to deliver him from the rest of his bad memories.

"Anyway, Asshole went all-in too and the cards were turned over. Now, the funny thing is, I had known he had a better hand than three-seven. That's why I was trying to fold before the flop."

Celia was on the edge of the table with excitement. "So what did he put down?"

"Pocket aces."

"Oh, man!"

"Like I said, it wasn't hard to guess he had something good. It was written all over his face. So the dealer announces both hands and Asshole makes a big show of his, waving his arms to pump up the crowd that had gathered around the table. Serious show-boating."

"I bet you were pissed."

"Yeah. I had a lot of pride in my game. I was okay with a loss, but not a three-seven against pocket aces. That just made me look like a damn rookie."

"So let me guess, you got all sevens on the flop, right?"

Trent laughed. "No, that would have been interesting. But I think what happened was even worse. Dealer starts turning over cards. The flop comes out three-spades, six-diamonds, and I think there was a ten or something."

"So, Asshole—"

Trent frowned at her.

"Sorry." She rolled her eyes. "The 'big mean nasty guy'— that better?" She grinned at him.

Trent smiled.

She continued, "So the guy has pocket aces and you've only got a pair of threes?"

"Yeah. Dealer turns over fourth street and gets another ace, spades I think. Asshole wasn't even nervous. I had a low pair against his three aces. He was already shaking hands and dancing around the room like an idiot. That's when the dealer went to turn over the last card.

"I had a pair of threes and a useless seven in my hand. But before the dealer can turn fifth street, there's this huge bang and a casino spotlight drops onto the table, totally out of nowhere, lands right on my cards. Chips scatter all over the place. The whole room goes nuts. Jack Mars tries to declare a re-do but the Asshole won't have it. He wants to win with his pocket aces. Jack asks him if he's sure, but the guy insists."

Celia's eyes went wide.

"Strangest thing. I'm sitting there in my chair, knowing I should lose this hand, lose the game, knowing Jack will do something terrible if I win, but all I could think of was Susan. Some part of me wanted to win, wanted to take this hand, to show Asshole up and walk home with enough money to retire, to give Susan the life she really wanted, just us and a nice house somewhere..." Trent stared at the cold walls of the old kitchen, quiet for a moment.

"Anyway," he said, "I could have sworn I had a three-seven in my hand, but when they lift up the spotlight, there's a three-six sitting on the table."

Celia's mouth dropped open. "So you had two-pair, not one. Pair of threes and a pair of sixes!"

"Yeah, but still doesn't beat three aces—"

"But there's fifth street! The dealer hasn't turned it over yet, right?"

Seeing the excitement on the teenager's face made Trent feel better, somehow.

"Exactly. Except Jack tries again to declare a re-do when everyone sees the six. But Asshole won't have it. He still sees three-aces against a low two-pair and is dying to take down the 'unbeatable gambler.' Everyone quiets back down, the dealer turns fifth street, and—"

"Another six!" Celia exclaimed and clapped her hands together with glee. "Full house beats three aces!"

"Yeah, except he's got a full house too, aces over sixes. Beats my sixes over threes. Or at least that's what everyone swore he had. That's when we notice there's no ace on the table. Never was. Just another ten. So he's got two pair, aces and tens, but no full house."

"So you won!"

Trent nodded. "'Course, Asshole starts screaming, demands a re-match, accuses the dealer of cheating, accuses me, Jack, God, the Pope, you name it."

"So that's why Jack wants to kill you?"

"Yeah, he was pissed because it turns out Asshole was gonna sell Jack a bunch of property on The Strip. Jack would've been able to make the next huge resort-casino. Worth a fortune. But now the deal was off. Asshole backed out, screaming that Jack was a cheat and a liar. If it hadn't been for all the TV cameras, Jack would've killed me right there at the poker table. Instead, he dragged me into the 'Discussion Room' and..." Celia was eating up the story. "Well, I got away." He decided to omit the part of the story where Jack nearly tortured him to death.

"So that was my last game," he said. "Susan and I tried to retire, but Jack got the GCB on me and they slapped my name all over the blacklists. No more poker."

"Until tonight," she said.

"Funny how things work out, huh? You always think that being the luckiest man alive would be a *good* thing."

Celia stared at him. One eye narrowed slightly and she cocked her head to the side. She eyed his face carefully and then spoke, with the utmost seriousness.

"I don't think you're very lucky at all," she said.

His smile vanished. Through the telling of the story, he had gotten himself worked up, excited by the adrenaline rush his lucky wins used to bring. Now he found himself spiraling back down, plummeting back to the firm ground of despair. He forced a fake smile to cover up the sudden loss of the real one.

"Neither do I," he replied.

Celia wrapped her arms around him and buried her face in his neck. Trent's heart felt hollow, empty. He had been dead for so long; ever since the crash. Only the moments with Susan had made him feel that spark of life, and now she was gone too. He knew that he would do anything to get her back, if he could. He wished for a moment that he could reverse time and set everything back the way it had been, before Celia and the hospital, before Salvatore, before the black shadow-thing.

But I guess that's what life is, he thought. *A series of moments that slam into you whether you're expecting them or not. It's a crapshoot, and everyone's just hoping to get lucky.*

He ran his hand through Celia's hair and thought about his own little sister, who had died in a car accident the year before. It was as if life had moved on around him after he'd fallen from the plane. As if he'd already died but no one had figured it out yet. Only Susan had stayed. Only Susan had kept hold of his hand all this time.

And now there was just this teenage girl, a sudden orphan who desperately needed a real father, not an old, washed-up gambler on the lam. He looked around the kitchen. Celia needed a real life, but they wouldn't find it in an empty casino kitchen. And if they kept running, they'd be running from death forever.

He gritted his teeth as she rested her head on his neck, eyes closed. She needed a better life than this. The running had to stop. He needed to set things stable, once and for all.

18

"OH, WELL WONTCHA LOOK AT that, guys? How sweet!"

Trent snapped to attention as a scrawny, pasty-faced fellow came in through the back door. Others followed behind. The scrawny man had an angular face and a shock of thinning hair that rested uneasily atop his scalp, a sort of oily black hair-creature, ready to escape backwards off his head at the next opportunity. His face was screwed up into a mocking sneer.

"See, I told you guys." He looked over his shoulder at the others and then pointed at Trent and Celia. "Guy has some dark secrets in his closet. I just didn't figure pedophilia was one of them."

Celia glanced at Trent with a hurt look on her face. He responded by rolling his eyes. He untangled from her arms and hopped down from the stainless steel kitchen table.

"She's my niece."

"To each their own, I always say." The scrawny guy shrugged and approached. "Sins can be a lot of fun, right?" He extended a hand, offering a handshake.

Trent didn't take it. "Let's just play some poker. Get this over with."

The scrawny guy clapped Trent on the side of the arm. "Just playing with ya, friend. If you say she's your niece, then she's your niece." He gestured behind himself. "And I guess you could say this is *my* extended family."

The last of the players had come in through the back door. He was a huge guy, muscle-bound and bald, with skin as black as night. He shut the door and locked it. From the opposite side of the kitchen, Jack Mars' voice floated through the cold air.

"Gentlemen!" he announced. "And lady, of course—" He bowed as he approached, then took the hand of the one female player, a voluptuous, red-haired beauty. Jack's tone grew quieter and he kissed the woman's hand. "You so rarely grace us with your presence, Miss... Barrister, is it now?"

The woman raised an eyebrow and nodded. Innuendo floated across her expression like a pianist's fingers across a grand piano.

Jack coughed, straightened his collar, and placed a hand on Trent's back. "Meet Trent Hawkins, everyone. I'm sure you've heard of him."

No one smiled. Nothing was said. The sudden quiet set Trent's nerves on edge. He broke it by introducing Celia.

"...his *niece*," the scrawny guy added, shooting Trent a wink.

Jack continued with the introductions as he collected jackets from each of the players. "Of course, this is Tricia Barrister."

The redhead smiled and held out her hand. Instead of taking her hand, Trent reached up and tipped his hat. She looked a little put-off as she withdrew her dainty fingers, instead using them to slide her black, fur-topped long coat from her shoulders.

Jack draped it over his arm and nodded to the giant man, who wasn't wearing any sort of jacket, just black slacks and a mustard yellow dress shirt that seemed about to rip under the strain of his incredible musculature. Trent figured he had to be a boxer or weight lifter.

"Damon Parrish," Jack said.

Trent reached out a hand, which Damon grasped. His fingers were as cold as metal.

"Most call me Steel."

His voice came out rough and filled with chunks of iron that rattled together as he spoke. The nickname made Trent imagine him as a steelworker.

"This," said Jack, giving a short bow to a thin, old, bald man in a three-piece suit, "is the most esteemed Sir Vladimir Nikoli Chyrmov."

Vladimir nodded.

"And finally—" Jack moved over next to the scrawny guy. "You've already met Snake."

"Snake?" asked Trent.

"That's my name, lucky boy. Ladies love it."

"Nice to meet you."

"It's an honor," Snake replied. His tone seemed less than genuine. "Are we gonna gab all night or play some cards?"

They headed for the front of the casino. Trent held back.

"I can't go out there, Jack. The cops—"

"The cops won't see a thing," Jack explained. "I've made sure the security systems are off and the undercover cops that normally work the place have been paid to turn their backs, just for tonight. Just don't tell any of my other guests. I wouldn't want anyone to get any ideas."

Trent felt a wave of paranoia rising. He had never expected Jack Mars to have that level of power. Sure, he was a successful casino owner, but paying off undercover cops? There was more going on here than Trent had assumed.

The table they finally settled on was a lush, real wood-paneled affair—not the standard synthetic wood or even plastic like most of the other tables. The felt surface was crisp and fade-free. It looked new. Every hair of felt was aligned just so, as if it had been hand-combed. The dealer was a tall, middle-aged man with a blond moustache and goatee.

"Gentlemen," he welcomed. "And Lady." A slight nod to Tricia. She took a seat.

Trent looked around the table as he pulled his chair up. He noticed that Celia, who hadn't left his side but didn't have a chair, was eyeing the other players. Tricia had seated herself to Trent's left, a little bit closer to him than comfortable for a table of this size. Snake had pulled up a chair backwards and was leaning over the top. He was on Trent's right. Next to Snake was the muscle man, Steel. His mouth was an impassive, thin line. Directly across the table from Trent, to Steel's right, was Jack. Trent was surprised to see him taking a seat. He had never seen Jack play. He wondered idly if Jack was any good at poker, or if he was filling in for someone who couldn't make it. To Jack's right, completing the table, was Vladimir. His old, frail form looked comical in the high-backed chair, and his upper body slumped forward ever so slightly. Trent wanted to reach over and straighten the old man up, but resisted.

Vladimir spoke first, as the dealer shuffled the cards. His voice was a weak, quiet rasp that made Trent lean closer. "Trent, I should explain that Mr. Mars would not normally be playing, but over the last several years, our good friend Ramón has found that he is increasingly less capable of joining our little game. We like to keep a fixed number of players, so Mr. Mars was kind enough to fill in."

Trent shrugged. He wanted to ask what had happened to Ramón, but he decided to leave it be. "Sure."

Vladimir stared at Trent for a moment and then said, quietly, "Please remove your hat at the table, Mr. Hawkins. It is—" He paused for what seemed like an eternity, as if he were searching through thousands of words for the perfect one. He finally settled on, "—inappropriate."

Trent, flustered, mumbled out an apology and pulled the cowboy hat from his head. He handed it to Celia and whispered that she should go sit in one of the chairs farther away from the table. Celia grumbled, but acquiesced.

"Now," Vladimir continued, with a weak smile that reminded Trent of a corpse in repose. "Let us begin."

The dealer introduced the rules: no limit Texas Hold 'Em with a standard double blind. All of the players except Vladimir and Trent reached into their pockets and produced some form of money. Tricia produced a crisp stack of bills and placed it delicately in the center of the table. Jack did the same. Snake, however, pulled out a small brown leather bag. He tossed it onto the table and it landed with a jingle that suggested coins. Everyone glanced at him. Vladimir raised a withered eyebrow, the folds of skin around his eye pulling up with it.

"What?" Snake responded. "They're worth a million. Count it if you don't believe me!"

"No need," said Vladimir. "We will trust you." He narrowed his eyes. "This time."

Trent thought it was an odd exchange, but was even more shocked to see Steel's payment, a pure, crystal clear diamond, cut to perfection.

Tricia's smile grew and her eyes widened. "Very nice, Damon. I should like to take that with me tonight."

Snake interrupted, "Yeah, not with your poker skills, gorgeous."

Tricia gave the scrawny man a look that might have set his wispy hair aflame.

They all stared at Trent.

Jack Mars spoke up on his behalf. "Mr. Hawkins has offered a collector's-grade handgun as collateral."

Snake shot back, "Well that gun better be made of solid gold! Come on, I thought he was a rich gambler?"

"Ex-gambler," mumbled Trent. He looked at Jack, who ignored him.

"Trent is my guest tonight. Besides, that isn't why we're here together, now is it?"

"No," answered Vlad.

Jack tossed the Desert Eagle onto the pile of objects in the middle of the poker table. The cold metal grip gleamed beneath the bright table lights.

Snake shrugged. "Yeah, money's not important. That piece of shit will do fine, Hawkins." He shot the ex-gambler another shit-eating grin.

"Great." Trent reached into his shirt pocket for his cigarettes. He realized with some surprise that he hadn't had a smoke in hours. He also remembered that his cigarette pack was gone.

Jack saw him fumbling and offered him one from a small silver case. "On the house."

"Thanks." Trent took a puff and blew smoke through his nostrils. He chuckled. "Never thought I'd hear those words from you."

"There's a lot you don't know about me."

"Yeah?"

Jack ignored the question and turned instead to the table. "Let's begin."

The dealer fed them round one. Each player got two cards, facedown. Then there would be some betting and three community cards dealt face up, called the 'flop.' More betting, then a fourth card. Finally, more betting, a fifth card, and the final round of bets. It all added up to a lot of money, especially in a no-limit game.

Each player received one million in chips. Trent figured it would get interesting real fast.

He peered under his two facedown cards. A king of clubs and a seven of diamonds. Not a great hand, but the king might be playable. He decided to stay in, at least until the flop.

Steel, his face an impassive mask, folded immediately. Everyone else stayed in and the flop was dealt. The dealer announced it: "King of spades, four of clubs, jack of clubs."

The king on the table made Trent's hand a strong one. "Raise two-thousand," he announced.

Snake laughed and rolled his eyes. "Come on, best you got is a pair of kings! You know I have pocket jacks and there's one on the table. But hey, if you wanna gimme money..."

Snake called.

Trent figured that if Snake really had something, he would've raised. The little bastard was bluffing. And, as Trent predicted, everyone else folded out. No pocket aces in this crowd.

The dealer flipped over the fourth card and announced: "Fourth Street. Four of hearts."

It would have been a nice turn for someone holding onto a four, but everyone had folded. Everyone but Snake. He was the question mark. Trent decided to goad him a little.

"If you wanna back out now, Snake, go ahead. I won't tell anyone."

"Well, look here!" Snake feigned surprise. "We've got us a table funny-man!" He nudged Steel. "Did you see that, buddy? Mr. Hawkins thinks he's a fucking comic! I'll raise you four thousand!"

Steel didn't respond.

Snake had made a big production of his raise. Trent was increasingly certain that the smaller man didn't have much of anything. "See your four thousand," he said with confidence and pushed another stack of chips to the middle. "Raise another two."

Snake grew quiet. "See your two. Raise you four more, you fuckin' chump."

The sudden silence at the table made Trent nervous. Snake couldn't have pocket aces, could he? He decided to call, rather than raise. Best not to lose all of his money on the first hand.

The dealer turned over the fifth and final card: "The River. Six of spades."

Trent, still shaken by the quiet, decided to check. It was a coward move at this point, but he felt uneasy about the situation. Snake, naturally, took advantage of his cowardice.

"Check, huh? Here's a six thousand raise. You wanna just give me that money or what?"

"Call," Trent replied, sliding his own six thousand dollars worth of chips to the middle of the table.

There was a dead silence as Snake stared at him, willing Trent to show his cards first. Trent took the dare and turned his over. "Two kings, Snake. You got anything better?"

Snake grinned. "Six, six, and— Oh, look! There's a six on the table! I think that makes *three*, right?" He feigned a goofy cowboy accent and winked at Tricia in mock naiveté. "Don't three beat a pair?"

Tricia rolled her eyes and looked away, turning to Trent instead. "I'm sorry, beautiful. He's always like this when he gets a devil's hand." Her voice was sultry, whispering, but her breath stank of sulfur and kerosene.

Trent turned away, trying his best to ignore her. He was not mad at Snake, but he was definitely shaken. Playing in on a lowly pair of sixes was one thing, but holding onto it and re-raising all the way to the river? It wasn't just a gutsy move—in some circles, it was considered insane.

"You probably think I'm crazy, huh?" Snake replied as if he could read Trent's mind. "But you just bet against the wrong guy."

"Yeah?" Trent hadn't been mad before, but this was pushing it a little. "What makes *you* so special?"

"Simple. Oh, and let this be your very first lesson about these things," Snake glanced at his companions as if seeking approval for what he was about to say. No objections were voiced, so he continued. "Never, ever, *ever*—under any circumstances—bet against a demon holding a pair of sixes." He tossed the two sixes onto the table, where they landed neatly beside the third. "They'll never fold, and they'll *always* get that last six. That's just how it goes."

And that's when Trent realized that every pair of eyes around the table was staring at him. Each glowed a deep, blood red.

After a moment's hesitation, he reacted. He leapt from his chair and tried to back away from the table, but instead knocked the chair over and stumbled, crashing to the floor on his backside. From the corner of the room, Celia gasped, but remained motionless. Tricia reached down and placed an elegant hand on Trent's outstretched knee.

"Honey, don't be concerned," she said. "At least not yet." She winked.

Trent found himself immediately entranced by her eyes. Though blood red like the others, he could lose himself in that crimson sea and let his fear be carried away by the waters. He awkwardly returned to his feet and righted the fallen chair.

Steel spoke, his low voice resonating through the quiet air. "Aren't we here to play poker?"

"Yes, indeed," added Vladimir. "Take your seat, young man. There are many hands to be played yet."

Trent felt as though he were in a trance. He glanced at Celia. She had her hands clamped over her mouth in fear. He found himself unable to resist as Tricia laid a hand on his shoulder and eased him back into his chair.

"There, now. All is well, my beautiful man."

"Come on, come on! Stop jerking him off, Trish," whined Snake. "Dealer! Next hand!"

The dealer, oblivious to the goings-on, dealt the next round of cards. With a shaky hand, Trent peered beneath his two. An ace of spades and a ten of diamonds. It was a good hand, but all he could think about was demons, Salvatore, the shadow-spider, and those arms from the cloud that Celia had conjured, arms that thrashed and twisted and clawed at the air. The day, it seemed, had gone from bad to worse.

His voice shaking, Trent muttered, "Call."

Snake, disgusted, flipped his cards back at the dealer. One of the cards, spinning horizontal, bounced off the dealer's chin. He didn't move or make any indication that he had noticed the slight. Everyone else stayed in.

The flop came and turned up another ace, a king, and a jack. Tricia led the betting, but folded immediately. Vladimir, his face impassive, pushed ten thousand dollars worth of chips into the pot.

"Trent," he said quietly. "We have been watching you for some time."

Trent didn't know how to respond, so he kept his mouth shut.

Jack and Steel both folded under the weight of Vladimir's massive bet. It was back around to Trent.

Vladimir pondered his cards while he talked. "You seem... an *anomaly* to us. None were given the knowledge of fate and chance save Baraqel and Ramiel, and they fathered no children."

With a shaky hand, Trent pushed a matching ten thousand chips across the table to call Vladimir's bet. "I don't understand."

Everyone else was out of the hand, so the next bet fell once again on Vladimir. The dealer turned over the fourth card on the table.

"Ace of hearts."

That gave Trent three aces, a very strong hand. He watched carefully to see what Vladimir would do, though his own thoughts were still preoccupied.

Vladimir, without hesitation, pushed another ten thousand into the pot.

"Oh, but I think you *do* understand," he said quietly. "There is more to your 'luck' than simple chance."

Trent was amazed at Vladimir's play, although with an ace, king, and jack on the table, it was not out of the question that Vladimir had turned an ace-high straight right from the flop. It would explain the old man's—old demon's—tenacious betting. Trent called, matching with another ten thousand.

Vladimir smiled weakly, peered beneath his cards, and then locked eyes with him. "You know what I have. But yet, you are going to win this hand, aren't you?" He pushed another ten thousand dollars in, despite his statement.

Trent, still shaken, mumbled, "I don't know what you mean."

But he *did* know exactly what the demon meant. And it had occurred to him that this was a moment where he could put the fix in—where he could *take* the win, even if he didn't rightly deserve it. This was the kind of hand that he had won a thousand times over, when his chance at the win was virtually nonexistent. This was the kind of hand that had gotten him blacklisted.

"Call." He matched the ten thousand. Sixty thousand dollars in the pot. Not enormous for a million dollar game, but still not a small pile of cash.

"Dealer," Vladimir said quietly. "Let us see the next card."

Trent knew it could naturally go only one way if he were to win the hand. The dealer had to draw the sole remaining ace in the deck, giving Trent four aces. But yet, that was not how it was going to go. This was the unnatural anomaly that Trent had never been able to explain—the aspect of his strange luck that perplexed him, enraged opponents, and baffled casino security. His nerves on-edge, he waited for what was about to happen.

"Three of clubs," the dealer said, as he turned over the last card.

Snake mumbled something inaudible to Steel.

Vladimir frowned as he surveyed the array of cards on the table. He didn't bother to look at his own facedown cards.

"Perhaps I was wrong about you."

He pushed another stack of ten thousand chips into the pot. Trent knew then that he was going to take this hand. He didn't know how he knew, but he knew. He could feel the win, burning in his ribcage, but he didn't want to make a huge show of it, not this early in the game, and especially not with the unique nature of his opponents. Instead of a raise, he limped to the finish line with a call and quickly turned his own cards over.

"Three aces."

"I'm sorry, Trent. Perhaps your luck is not as it seems. Perhaps you are no longer the luckiest man alive."

Vladimir used a withered finger to tip his two cards over, face-up. A king and a queen. Vladimir only had a pair of kings, not a straight. As he viewed his cards, he raised a thin eyebrow in curiosity.

"Holy shit," said Snake.

Vladimir raised a hand for silence. His raspy voice came out quiet and slow as he addressed Trent. "You knew that I had the straight before, didn't you?"

Trent *had* assumed a straight in Vladimir's hand. Years of poker had left him with a knack for predicting the cards, but unlike most gamblers, Trent could actually do something about it. The one strange caveat to his odd luck was the occasional ability to affect change—the rare moment that surfaced when Trent found himself able to bend reality to his will. Normal gamblers never noticed, their minds seemingly content to accept the new reality without question. But these players—demons, apparently—could spot the change.

Trent shrugged. "Well, I guessed that's what you had. I didn't expect you'd bet so strong otherwise."

"He has the gift," said Steel. "The Prophecy is true."

He spoke infrequently, but when he did, it seemed to carry significant weight with the other players.

Jack Mars grinned. "See, Vlad. That's why I banned him. Don't know how he does it. Maybe Baraqel had some kin after all?"

"No," replied Vladimir without hesitation. "There have only been two creatures in twelve-thousand years who could command this manner of change. The Prophecy is impossible. Unless..." The old man seemed lost in thought.

The dealer had already pulled and re-shuffled the cards. He pushed the large stack of chips in front of Trent. "Congratulations, sir."

"Uh...thanks."

The dealer began to distribute the next round of cards.

Jack shook his head, still looking at Vladimir. "You don't think—?"

"It would be very unusual. But many things are possible."

Trent built up enough courage to ask, "What?"

Vladimir turned to him, his face deadly serious and his eyes glowing bright red.

"When we are done here tonight, there is one you should speak to. But we will discuss this more in time. For now, there are things you have earned the right to understand."

"Oh," was all Trent could think of to say.

The play continued around the table.

"This world is older than most believe," Vladimir began. "And far more dangerous. What have you learned of religion, Trent?"

Trent shrugged. "Not much. Just what they taught me in Sunday school."

Vladimir suddenly changed topic. "You seem to be traveling with a dangerous companion."

Trent glanced at Celia. He felt bad about all the things she had had to witness today, all the nightmares come true.

"Yeah, I guess," he replied. "That old man's been hunting her all day. And that spider thing is after me. One of your friends?"

"Oh?" Vladimir seemed surprised. He turned to Jack, "You didn't say they had been running from a Render."

"I thought they were just running from the cops and the grig," Jack replied. He looked at Trent. "You know, Metro thinks you're the kidnapper."

Trent nodded. "Yeah, I'd gathered."

"So, wait," said Snake, with a sly grin on his face. "She's *not* your niece? Oh, this gets even *better*!"

"Quiet, Snake!" Vladimir shot back. "If she is as I suspect, then you're running from Zamagiel. That is his true name."

Trent recognized it as the name Charlie had mentioned. "Goes by Salvatore now," he murmured.

Vladimir smiled. "In his current body, perhaps. I pity the poor, unfortunate soul whose life he has usurped, though I'd imagine he hasn't forgotten who he is, and who he was. But your fate is greater than his, Trent. If you are who you seem to be, then you will destroy him for us." Vladimir's red eyes narrowed to tiny slits. "And you will continue to do our bidding, to cleanse the world of more of his kind. The Prophecy foretells it."

Trent hated being told what to do. It was a character trait he had picked up from his adoptive father.

"I've already taken him down. He's bleeding out as we speak. And the only people I did it for was her"—he aimed a finger at Celia— "and my wife, Susan."

Vladimir shook his head. "He's not as easy to destroy as that." He frowned. "And what makes you think the death of Zamagiel will end all of this? Is revenge ever that simple?"

"It can't hunt us anymore if it's dead."

"But others will. Zamagiel and his associates are raising an army. An *army*, Trent. They intend to take this earth— from you, from us, from everyone. It will become a place of shadow, a place of unnamed horrors. They will bring about the End Times, and the Great War will leave this place in ruin. Everything you see, everything you love, will be gone."

Trent spoke quietly. "Everything I love is already gone."

"Gone, Trent? Or sacrificed?"

Trent snorted, but refused to answer. Instead, he opted to counter with his own question. "Then why don't *you* kill him— all of them— whatever? You're demons, right? You deal with this!"

Vladimir sat back in his chair and sighed. "There are rules. There have only been two wars in Heaven, and both were quite terrible."

The others stopped playing cards. Even the dealer stood back from the table. Trent noticed that Snake's head bowed slightly, his eyes closed. Tricia drummed her fingernails on the table, not impatient, but nervous.

Vladimir's eyes narrowed. "Many of us were destroyed for what we believed. And when the War ended, God decreed that no more would an angel be permitted to destroy another. The punishment is eternal execration in the places of shadow. Only when the next war comes will any of us willingly enter into combat with those of our own kind. For now, a mortal must fulfill the Prophecy. It has been written thus."

"So you think I'm your loophole, huh? You get me to fight your battles by proxy so you don't go to jail? That's honorable."

Tricia winked at him. Her voice was a whisper of nostril-burning cinnamon and rotten eggs. "We never said we were honorable."

Trent sniffed, trying to clear his sinuses of the pungent aroma. "So what if I say no? What if I walk away from all of this? What if I leave?"

"Do as you wish." Vladimir shrugged. "Zamagiel will cleanse this place in his mad quest to restore the Garden. And then the War will break upon the mortal shores. You and Celia will be running for the rest of your short lives, as will all of the others of her ilk."

"Others?"

Vladimir raised an eyebrow.

"You think she's the only one of her kind? Many of the *grigori* children are awakening. And every last one of them will be hunted and captured. Many will be killed. Those who are not will join in willing or unwilling allegiance with their Watcher ancestors. An army, Trent—they will first bring forth an army of power-hungry *grigori* and *abaddi*, the shades from the Realms of Darkness. And then the *grigori* will enlist their twisted children and scions of mortals weak-willed enough to bend to their seductive words. An army you will have to face, whether you like it or not."

"Why now? Thousands of years and you're just now getting around to starting your third war?"

"This war has been raging quietly for millennia. But true Armageddon looms when Man begins to lose faith. And Man has lost so much faith. Look around you. How many of your kind would bend to a voice that offers them untold power? How many of your kind followed Hitler? Stalin? Milosevic? Hussein? How many of your children slaughter each other in the streets? How many, Trent?"

By the end of his speech, Vladimir was nearly shouting and had risen a little from his seat. He relaxed and settled himself. His voice grew quiet and raspy again.

"I would imagine it comes as no surprise that things in this world have reached a tipping point. Your strange gift may permit you to tip things in the favor of your race, a situation that would also favor ours."

Trent spent a long minute considering. The others resumed play. He didn't like being used, and it was all a bit much to swallow. But after the things he had seen in only a handful of hours, it was hard to ignore Vladimir's words, and those red, red eyes.

They had reached the end of a round of cards and Trent quietly turned his cards over to reveal a pair of jacks. Everyone else at the table turned over theirs to find something only marginally worse. Trent eyed each of the demons carefully.

His voice was tired. "And why should I join your side, the side of the demons? How are you any better than the *grigori*, the Watchers? Or these 'shades?' And what about the angels? Some of them are left, right? Shouldn't I join *them*?"

"The Watchers have allied with the Realms of Shadow. Together, they seek no less than the destruction of your world. They will fill this place with black nothing, and the dark ones will pour across the face of the earth. We, the pride-fallen, are content with the current status quo. We see no purpose in destroying this place or its inhabitants."

Vladimir sneered. "And as for the so-called angels— I do not believe you will want to meet them. Your race has ruined the world they sought to preserve. I think you will find them far less *accommodating* than we. They do not trust your kind any longer."

"Doesn't God have something to say about all of this?"

"God." Vladimir paused for a moment, considering the question. "God, in His infinite wisdom, permits the cards to fall as they may. His purposes, His motives, are inscrutable and unknowable. And all of us have a hand to play."

The dealer finished shuffling the deck and began to distribute the final round of the game.

Vladimir continued, while peering beneath his newly dealt cards. "As is often the case in this world, you must play the hand that you are dealt."

Trent looked beneath his cards. He had been dealt a pair of sixes.

"There are things, Mr. Hawkins, which you will need to come to terms with if you intend to confront one such as Zamagiel." The old man pondered his cards. "And then there are the Realms of Shadow, which your prophets called 'Abaddon.' It is the only place between Heaven and Hell that God will not judge in the final days. It is the place where all mortals go upon death, before they are chosen to go above or below. Those who are not chosen, remain in the shadows forever."

"Purgatory?" Trent muttered.

"In a sense, yes, but it is more than simply a waiting room for mortal afterlife. There are things in that place that are truly incomprehensible. And the *grigori* have established deals with the Prince of Shadow, deals that enable them to bring the foul creatures into this world. And the Prince himself sends his own hunters to this plane—"

Snake interrupted. "You actually survived a fight with a Render?"

"Yeah. Two, actually."

Snake nodded, looking impressed. "It's a kind of shade. Things are really good at sniffing out *gibbori*, Watcher-kids." He gestured at Celia. "Like your chicky over there. Can smell 'em for miles away."

"It was after me, I think."

Vladimir cut back into the conversation. "I highly doubt it," he said. "But in either case, it must be destroyed."

"Will bullets work?"

To Trent's surprise, Steel answered, his iron-filled voice booming, "God created all things in this world. He left these things for Lucifer to name. Lucifer, preoccupied with his creation of Adam, failed at this task. Those beasts that went unnamed were lost to the shadows. But they are still creatures."

"They can harm it, can send it back to the Realms of Shadow for a time," replied Vladimir, frowning. "But they cannot end it. Only fire or an angel's blade can do that. Trent, you must understand fully what is happening here. As I said before, this is a war and you cannot fight it alone, no matter how many bullets you carry."

"So I should choose your side. You've made that pretty clear already."

"That choice remains to be seen. It is one you will have to make." He paused and then turned toward Celia. "It is a choice *she* will have to make as well."

From beneath the momentary silence, Celia cried out, her voice strained, full of anger and horror and grief.

"What am I?!" she screamed, her eyes squeezed shut, tears streaming down her face. "Am I a *monster*?!"

She began to sob, momentarily exhausted by the question. But another wave of fury rose in her, even as tears rolled down her cheeks. "Tell me!" she yelled.

The outburst shocked Trent to silence. All around the table suddenly seemed on-edge. All except Vladimir, who stood slowly from his chair and faced the corner of the room where Celia wept. He raised his voice louder than it had been at any time during the evening.

"My child, you are first a mortal. One of the Race of Man. But what you will become—" He paused, searching for the exact words that should come next. "That is for you to choose." He whirled on Trent then, anger in his eyes. "But know this! You have a part to play in this war, Mr. Hawkins. Whatever your choice, the Prophecy has been written, and you seem to fit the riddles. You are involved, whether you like it or not."

"And what if we don't want to be on your side of the war?" Trent stood up from his seat to face Vladimir on his own level. He leaned in. "What if I destroy Zamagiel and then walk away, from all of this, from you, from the demons, from the *grigori*, from your ancient war? What will you do to me then? Kill me?"

Vladimir's hand shot forward, striking Trent square in the forehead. The hand was withered, pale, and ended in claws. The blow to Trent's head knocked him backwards, sending the chair clattering to the floor and Trent with it. In a flash, Vladimir was above him, his desiccated grip wrapped around the fallen man's wrist.

"See, Trent Hawkins! Look at what you see!"

As Trent felt the cold, brittle nails digging into his wrist, he saw Vladimir's *true* countenance. He could see the glowing red eyes even brighter, and a distended, angular spine strained against the fabric of the old man's clothing. Worst of all was the smell. He could taste the odor of fire and smoke and ash emanating from him. The new vision struck a chord of primal fear. Trent yelled and squeezed his eyes shut as hard as he could muster. He wrested his hand from Vladimir's grasp.

When he opened his eyes again, all seemed normal. Vladimir looked human, though his eyes still bore the faint red tint.

"I have given you a gift, Trent. Touch the flesh and you will know the truths behind the masks. So many things in this world are not as they seem. Today, you have seen a creature of shadow, a *grigori*, a handful of demons and a *gibborim* child, though I assure you there are plenty more of each. And there are other sides to this war, sides you have yet to meet. This is more than simply the *grigori* hunting their children. There are those who hunt us and there are those who will be hunting you as well."

He growled from deep within his vein-laced throat.

"And they will have you, Mr. Hawkins. They will catch you and they will destroy you. And they will take her—" He pointed a finger at Celia. "—to places I would rather not discuss. Realms even such as we would dare not traverse. Do you understand?"

Vladimir's strike had drawn blood from Trent's bottom lip. Trent used his right hand to wipe away a smear of blood. "Yeah," he growled. "What do I do next?" His bravado fought against trembling fear, leaving Trent mostly paralyzed.

The anger drained from Vladimir's face and was replaced by a thin smile. "I have told you enough. The rest you must learn from Ramón. He has been waiting to talk with you for quite a long time."

Trent shook his head in frustration. "Alright, so where is this Ramón?" He realized then that Celia had made her way out of the corner and over to his side. Her head was down and her fists were clenched and shaking.

Snake spoke up. "Let's end the game. I'll draw you a map before we leave."

Trent grumbled, righted his chair, and sat back down at the table. Celia came over to stand by his side, still trembling with fear and anger.

Vladimir said quietly, "In a way, I feel pity for you both. This must be very hard to understand all at once. And I fear that Ramón will give you even more to consider."

Trent mumbled, "What is he gonna tell me that'll trump all this?"

"As I said before, sometimes you have to work with the hand you have been dealt. But this is a game to which you have yet to learn all the rules. Ramón will help you read your cards."

Trent went all-in, forcing everyone else to match him or fold out. They all stayed in. Somehow, he wasn't surprised when he pulled that third six.

"Yeah? Well I've been dealt a devil's hand, so fuck you."

Vladimir looked up at Trent then, his eyes sagging in their sockets. He looked sad. "As you see, sometimes things are not as they seem. And sometimes they are."

There was grumbling all around as the demons stood up from the poker table and the dealer collected the cards.

Trent turned to Jack and said, "Keep the money. Now I don't owe you shit."

Jack broke into an evil grin and turned away in order to escort his companions to the back door.

Snake lagged behind. He stared at Trent and Celia for a moment and then chuckled. "Knowledge is a real bitch."

Trent met Snake's snaggletoothed grin, but said nothing.

Snake shrugged. "Yeah, anyway, so here's a map to Ramón's place." He pulled a neatly drawn map from his pocket and shoved it into Trent's hand. He turned to leave and then paused, spun back around and tossed Celia an apple that had appeared in his hand.

"Here. You might get hungry later." He ran off, shouting, "Hey, wait up!"

Trent and Celia stood amidst the ringing cacophony of the casino. She stared at the shiny red apple in her hand. As a test, Trent closed his eyes and tried to summon the fiery sensation he had felt previously. He opened his eyes again, reached out, and brushed a hand across Celia's exposed neck.

His heart sank. There had been no hallucinating. Celia's form had taken on a new hue, her skin tinged blue-white. She stank of sea salt. Water. Always water.

Trent knew that Vladimir had spoken truth, though cryptic and likely incomplete. And now, he had the ability to see the truth whenever and wherever he needed. He thought it the sort of enlightenment that only a fool might desire.

He turned to Celia as the last of the players disappeared through the back door of the kitchen, leaving only Jack Mars standing there alone. Her face was streaked with red, but her expression had slowly changed from despair to resolution.

"I don't know what I've gotten you into, Celia," he said quietly. "But I'm sorry."

Celia didn't answer. She seemed to be struggling with her thoughts.

Jack Mars wandered over and Trent noticed he was carrying the Desert Eagle. Jack approached and offered it. "Here," he said. "You gave me the cash so I'll let you keep your gun. Besides, sounds like you're going to need it."

"This mean you're lifting the death warrant on my head?"

"Not necessarily." Jack smiled. "Gotta keep it interesting, right?"

"It's not interesting enough already?"

Jack chuckled and started to walk away. "Oh, hey," he said, pausing mid-stride. "You should probably go see Ramón tonight. He's been expecting you and he's not the kind of guy to keep waiting."

"Yeah," said Trent. He turned to Celia. "I don't know how this is going to end, kiddo, but I say we go talk to this

Ramón, see what he has to say. If he can tell us how to stop Salvatore, then maybe we can get you out of this mess."

Celia nodded. Her hand went instinctively to the Book in her jacket pocket.

Trent saw the motion and felt pangs of worry. The way Celia had become attached to it scared him somehow, and the fact that he didn't understand his own fears made him worry even more. "What is that book, Celia?"

She looked up at him, fear in her eyes. She obviously didn't want to say, but Trent needed to know.

He pressed the issue again, more insistent this time.

Finally, she lowered her gaze and answered. "Its name is Raziel. It's trapped in The Book. It's helping me understand the words in my head." She held up her hand and ice began to form across the surface of her skin. It made a sharp crackling sound as it appeared. "I can hurt people." She looked deep into Trent's eyes. "I'm afraid, Trent. My parents are gone. I don't have anything left but this—" She held up her icy hand. "I don't have anything at all."

Trent thought for a long moment. "Let's see what this guy Ramón has to say first. Things are bad, I know. Both of our lives are going to be real different from now on. But just hold on, okay?"

She nodded. The ice faded back into her fingers and was gone.

Trent grabbed her hand and took a step toward the casino's back exit, but it exploded open, admitting the roaring sounds of a blizzard outside and two men in gray business suits, blond and strangely beautiful. Behind them, the two bouncers lay unconscious, or maybe dead.

Celia shrieked and began moving backwards, away from the two men. Trent stood frozen for a moment, paralyzed by the unexpected entrance. And that's when he noticed they both carried guns.

On instinct, Trent raised the Desert Eagle from his waistband, aimed and fired at the nearest advancing suit. He squeezed the trigger and felt the massive gun unload, the recoil nearly throwing his arm out of its socket. The bullet missed. Trent was sure his aim had been good.

Goddammit, where's my luck now?

He fired again, and then a third time. None of the bullets hit home and he took a step back, away from the still-advancing suits. People in the casino behind him had begun screaming, panicking, fleeing to the front lobby and the exits.

"Run!" he yelled to Celia and then turned to flee back into the casino proper. Celia, though, stood still, fixed in place with her eyes glued to the oncoming men. Trent skidded to a stop a few feet away and looked back. "Come on!" he screamed, but it was too late.

One of the suits stepped right up to her and grabbed her around the waist. The other kept on toward Trent. Celia shrieked as the man picked her up and jammed her palm against his face. Steam rose from between her splayed fingers and the man gritted his teeth in pain, but didn't falter. He turned and headed for the back exit.

"No!" shouted Trent as he barreled back the way he had come, gun raised. He ran straight up to blond man and stuck the barrel of the gun in his chest and pulled the trigger, but the man was too quick.

In an instant he had Trent's wrist in a lock and yanked the arm upward, pointing the Desert Eagle at the ceiling. The bullet plowed into the overhead tiles, creating a shower of dust. He then put his other hand palm-first into Trent's sternum and the blow sent him careening backwards through the air, doubled over with pain. Trent crashed through the glass doors that led into the casino proper and collided with a security guard that had just rounded the corner. They both tumbled to the floor in a heap of blood-spattered glass. The gun did a midair somersault and landed neatly in the blond's outstretched hand. Trent, gasping for air, looked up just in time to see the other suit leave out the back exit with Celia struggling in his arms.

"Things must be as ordained," said the remaining suit in a calm, melodious voice as he moved toward Trent and the now-unconscious guard. "We want our Garden *back*."

Trent raised an arm weakly in a futile gesture of protest. The blond stopped, lowered the Desert Eagle and trained it on Trent's panicked face. And fired.

A wave of nausea washed over Trent then—a black, sickening miasma that poisoned his subconscious mind and made the air around him smell instantly like aged dust. He felt his heart skip a full beat, leaving behind a sinking feeling, a terrified pit. Blood sprayed onto his arm but he didn't feel the bullet pierce his skin. He realized his eyes were closed and opened them.

The bullet had buried itself in the neck of the unconscious—now dead—security guard beneath him. At near point blank, the blond suit had missed, had killed the wrong man. Trent watched a look of confusion spread across the blond's beautiful face, a look that changed abruptly when another gun went off nearby.

The blond turned to look at the source: Jack Mars, with two guards backing him up. Jack lowered his rifle and aimed the barrel at the man in the suit. "You're not welcome here," he growled. "I've already thrown you out once today. Get out, now!"

The blond grinned and stuck Trent's still-smoking gun in his waistband. "You wouldn't," he said. "There are rules."

"Yeah," said Jack, with a grin, "but they would." He made a head gesture and doors opened on either side of the blond. Men stood in the doors—two each—bearing rifles trained on the interloper. "Regular folk," said Jack. "No rules for them. How fast can you move?"

The blond scowled and looked back at Trent. He waved the Desert Eagle at him. "I'll be keeping this," he said with a wink. Then he left, head held high. As he stepped through the broken glass door, heading for the rear exit, he muttered, "I'm sure we'll meet again, Mr. Hawkins." He left the casino and closed the door behind him, muffling the sound of the blizzard outside.

Trent grunted, gasped for breath, and finally pulled himself to a seated position. His mind was racing, trying to piece together what had just happened. Blonds. Guns. Celia gone. Celia!

"Where's Celia!?"

Jack lowered his eyes. "I'm sorry, Trent. I couldn't stop them."

"Why the fuck not? Who was that? Why couldn't I shoot them? He took my goddamn gun!"

"Angels. Cherubim. Pretty minor, but they move quick. There are still some left, working their own agendas."

"And you can't shoot 'em when they crash your place?"

"Rules."

Trent sneered. "Fuck!" He struggled to his feet, brushing the glass off his jeans and torn dress shirt. "Where did they take her, Jack?"

Jack shrugged.

Trent walked over and grabbed Jack by the shirt lapels and shook him, hard. "Listen, you little shit. After the things I've seen today, I'm not the slightest bit scared of *you* anymore, so throw me a goddamn bone! If you don't know where those angels took her, then tell me who does."

Jack pulled himself away from Trent's grasp and brushed off his sport jacket. "We've already told you who has the answers."

"Ramón."

Trent took a deep breath, stared at the ceiling of the now-vacated casino, and then exhaled slowly as he watched the violent sprays of snow machine-gunning against the glass windows around the casino floor. He picked up his gray Stetson and brushed off shards of glass and then put it back on his head. Without another word, he walked out into the blizzard through the front doors of the Inferno, his snakeskin boots crunching on fallen plastic chips as the neon lights cast him in various shades.

Trent stepped out the casino door and into a winter maelstrom. He gasped. The earlier snowfall had been startling, but the scene before him now was both breathtaking and horrific. The wind screamed violently down the street, picking up bursts of snowy drift from the thick blanket of white that had settled during the poker match. The icy spray battered the unlucky—or idiotic—few people that still lingered outside. Most had their hands up, blocking their faces as they trudged through the blasting snow.

"Fuck," Trent exclaimed, more sadness than anger in his voice. He wanted to laugh, or maybe cry, or something. His emotions felt jumbled. Everything had gone south. He felt lost and pressed his fingers to his temples to try to still his thoughts.

He leaned up against a gaudy marble statue of a cartoonish devil and used it for cover from the snow gusts as he watched looters trudging through the snow across the street, carrying televisions out of the destroyed façade of an electronics rental shop. The whole situation was spiraling out of control. It felt like a metaphor for his life. Everything always spiraled down like this. The plane crash, the gambling career, his life with Susan. He punched his fist into the statue, bloodying his knuckles.

He stared at the black Ducati, waiting quietly for him on the street, rocking gently with the buffeting gusts of ice-laden wind. A pair of looters wandered over and began to examine it. Trent eyed them warily.

"Touch that," he shouted, "and you'll be picking your fingers out of your ass."

The two men looked up at him, fists raised, then met his gaze and backed down. Quietly, they slunk off into the howling gray to join their compatriots at the electronics store.

He shook his head. Maybe he had been wrong to drag Celia around this city, this horrible shit-filled pit. Just like with Susan, he was all talk and no action. He could see the bad, the nightmares, in everything, but when was the last time he had stopped to do anything about it? Now he was standing in a freak blizzard in Las Vegas, blindly running from a shadow-monster and an old man with supernatural powers. A pair of angels had stolen the only thing he had left to protect. Forces were acting against him on every side and he was the only one not playing the game. He was just running scared. It wasn't about to end as far as he could see; at least not on its own. He had to take the initiative, had to sit down at the table and push his money in and take his chances. But he needed to figure out the other players first.

Poker's not a luck game, he thought. *Not by a long shot. And if this guy Ramón had some answers, maybe he can teach me how to play my hand.*

19

SALVATORE LAY BROKEN IN A trash-filled alley, shielded from the falling snow and blasting cold wind by the old, torn-up awning over the back entrance to a now-closed strip club. His new domain was one of broken bottles, plastic wrap, and filled trashcans, rotted and stinking and buzzing with the few flies still struggling against the dropping temperatures. From the litter Salvatore had painfully arranged a crude nest, a bed of filth. With a child's discarded, cigarette-burned blanket, he had attempted to tourniquet his leg. Oozing tendrils of ravaged, scorched flesh hung from the inexpert wrapping like half a gutted fish in butcher's paper. He stared, unblinking, at the pulsing wound as it disgorged ever-greater quantities of blood into the bed of trash.

His mind reeled with thoughts. It felt to Salvatore like a dark and horrible past that he had been running from had finally caught up to him. Things that had lay buried, deep in his mind, had come unburied. He thought about his lost wife and wondered if he had—

No, he thought. *Not possible.* He shook his head and balled his fists and moaned like a wounded animal as another wave of pain traveled up his leg and settled dimly in his brain.

An angel? A demon? Inside me? He could scarcely believe it, but then he knew it to be true. The recipe, the pasta sauce he'd be trying to replicate for years—whenever he had tried to access that place in his memories, he had felt a blockage, an obstacle, as though some great, dark thing had obscured that information. And so he had fought against it by working the recipe over and over, trying to pry out that last glittering gem. Much of his previous life had gone dark after the fire; the brilliance of the flames burning away what happiness he could remember of his wife and his daughter, Fiamma. The memory of that single recipe had gone too.

Dwelling on those painful thoughts suddenly dislodged a forgotten bit—the smell of gasoline and match smoke, untethered to any visual or other remembrance, just the memory of the smell. *Those men,* he thought, with anger rising in his gut. *Those foul, godless creatures with* blond *hair, talking voodoo and demons. They killed my wife! They burned my house and my life and my little girl!*

Salvatore's fists clenched tight and he gritted his teeth and tried to drag himself from the bed of trash, to pull himself up from the filth in which he was mired, to regain his stature.

"No," he said out loud, perhaps to himself and perhaps, he thought, to the demon sharing his flesh. "No, this is not the work of the Lord. This I will not do!"

He knew he was talking to the demon now. "I resist you!" he yelled, his voice hoarse and muffled by the stinging winter winds. And for a moment, he waited, as though he might hear the demon's voice in reply.

After a few seconds, he did.

A few seconds beyond that, Salvatore Cortina died. His corpse lay motionless and ruined amidst the trash in the alleyway, slowly collecting a fine layer of snow and ice as the body cooled. His soul passed on to the Realms of Shadow.

Salvatore's vision settled warily on the impossible landscape of a realm outside existence. It was a black place, not from pigments in the soil or shadows cast by distant radiance, but from the lack of it. It was the ash from fires long dead, from light that had failed to fall and objects that had not ended their existence, but rather had never *been* in the first place, and Salvatore knew that his eyes did not see anything there. It was a place he could witness without human senses, for he had none. It was the domain of the unnamed, a realm of shadow, one of many, separate and unified at once.

It had a name, given it long ago.

Abaddon.

Salvatore moved carefully through the black, guided by the unwavering, invisible tug of the fallen angel that had passed into that place alongside him. He quaked as he sensed the presence of the *unnamed*—creatures that had never come to exist. Creatures left to rot in the black that hungered mightily for form. Shades, the demon called them. Salvatore averted his gaze from them and looked at the landscape instead, and blanched at the image of towering spires, gleaming black, curved and sharp as knives, fifty-feet tall and looming over the ashen terra firma, claws over cowering prey.

"It is not the domain of God," came the demon's voice, loud and resonate in this place, though without discernible source.

"It is Hell," answered Salvatore, though he knew not how he produced sound or to whom exactly he was speaking.

"No," said the demon. "It is nowhere."

"Why are we here? Am I dead?"

"Yes," said the demon. Its voice was a fading whisper. "We are here to see the Prince. Your frailty has cost us much and I fear he has no more patience."

"Who are you?"

"Zamagiel."

"Who is the Prince?"

"He is this place and everything in it." A dust-black cyclone meandered across the horizon. Zamagiel added, "He owes me one last chance."

"Why?"

"Because I once did him a favor. But if I fail again, I will remain here forever."

"Forever?"

"Yes."

"And I?"

"You are already here. You are dead."

Salvatore thought on this for a moment. "How can you return without me? Don't you need a body?"

There was a long, seemingly endless, silence, broken only by the distant whispering of cyclones traveling the horizon, and the much closer sound of claws click clacking in the shadows nearby.

"It is my body now. You have failed me. You have even obstructed my holy cause. I once believed that, together, we would restore the Garden and rid it of the sin and vice that had overtaken its soil. If the Prince grants my last wish, you will only accompany me as a necessity for the body's functioning."

"It is *my* body!"

"It is no longer yours to command. Unblessed, unsanctified, it belongs to the Prince now. It is his to do with as he would, until consecration or flame. The fact that you are needed to operate it is... an irritation."

There was another long silence. Salvatore's feet plodded through the swirling dust. He shielded himself as a howling vortex ripped past and through him. Then, he heard the demon's voice for the very last time.

"How we return is left to the Prince to decide. I fear it will not be pleasant."

20

TRENT HAD EXPECTED SOMETHING BIG, ostentatious and imposing. Instead, he stood before a medium-sized villa in Spanish adobe style. Vines adorned the arch-shaped entranceway, though most of them had all but blown off in the raging snowstorm. In their place, a thick layer of snow made the house look strange and foreboding, despite its small stature.

Unflinching, Trent passed through the arch and made his way past snow-buried gardens and frozen statuary. One that caught his eye looked like a Franciscan monk, hands together and head bowed in prayer. The snow had coated his bald pate, forming a white cone that made the statue look comical, like a white-capped yard gnome.

He made his way up the cobblestone path to an old-fashioned front door, made from weathered wood planks. Everything about the construction of the adobe home—the wooden door, the stonework, and the gardens—seemed natural and non-synthetic. It was unusual and a stark departure from the common pre-fab construction of the suburbs that dominated most of the city. Trent raised a frostbitten hand and banged on the door. It opened almost immediately, seemingly of its own accord.

"Come in, Trent," intoned a voice that immediately struck chords of remembrance in his mind. The speaker's identity rested on the tip of his tongue, like a word long forgotten.

Trent stepped inside and was greeted by an imposing amount of warmth from a blazing fireplace near the front entrance. In fact, nearly every room he could see from the foyer sported a beautiful stone fireplace, all of which were contributing heat to the dwelling. It wasn't just warm in the mansion—it was almost hot. Trent figured that if Ramón was another demon, then that made perfect sense. He walked into the foyer and the door shut behind him, again of its own will.

"I'm in the kitchen. Let yourself in. I reckon we got some things to chat about."

Trent was taken aback by both the matter-of-factness and the friendliness of the voice. He walked past the entranceway to a large room with a vaulted ceiling that apparently served as an indoor arbor of sorts. The center of the slate-tiled floor was broken by a large live oak that stretched to the zenith of the twenty-foot ceiling. Behind it was a fountain that poured down from the second story, obscuring one of the ubiquitous fireplaces. Steam drifted from the warmed water as it made its way via cracks in the floor to narrow channels that ran along the lengths of every wall. A set of cast-iron stairs near the entranceway led to the second floor, where Trent could see closed wooden doors, similar to the front door, all of which looked out over the great hall with the oak tree. Trent found himself transfixed.

The voice intoned again from the kitchen, somewhere around the corner of the arbor to Trent's left. "I'm brewing some coffee. You want a cup?"

Trent muttered, "Sure."

"I'm sorry?"

Trent realized that the sound of running water from the fountain probably made it hard to hear anyone speaking in the arbor. He proceeded forward past the tree and turned left into what he assumed would be the kitchen area. As he rounded the corner, he repeated himself, "Sure, I'll have some coff—," he stopped mid-sentence.

Standing only twenty feet away, retrieving coffee cups from a cabinet, was the man that Trent had seen so many times in so many nightmares since the airplane crash. He was dressed in tight blue jeans and had a brown belt that cinched them around a tucked-in, western-style blue dress shirt with a faint white flower print. His skin, tanned and leathery, bore many wrinkles, and his long black hair had developed quite a few strands of gray. His sleeves were rolled up to the elbows, showing off massive iron cross tattoos on both forearms.

It was definitely the man that Trent had seen in his dreams. It was the same man he had watched fall to his death, arms outstretched like a skydiver caught in a moment of absolute bliss. It was the same man whose body had saved Trent's life. It was the old Mexican.

He turned to face Trent, coffee cups in his hand. One was black and the other white. The Mexican smiled and shot Trent a brief wink.

"So you still remember me, huh?" He pulled the carafe from beneath the coffee maker and poured out one cup, then the other. As he watched the near-black liquid pour into the ceramic mugs, he added, without looking up, "And I see you stole my hat."

Unconsciously, Trent reached up and touched the brim of the gray cowboy hat on his head.

Ramón chuckled and set the coffee carafe back in its place before turning to approach Trent with an outstretched arm holding a steaming mug.

"It's alright. I don't need it. Got a whole rack of hats upstairs." He handed the mug to Trent, who took it without hesitation. "Besides, it looks good. Fits you nicely. I've always said that a hat judges a man, not the other way around. That one judges you just fine."

Trent's thoughts swam as he stood in the dining room of the strange Spanish-style mansion, taking coffee from a Mexican who both caused and prevented his death. Unable to think of any proper response, he lifted the coffee to his lips and took a sip.

"This coffee is really good," he said, meaning every word. It was the best coffee he had ever tasted.

"Jamaican Blue Mountain," Ramón replied. "Tried it once and never could go back to drinking anything else." He shrugged. "Call me a snob, but it's damn good."

"Ramón," Trent said, repeating the name over and over in his head.

"So they told you my name already," Ramón took a long sip of his own drink. "That's good. One less thing to explain."

"Okay."

Ramón laughed. "Look, son, just because every bone in my body wants me to kill you and fill the front fountain with your blood, now that don't mean you have to act all shy. Loosen up a little."

Trent blinked. The sentence was filled with such an odd mixture of friendly intentions and clear, horrifying malice.

"Besides, wouldn't do me no good to kill you anyhow. Such as things are."

Ramón started walking—limping, really—toward a small hallway that curved back around the arbor and fountain. He gestured for Trent to follow.

"Let the ice melt out of your boots and bring the coffee to the study. We got some things to discuss."

Trent watched Ramón wander off beyond the gentle sounds of the fountain, toward a room in the back corner of the mansion. Trent surveyed his surroundings.

The kitchen was neat and clean, but clearly stocked for a sole resident. A bottle of imported Tequila stood on the countertop next to a vase of red and purple flowers and a green curvy glass bottle filled with olive oil and red peppers. The coffee machine was already brewing away, refilling its carafe – one of those automatic models that ground the beans and started the brew when it sensed an empty pot. On the far side of the kitchen was a glass door that looked out onto a stretch of empty desert, broken only by a set of stone furniture arranged around a stone table under an umbrella. The umbrella had blown over and lay twisted around the base of the table. Snow battered against the window, diving into the light from the darkness of the blizzard-ensconced desert. It seemed as if it was trying desperately to force its way inside, only to be denied by the glass.

Trent steeled himself and took a deep breath. He knew there would be more answers to be found here than he had even considered—answers about more than just the secret wars of angels and demons. There were answers here about himself.

The study was immaculate and sparsely furnished. The colors were simple, in light browns and oranges, with white stone-block walls and a bamboo floor. A painting of a white horse standing against a fiery sunset graced one wall and small wooden shelves holding flowerpots graced the opposite wall. Above Ramón's large oak desk was a small window that looked out onto the snowstorm. In the corner near the doorway stood a modern floor lamp and next to it on the wall was a candelabra. The combination of the two left the room basking in a warm, quiet glow.

Trent carried his steaming coffee mug to the couch beneath the flowerpot shelf. He sat down and faced Ramón, who was sitting in his desk chair now, absently watching the snow rage outside. Trent ran his fingers over the couch. It was black and leathery, a strange sort of leather with numerous rough patches. Trent had never seen or felt anything quite like it.

Ramón broke the silence without turning to face the younger man. "So I suppose you want to know a lot of things. I suppose you're just full of questions and probably a few worries, too. And this blizzard ain't helping matters much. Am I right?"

"Yeah," Trent answered.

"You think I can answer all your questions?" Ramón finally turned to look at the gambler. "You think I can smooth over all your worries? Tell you that things are gonna be okay?"

Trent scowled. "Tell me how to end all of this."

"Right to the strategies and tactics, huh?" Ramón grinned. "Son, you got things to worry 'bout now that I haven't had to think on for a long time." He paused and looked at the ceiling for a moment. "Well, at least it would be a long time to you, I guess. For me, it seems like yesterday."

"The crash."

"Good a place to start as any."

"You didn't die."

"Now that's not exactly a question, is it? Come on, Trent. Ask what you really want to know. There's a question that's been eating you from the inside." He smiled and winked. "I'm the guy to ask." He took a sip of his coffee and waited.

Ramón was right. Trent had been fighting the question every second of every day since the crash. It was a question he had seriously entertained only in the darkest hours of the night, only when Susan was safely asleep. It was a question that had kept him awake, a question that had given him nightmares.

"How did I survive that crash?"

Ramón took an excruciatingly long sip on his drink. "Well," he answered, "in a way, you didn't."

Trent's heart sank. He had always known the answer, and in the past hours it had grown in intensity, lingering at the back of every one of his thoughts. But he had always wanted it to be a lie. He was not sure exactly what the resolution of that question meant for him, but he suspected it didn't mean good things. "What am I, then, some sort of zombie?"

Ramón chuckled. "Hell no, son. If you were one of them, I wouldn't have let you through my front door. Even limping around like I do nowadays, I could still take a walking corpse."

"Then what am I?"

"Well now, that's a tougher question to answer. The better question would be to ask what *I* am."

"What are you?"

"Glad you asked." Ramón smiled. "I'm a fallen angel with a mortal soul—yours, to be specific."

Trent choked on his coffee. Oddly, he mused, it wasn't the angel part that had made him swallow the coffee down the wrong pipe.

"And you, my friend, are a man without one. But, see, that's the problem." He took another sip. "I've got something of yours, and you've got something of mine."

"What?"

"I just told you."

"But that doesn't explain how I survived—"

"Me." Ramón poked himself in the chest. "You survived because you fell on me. Thing is, when that happened, somehow—and frankly, I don't know exactly how—but somehow, you took the essence of what made me an angel."

"You mean a demon," Trent corrected, knowing as he said it that he was making a serious conversational gaff.

Ramón waggled a finger and shook his head. "Now now. I'm all for calling a rose a rose, but falling out of the Lord's favor—" He made the symbol of a cross in the air. Trent noticed that Ramón's hands bore several silver rings, all adorned with strange symbols. "Falling out of the Lord's favor didn't give me any special talents, just a new office environment. I brought all my talents with me."

"But now I have them," Trent offered. It was both a statement and a hesitant question.

"Not all, but some." Ramón finished the coffee and set the mug aside on the desk.

He leaned forward in his chair, a few strands of long gray hair slipping from his ponytail to cascade down over his face. He clasped his hands together, fingers intertwined. Trent realized that Ramón's eyes were beginning to glow a faint yellow and he couldn't resist the temptation to see this creature in his true form. Ramón offered a handshake.

"Look at me, Trent. See what I really look like and understand one thing—"

Trent reached out, took the hand in his own, and saw the angel's true form. It was horrific. Where two eyes had been there were now hundreds. Where there had been two arms, there were now a dozen, covered in scaly, jaundiced flesh, sporting a dozen broken wings of brown feathers. The creature's body was twisted and malformed, and its jaws bore several rows of razor-pointed teeth that proceeded back into the blackness of its maw. This was no mere fallen angel—it was something far more powerful. In its yellow eyes burned a hatred that Trent could almost taste. The smell of ozone shot up Trent's nostrils, forcing him to choke out loud.

Looking at Ramón in this way had given the creature's voice a new tone. It was rough, guttural, and its jaws dripped with fluid as it barked out every word. "Understand that if I could, I would kill you right here, right now. I wouldn't spare an inch of my mercy on your weak little existence. God delivered his wrath down on me thousands of years ago, and I would do likewise to you. Understand?"

Trent nodded, closed his eyes, and pulled the hand away. He could not stand to look upon Ramón's true form any longer. The hideousness of it raised in him an ancient, primal fear. At least in human form, the old man was bearable to behold.

"Then why don't you kill me?" Trent asked, weakly.

"Can't." Ramón leaned back in his chair and smiled with one corner of his mouth. Seen in human form again, his voice had regained its friendly, southwestern tone. "I said that you and me had some things to discuss. We're four halves to two wholes, but we're all mixed up. If I kill you, your soul turns me mortal. And I've lived way too long to be turning mortal now. You'd be lookin' at a pile of dust in this chair." He paused and then added, "Well, you wouldn't, 'cause you'd be dead." He chuckled.

Trent fought the urge to ask the complementary question, but lost out in the end. "And if I kill you?"

Ramón raised an eyebrow in surprise. "If you killed me, Trent, your soul would die."

"So?"

"Only reason you're still walkin' and talkin' is cause your soul is still hanging around. So maybe it's hanging around in the wrong guy, but its still here." Ramón tapped his chest. "But with it gone, you'd go to that same place that all the dead go to." He glanced out the window, watching for a second as the snow swirled against the glass pane. "And you'd stay there."

"Hell?"

"See now, those so-called 'friends' of mine just didn't tell you anything, did they? No, not Hell, I'm afraid. That's a place you get to go by invitation only. And you gotta have a soul to get past the bouncers. Heaven's the same way. If you show up soul-free, you just stick around in the dark for the rest of time."

"The dark?"

"Realms of Shadow. The Night Lands. Purgatory. Abaddon. Whatever you wanna call it. You stay there. Trust me... Hell's a vacation in comparison. At least in Hell, you got something to do."

Trent wasn't entirely certain of the last statement, but the thought of death was enough to stave off any thoughts of attempting to take the life of the demon sitting in front of him. And that assumed he even could. Trent wasn't so sure that Ramón was as powerless as he implied.

"So exactly what *are* you?" Trent asked.

Ramón smiled. "Now that's where things get complex. We're all angels, except you folks," he paused and scowled. "And the shades, of course.

"We're all angels, like I said, but some of us took different paths. The demons—they call themselves the *nephilim*—they started the First War in Heaven. They were prideful, figured they certainly were better than a bunch of lame mortals made from mud and dirt. God didn't quite see it that way, so Samael and his friends end up in Hell. The higher-ranking folks, like your poker buddies, spend most of their time top-side, messing around in human affairs, but the rest of the demons—and their various minions—are still stuck in the fires below." He looked thoughtful, then shrugged. "Or what's left of them."

"And you?"

Ramón seemed to ignore the question. "After the nephilim, you get the *grigori*. They're a whole different breed. Started out as angels, just like the rest, but they got thrown out later, after Samael and his friends had already taken off. The *grigori* thought that God would like it if they consorted with the wives of man, if they infused angelic blood into the human bloodlines."

Trent nodded. "Guess they were wrong."

Ramón agreed. "God wasn't too happy about that. In fact, He seemed even more pissed about that than about Samael's pride. The demons at least got a kingdom to rule over. The *grigori* got nothing but chains. He bound them to Earth. I guess He figured if they liked humans so much, then He'd make sure they get to stay with 'em. Permanently. And the *grigori* had poured so much of their celestial power into human blood that they were little more than humans themselves at that point. They become known as the Watchers, because that's all they could do. Watch. For all eternity."

Trent's mind reeled with the information, before he realized that Ramón had never answered the question.

"So what are *you*?" he asked again.

Ramón stared out the window at the blizzard.

"I'm the only one of my kind. Not a demon. Not a *grigori*. But not an angel anymore, either. I'm something else."

"What?"

"More coffee?" Ramón asked.

"What?" The sudden change of subject confused Trent.

"Can I get you some more coffee? Your cup looks empty."

Trent looked down at the mug. He hadn't really noticed that he had drained it clean. He frowned. "You still haven't answered the question. And why were you on that plane?"

Ramón leaned back in his chair, glanced again at the snow-filled window, and then said, "You sure you don't want some more coffee? This might take a while."

"I'm fine. Answer me."

Ramón shrugged. There was a long pause, and then he began to speak, his voice taking on a subtle, but different, tone. His words seemed *older* somehow.

"You see," he began, "In the beginning, there existed but one God..."

"In the beginning, there existed but one God, who created Lucifer, the light-bringer, so that he might bring the Light of God to the world. From that Light, a shadow was cast, and all things were pulled from it to form this world. And those things that were named became all that we know—plant and beast and earth and sky. But the things that remained nameless became unto themselves a place of shadow, a realm of utter darkness and despair, where all things go after the Light of God no longer shines upon them. And a domain for those things upon which God's light has never shone.

"And from the shadows Lucifer pulled the angels, drawing their shapes and forms and giving them all divine gifts from God Himself. And then, in order to please God, Lucifer formed a creature in His glorious image—a creature Lucifer named Man. But Lucifer, though he was the light-bringer,

could not imbue his new creation with the true Light of God–
-and so God took pity on Man and breathed into him a soul,
that Man might live in the everlasting grace of the Holy
Father.

"God, in His infinite wisdom, also sought to give another
gift to angel and Man alike—the gift of free will. No longer
chained to God's almighty will, angel and Man could shape
their own destinies and make their own choices. But Samael,
the most powerful of God's angelic soldiers, the leader of an
army whose purpose was indeterminate, came to God,
doubtful of the Lord's omnipotence, and questioned that
Man's choices and fates should be unknowable. And so God
created an entire host of angels to guide and shape Man's
destiny.

"God created many angels, who held dominion over every
aspect of Man and nature. And then, God created me. I was
known then as Ramiel.

"I held dominion over prophecy and fate. I was given
charge over the souls that would come for judgment in the
final days. I saw the past, present, and future of all things. And
I stood beside the throne of God, one of His most cherished
advisors. And my wisdom came to take precedence over even
Lucifer's, who then fell into the shadow of the Heavenly
Kingdom.

"God bid me show fate and future to early man, that he
might record prophecy in tomes and scriptures. I was the first
Prophet. God bid me show Man the consequences of actions
and the dangerous duality of free will. And I did.

"Then, it came to pass that the angels of heaven began to
plot. Some, under the direction of Samael, sought to

challenge God himself for the throne of heaven. Others, led by Semyaza, had begun to find in their hearts lustful desires for the Race of Man. Worried, many of these angels sought my counsel that they might know of their own futures. At first, I was hesitant to do so, but soon I found the demands of so many thousands of angels overwhelming, and I ceded to their wishes.

"Angel after angel came before me, seeking the knowledge of their fate. And those who had true reason to worry did indeed see the consequences of their actions in the visions that I bestowed upon them. They saw the fiery wrath of an angry God looming in the distance. They saw the War and the fall from Heaven and Holy Light. Those under Semyaza's influence saw the mutual execration and the binding to Earth for all eternity. And all who came before me were distraught.

"Finally, Samael himself bid me come to his chambers, asking for a vision of his future. I gave without hesitation, for at the time I did not know of Samael's hatred and malice. To me, he was the holy light-bringer, greatest of all archangels, and his command unto me was like that of God Himself. In the vision that I presented to Samael, he saw himself indeed as ruler of a mighty kingdom. But it was not as he might wish. The kingdom he would command was not Heaven, and the angels he would rule over were no longer glorious in their beauty. He saw a vision of the first War. He saw his glorious, shining armies dashed upon the shores of Heaven. And he saw a vision of Hell.

"Frightened by the vision myself, I quickly left the chambers of Samael and fled to my own. Never had I seen such horrors as were to come and I found myself stricken with sorrow. For a century I remained in my chambers, silent, heeding not the calls of angels or even God Himself, a decision that would ultimately bring me out of God's favor. The prophets of Man were spoken to by others, then, who told them sometimes truths and sometimes lies. And all the while, Samael's hatred for me grew.

"Finally, Samael devised a plan to remove my visions from his mind. He desired that I be destroyed outright. He beseeched God to banish me from the Light for telling the lies that he believed I had told. But God refused.

"I believe that that was when Samael first found himself truly skeptical of God's omnipotence. To Samael, whose pride was greater than his reason, my visions were clearly untrue, and God was protecting me because He favored me. Samael devised another plan.

"Into my chambers he burst, his holy visage bearing tidings of sadness and shame. I did not know then that it was all an act and I asked him immediately of the cause. He informed me that God was pleased with the visions I had shown to the angels, but that He wished a greater test for his celestial children. He said that God wished I should tell the angels otherwise, that my early visions had been false. He said that God wanted to test their faith.

"I was unable to refuse an order that had come from the captain of God's angelic legions, even with the visions I had seen of Samael's fate. God had seen fit on many an occasion to test the faith of Man, so it seemed natural that He would do so with the faithful of heaven as well. I spread my lies among the angels then, telling them of my errors, telling them that I—who had dominion over all true visions—had been wrong.

"The hatred of me grew and the name 'Ramiel' became a curse among the celestial host. The angels who had once succumbed to worry were bolstered by my disgrace and sought to begin their scheming anew. Samael seeded them with the lie that if I had been wrong—one of God's direct advisers—then perhaps God was no more omnipotent than I. And as unbelievable as it might seem, the Prince of Lies planted a seed that sprouted true.

"I do not know if Samael ever came to believe the visions I had shown him. In some ways, I believe that perhaps he did understand, but his pride refused to accept his own fate. In any case, as with many prophecies, his was self-fulfilling. When Samael and his armies rebelled, the War in Heaven was horrible. It was a time echoed on Earth by the most fearsome of storms and the most horrific of plagues. And as the rebel angels fell, their names became demon, but never again angel. And for that, Samael cursed me with the last of his holy words, that I should never again see the Light of God myself. And his curse rang true.

"For a thousand years I toiled in heaven, unable to see the Light or hear the words of the Lord God. I held council with the young angel Semyaza, who had concocted a new plan to win back the Lord's graces in the wake of Samael's fall. I attempted to convince Semyaza of the error of his ways, for he and his kind believed that God would find favor in angels if they would take upon them the wives of Man. He believed that Man with the blood of angels would be a greater creature, even closer to God than the base Man that walked the earth.

"This is what Semyaza spoke to me, and to his fellow angels. He and his followers were jealous that Man could produce more of its own kind, an ability no angel possessed. And with the demons banished from God's sight, the angelic host had grown smaller by a third. Many of the *grigori*—for that is what Semyaza's converts would come to be called— acted out of fear more than lust.

"But I truly believe that, at the core of Semyaza's being, his motivation was one of lust, and nothing more. Regardless of his motivation, all who acted were judged accordingly.

"When the *grigori* took mortal wives and produced their children, the peoples of Earth cried out. The children of the *grigori* were mightier than the mightiest man, for they bore angelic blood and divine power, and this power served to corrupt and twist many of their desires. The pure of the mortal lines became oppressed beneath the heels of the mighty half-breeds and they beseeched God, through the mortal prophet Enoch, to destroy their oppressors. And God, for the second time, administered His awful punishment upon his own celestial children.

"God bound Semyaza and his kind, the *grigori*, not to Hell, but to Earth, that they would be chained to the firmament for all eternity. And Semyaza, remembering my warning, sought to punish me as had Samael—for a drowning man often attempts to take his companions with him into the deep.

"In their last conversations, Semyaza told Enoch, who was to later become a great prophet at the side of God, that it was I, Ramiel, who had told the angels that their futures were of glory and righteousness. It was a lie, of course, and one that God would know.

"But in His inscrutable wisdom, He heeded Enoch's words and did indeed move to banish me from the Kingdom of Heaven. He stripped me of my rank in the heavenly host and threw me from the Light. Not chained to Earth like the *grigori*, but unable to enter Hell—for Samael bears a mighty grudge to this very day—I found myself in the one place that all things go when the Light is no longer upon them—the places of shadow, suspended between Heaven and Hell for all eternity.

"I was bound there, languishing in the everlasting darkness for many ages as they passed across the Earth. I witnessed not the Great Flood, nor the rebuilding of the race of Man. It was only when the *grigori* entered my dark prison that I saw a way to escape.

"It seemed that Semyaza, never content to abide by his earthly chains, sought and discovered a secret way to move between the realms of shadow and the mortal world. I watched the *grigori* come and go for many of your mortal years before I chanced my escape. The places of shadow were—and still are—no easy realms in which to survive. The very natures of the places seek to strip one of all remembrance of things past and all hope for things of the future. It is a place where dreams die, nightmares are born, and death waits ever-patiently for the end of all things. It is a purgatory for mortals who are lost after death. A prison for angels upon whose wings the Holy Light shall never again shine. The realms of shadow are filled with those creatures that never received names, and they harbor eternal bitterness over that fact. I spent many ages walking in the unending black, hiding and staving off attacks from the nameless ones as they attempted to rend away my existence. And so I planned my escape carefully.

"After Semyaza had come and gone, I made my way to the place within the shadows where he had entered, hoping he would return there once more. The places of shadow do have a sort of geography, though it is ever-shifting, and the points of entry from this mortal world seem to be fixed in the shadows where unnatural death has reigned, at least for a time. My assertion was correct, and the king of the *grigori* did, indeed, return.

"My mind filled with the fury of what Semyaza had done to me. I attacked with all my strength, tearing his blackened wings and leaving him broken upon the shifting landscape of the shadow realms. And then, my murderous deed completed, I came back into the mortal world for the first time in millennia.

"Though I had defeated the king of the *grigori*, it had taken all of my strength and had been no easy battle. I decided it was better that I should hide in this world for a time, and so I did. Only a few mortals, and none of the fallen host, knew of my residence in this realm for yet another age. And then, on a cloudless night in the middle ages, I heard the voice of God once more.

"God spoke to me in a dream and His voice was cold, distant, and pained. He told me of the Flood and the sins of Man and angel alike. He told me of His concern for the realms of shadow, for things that were left unnamed seek always to return to this place, where all things have a title. He instructed me that I should begin a hunt—a hunt for those things that had tormented me in my captivity in the dark, a hunt for the angels who had told lies in my name—and that I should never cease until another took up my cause. I had become His angel of retribution, though I still know not of the fate of the angel Gabriel, who had held that position before me. I took to my task with eagerness and ferocity. I took it upon myself to protect His children, the race of Man.

"For centuries, I hunted the creatures of the dark realms—the shades—and those *grigori* who would seek to gather their foul assistance. I had mastered the means of their destruction and learned many of the secrets they kept, even from God Himself, though I doubt anything is truly kept from His eyes. But as the centuries wore on, I found that my divine gifts, though still mostly intact, had been changed during my times in the shadow realms. No longer could I tell the future of a man and my visions became increasingly sparse. In their stead came a gift for changing fate, rather than knowing it. And I used this new talent as my weapon of the hunt.

"That was, until you stole it from me, Trent. Now, I sit here, in my house, waiting for the days of judgment, at which time I believe God will take me back to His side, for I have done as He desired, and I have given up the hunt now that another has arrived to take up my cause. It is as He said it would be, and I—of all of the angels—still know the truth of prophecy."

Trent sat in stunned shock. At first, he didn't know how to respond to such a tale, though he had a number of burning questions. Finally, he selected one and posed it to Ramón—who had once been called Ramiel.

"So you think I'm the one to take up your hunt? To kill shades and *grigori* and the angels who cheated you?"

Ramón lit a cigarette, took a long puff and looked out the window at the blowing snow. Where his voice had taken an almost regal tone in the telling of his tale, it now slipped back to the friendly colloquial that Trent had become used to.

"I don't *think* you're the one, son. I may not see the true visions anymore these days, but I know a working prophecy when I hear one. It was written that you would come here." He smiled. "And here you are."

Trent thought for a moment. "The guys—the demons— that I played poker with tonight. They told me I should come here. They wanted me to start hunting, too. But I thought the demons hated you?"

"Things change over a couple thousand years. There's a handful of demons—angels too—that have come around to my way of thinking. A lot of 'em are getting downright nervous with the way things are starting to go. They figure if I was right the last time, maybe I'm worth believing this time."

"And you trust them, after what they did to you?"

"Trust is a difficult word, Trent. First off, you never trust a demon. Just ain't smart. But that doesn't mean they can't still work at your side. You mortals have always been so fond of putting everything in the black or the white. But it just ain't so. There's a lot of gray out there." He looked toward the small office window and watched the white snow blow mindlessly against the black night.

"Okay, so let me see if I understand." Trent paused for a second to sum everything up in his mind. "I've lost my soul. I have your powers. I'm supposed to take up your job. And I'll probably have to buddy up to demons to do it."

"That about sums it up. Not just demons, though. You'll have to work with demons, some of the *grigori*, even some of the remaining angels. And other mortals, of course. It's not an easy job."

"But somebody's gotta do it, huh?"

Ramón inhaled from the cigarette and winked.

It was a lot to take in, but Trent had gotten used to that over the course of the day. Susan's loss had sent him down an unclear path; any kind of direction that might clear it up was welcome. Another question crossed his mind.

"You said your powers changed in the places of shadow, right? You couldn't predict the future anymore, but you could mess with it?"

Ramón nodded.

"So does that mean I *am* the luckiest man alive? I've been changing my own future all this time? Fixing the deal to get the best hand?"

Ramón frowned and shook his head. He took the cigarette from his mouth and leaned forward a bit in his chair.

"Sorry I have to be the one to tell you, Trent, but you got it all wrong."

"Just tell me the truth," said Trent.

"There was a creature that I fought with once, in the shadow realms. It was the only shadow creature I never defeated. Escaped before I could kill it. Damn thing actually managed to hurt me, something that no creature had ever done or has ever done since." He smiled. "Well, except you I suppose.

"The damage it caused affected my celestial gifts and they were never the same after that. The creature was called a Bringer of Nightmares, and in damaging me, its nightmares twisted my own abilities. I couldn't see true visions anymore, but I could *make* something else. I could bring some twisted version of the future and make it true."

Trent's eyes widened. The notion that Ramón was getting at had begun to seep into his thoughts.

"You're the bringer of bad fate, Trent. Corrupt karma. Evil mojo. Bad vibrations. Whatever you wanna call it."

Ramón took a long puff and exhaled the smoke toward the ceiling, where it lingered as a fine gray cloud. His face betrayed a deep sadness.

"Trent, you're walkin' doom."

A long silence passed between them while Ramón watched the snow outside the window. Trent considered the ramifications of his new knowledge. If he hadn't been lucky, then that explained a lot of things that had always bugged him—like how he could turn opponents' hands bad even when he had nothing in his own cards. Why he could never win at the slots. It also raised in him the worry that a number of other things were, in a sense, his fault. He thought about Susan's death at the hands of the Render and felt a cold, numb feeling seeping into his chest.

"What about Celia? And Zamagiel?"

Ramón raised an eyebrow and stubbed out the cigarette in a nearby ashtray. "I know Zamagiel, but who's Celia?"

Trent stammered for a moment. He had just blindly assumed Ramón would know everything.

"Celia. The girl I rescued this morning. Salvatore— Zamagiel—was trying to kill her."

"Oh, I get it. She must be one of his kids. So you wanna go down to the Luxor and take him out, save her life? Good. I tracked him here a year ago. Couldn't help myself. Then I realized I couldn't do much about him with half my powers in you."

"The Luxor?"

"You know, big black pyramid hotel on the end of The Strip—"

"Yeah, I know what it is."

"That's where he's been hidin' out."

"So how do I kill him?" Trent asked.

"Zamagiel? He's just like any other angel. Hard to kill, but it can be done. On Earth, we have to use host bodies, infect the weak-minded living and take 'em over. Kill the body, we have nowhere else to go, and we're stuck. If you bury the body with an angel still inside— Well, you get the picture." He paused to consider things. "I guess you can burn the body too. That's the only real way to actually get rid of an angel for good. Well, for a while at least. Why do you think some religions like burning dead bodies so much?"

"But how do I take him down in the first place?"

"Well that's just something you'll have to figure out. Part of the fun of it. 'Course, now that you know what you know, maybe that'll help some."

Trent nodded. He noticed that Ramón was glancing more frequently now at the snow-filled window above the desk, as if nervous about something.

"What do I do next?" Trent asked.

Ramón looked through the office doorway, toward the kitchen. Without turning his head to face Trent, he said, "Well, it looks like we've got some friends outside. I suppose you're going to have to deal with them, first." He raised an old hand and pointed toward the kitchen.

In a panic, Trent whirled around in his chair and looked through the office doorway. His gaze traveled down the hall, past the arbor, over the ornate dining room table, past the now-refilled coffee carafe, until it finally settled on the large glass window on the far side of the kitchen. Standing only inches from the glass were the two tall blonds in their impeccable business suits. Their faces were impassive and still, marked only by eyes with no corneas, just huge black pupils staring back at Trent, twin voids of absolute nothingness.

"Shit!" he yelled and jumped from his seat as he reached for the gun no longer in his waistband.

Fuck.

"Whoa! Hold on there!" barked Ramón. "They can't come inside. There are rules. Just settle down."

Trent calmed some, but all of his nerves burned with tension. A dead sensation began to drown him like a thick, gray fog. It filled his chest first, then his throat, and then slowly oozed its way into his face and skull. He clenched his fists tight.

"Just settle down, *vaquero*. One last thing you need to understand before you head back out there." Ramón got up from his chair and walked toward the kitchen, gesturing for Trent to follow.

"Yeah?" Trent's voice had turned low. His gaze never left the unblinking stare of the two blonds outside.

"If you don't listen to a damn thing I've said all night," said Ramón, "at least remember this piece of advice: demons lie."

Trent nodded. Then it struck him that Ramón was a demon, or at least something close. "Then that means..."

He trailed off without finishing the sentence. He didn't need to. A lot of what Ramón had told him was probably true. It was up to Trent to decide which things happened to be lies. He realized it for what it was: not an explanation of fact, but a test of faith.

"What's with their eyes?" Trent asked.

Ramón glanced toward the door.

"The angels? Pupils don't need to dilate. You don't need to squint if you can stare at the Light of God."

Trent watched the two men outside the window. They stood, unmoving, staring with their unblinking all-black eyes, hands clasped behind their backs. It unnerved Trent.

"Ramón," he said, "tell me one thing true before I go. "

Ramón shrugged and took a sip from his own fresh cup of java. "Shoot."

"When we were falling from that plane, you stopped struggling and stretched your arms out. I remember your smile. Why?"

Ramón took another sip, cocked his head slightly to one side, and regarded Trent for a moment before answering. "Lost my wings when God threw me from Heaven. Been falling ever since." He considered the ceiling. "You know, Trent, there's a big difference between falling and flying. When you're flying, you're the one in control, even if you're going straight fucking down."

21

THE TWO BLONDS LEFT AFTER giving Celia into the custody of the Metro Police officers, who did not seem too happy about the interjection of authority. One officer, a skinny black guy with a neatly trimmed moustache, handed Celia the apple that had originally been taken from her jacket. He said she could keep it since dinner was already past and they would not be giving her any food until morning. When she replied with a question about how long they'd be keeping her, the black cop had shrugged.

"This one's above us. Agents said you're being held for your own safety."

The other officer, a pale, younger man with way too much fat on his frame and a double-chin below too-close, piggy eyes, had said, "They said it was only temporary, so don't worry. Something about you being let free when the time was right and we don't gotta worry about it." He snorted. "Whatever that means."

So now Celia sat on the dingy, concrete floor of her cell—a lockup normally reserved for drunks, prostitutes, and wife-beaters—with no food save an apple, and a phone call she couldn't use because there was no one to call.

The cops occupied a table just outside her cell, playing cards and talking about things she'd rather not be privy to, such as the size of a fellow officer's tits, or how officer so-and-so had caught the clap from a prostitute last week that he had arrested the week before.

Celia's first instinct was to cry, but she felt the emotional center of her mind receding. The part that was at the forefront screamed *"No crying!"* Instead, she looked down at the shiny red apple in her hand. She felt hungry, but something about the apple made her hesitate. It wasn't that she distrusted Snake, though she didn't trust him to any great extent. It just didn't *feel* like the right time to eat the thing.

"Yeah," said the black cop, holding his cards way too far in front of him.

At any real poker table, Celia thought, *he would be showing his hand to half the people in the room.*

"So, I dunno about you, but those blond guys freaked me out," the cop said while chewing on his moustache.

The subject of the two blonds hadn't come up before now. Celia found that strange considering how unhappy the cops had been at the intrusion on their turf.

The other officer shook his head and neatly folded his hand facedown on the table. Then he leaned across toward his companion while glancing around to be sure no one was watching. "I think they're maybe NSA or something. You know, government spooks."

"NSA? Why the hell would NSA be messing with a little girl?" Moustache shook his head and gestured toward Celia with his thumb. "Nah, I'll bet she's one of those rich kids or something that got kidnapped by that dude. Maybe they finally got him on the run. Those guys probably work for her folks or whatever." He paused. "And you know, there's that syndrome or whatever that happens when you get kidnapped. Can't remember what it's called but you get all attached to the guy, don't wanna leave, so we gotta keep her in there." He gestured toward her cell.

"That's messed up, man."

"Yeah."

"I still think they're NSA."

"You think *everyone* is NSA! You probably think your old lady is NSA, working for some kinda underground fat-lady espionage team. Like Charlie's Fat Angels or some shit." Moustache laughed.

Pudgy didn't look too amused. "Fuck you," he said, and laid down his cards for a second insult.

He had three kings, easily enough to beat Moustache's pair of eights.

Moustache turned in his chair to address Celia, who was sitting on the floor cross-legged behind the cell bars.

"Hey, kid. You rich or something?"

Celia's first instinct was to shrug and tell them no, but then a different idea wormed its way into her head. "Yeah," she replied.

"No she's not," said Pudgy. "She's just messing with you."

Moustache considered this for a minute. He needed more evidence to make his point. "Whose daughter are you, then?"

Celia considered for a moment, but her mind was moving quickly and it didn't take long. She tossed out the name of one of the wealthiest casino barons in the city. "Jerry Warman, you know who that is?"

Moustache's eyes lit up. *Bingo*, she thought. "Yeah, yeah! He's the guy owns all the casinos, right? I didn't know he had a kid..."

Celia decided to add on a little extra. "Yeah, he doesn't talk about me much. Oh, and you should hold your cards closer when you're looking at 'em. I could tell you had a pair of eights from all the way over here."

Moustache looked embarrassed. "Oh, yeah. Thanks."

He scowled and then perked back up and turned to Pudgy. "See, I told you she was rich. Damn I'm good. They should set me up as detective. Fuck this street patrol bullshit."

Pudgy still wasn't convinced. "Man, she's just yanking your chain. Everybody knows Warman, so she's just telling you what you wanna hear."

Moustache looked annoyed. "Dude, you are one paranoid little fatty. Think everybody's always lying to you."

"I'm a cop! Everyone always does!"

Celia was waiting for the next part. She could feel her hands trembling.

Moustache turned around in his chair again. "Kid, you got some ID to prove that?"

Celia let out a long exhale to calm herself. She smiled, "Yeah, bring me my jacket."

Moustache, caught up in his theory, didn't even hesitate. "Sure, which one?"

"Black. Leather."

He jumped up from the table and went over to the set of cubbies they used to hold prisoners' personal effects. Celia's jacket had been stuffed unceremoniously into one of them. Moustache yanked it out and headed back toward the cell. He didn't even bother to search the jacket himself for the ID. It was his first mistake.

"Thanks," Celia said as she took the jacket through the cell bars.

Instinctively, her hand went into the inside pocket and, sure enough, there was The Book. Its surface warmed instantly to her touch. She pulled it out and carefully set it on the floor next to her, though even removing her fingers from its surface was near unbearable. She reached back into the jacket as Moustache watched. Celia made a show of searching the pockets, then shook the jacket, and then finally made a sour face.

"Those guys must have taken my ID."

"Dammit! They can't take evidence out of here!"

"Fuck man, they're NSA. They can do whatever they want."

"I'm calling the Chief."

"I wouldn't do that. If you're wrong and they *are* fed spooks, you'll be naked, hanging upside-down by your feet in South America by next week."

Moustache considered this piece of advice—albeit bizarre. "Yeah, fine. I'll give 'em a couple hours. They don't come back with that ID, I'm gonna raise all hell."

Pudgy shook his head and dealt the next round of cards. Moustache turned back to Celia, gesturing for her to return the jacket through the bars.

"Can I at least keep my book? It's really boring in here."

Moustache was too pissed off to worry about it. "Yeah, whatever." It was his second mistake.

Celia handed the jacket back through the bars and then took The Book and shuffled to the small bench seat at the back of the cell, where she opened the green-bound paperback beneath the dim light of the buzzing half-broken fluorescent bulb. Moustache returned to his seat at the card table, grumbling all the while.

"Damn, man, it's getting cold in here," said Pudgy, rubbing his arms for warmth.

"Yeah, this weather is crazy. Never seen anything like it."

"Somebody leave a door open or something?"

Moustache shrugged.

Celia read furiously. She didn't know when—or even if—the blonds were coming back, but she wanted to make sure she wasn't around when they did. At first, she wasn't sure where to look or how she was going to use The Book for her escape, but as her fingers thumbed through the pages, a cold, malevolent force filled her heart.

The text on some pages of The Book had been written in an odd, intricate script, all sharp lines and tiny circles at the corners. These pages felt dangerous, somehow, and powerful, and Celia knew instinctively that her escape could be found there. She did not bother to consider what that freedom might cost.

Finally, she settled upon one page with only a small amount of the unusual script. Though Celia had never seen this writing before in her life, it made immediate sense to her. She began to read it aloud, her voice strong and unwavering.

"Hey, quiet over there!" shouted Moustache. "I said you could read, not talk."

Celia did not stop. Her voice grew louder as she read, and coupled strangely with an increase in the volume from the buzzing fluorescent bulb above them.

"What the *fuck*?" Moustache got up from his chair, annoyed. It was his third, and final, mistake.

As soon as Moustache touched the metal bar of the cell with his hand, the iron turned ice-cold, throwing waves of steam into the air. His skin welded to the icy bar like a kid playing on a frozen jungle gym without gloves. He screamed, trying in vain to pull his aching flesh from the hissing metal.

Pudgy fell backwards out of his seat in an attempt to get up and help his fellow officer. "What's wrong, man?! Holy shit!"

"My hand!" Moustache screamed. "Oh fuck, my hand!"

He looked through the bars then, and locked gaze with Celia, who stared right back at him, unblinking, unwavering, lips still moving with the strange sounds and words.

Moustache panicked, and in a final desperate move, pulled with all of his force against his frozen hand. The majority of his palm flesh remained grafted to the bar, and he pulled away with a handful of blood and torn skin flapping wildly as he writhed in pain, grasping the wrist with his good hand.

"Oh, fuck!" he yelled, over and over.

Tears were streaming from his face as he doubled over and slowly dropped to his knees. Bloody handprints were soon smeared across the cold cement floor.

Pudgy wasted no time in scurrying out the door of the lockup area, screaming for help as he went.

His face streaked with tears of pain, Moustache looked up to watch his friend go, and then turned his gaze on Celia. She stood up from the bench seat, The Book open, floating impossibly above the palm of her left hand. She walked toward the cell bars and the writhing, moaning cop. The fluorescent bulb buzzed violently and then popped as she moved beneath it, casting the cell into darkness.

"Please, no. Please..."

Celia continued to smile as she reached out her right hand and grasped the bar that had taken some of the cop's flesh. A second mass of ice crystals formed across its surface as she held it and then, with a quick motion, she snapped the bar at its center. Like a broken icicle, it crashed to the floor, shattering as it struck. To the bar next to it, she did the same.

"Oh God, help me," Moustache groaned, trying to push himself across the floor with his feet, trying to escape the quiet, smiling thirteen year-old. "Please, God, no..."

Celia walked slowly to the fallen cop and, before he could scream, touched one finger of her right hand to his chest.

His eyes wide and bloodshot, the cop shuttered and blinked several times. He tried to cough, but could not. His body shuddered, and then he closed his eyes and was gone.

Still smiling, Celia stood, turned, and walked over to the cubbies were she retrieved and donned her jacket. She closed The Book and placed it in the inner pocket and then headed for the door.

She stopped.

A tiny, almost imperceptible voice in the very back of her mind was calling out. It was a voice that said she had forgotten something. She looked around the cell until her eyes rested on the shiny red apple, sitting quietly upon the concrete floor. She strode over, picked it up, and jammed it in her pocket.

The police station had burst to life. People yelled frantically and she could still hear Pudgy screaming for help. A siren had been set off somewhere in the building.

The first cop to come around the corner was an older Hispanic woman, her gun drawn and ready. She clearly hadn't been expecting someone to be right around the corner, and she collided with Celia. The young girl didn't budge as the older cop staggered backwards. Celia wrapped her fingers around the outstretched gun, and steam burst from its surface. The woman tried to pull the trigger, but the gun crumbled to pieces. Shards of frozen crystal tinkled across the floor.

Celia stepped past her and proceeded toward the station exit at the end of the long hallway. As she walked, the fluorescent bulbs above her popped and died, one by one, as if her passing demanded darkness. Celia, still smiling, moved on.

The second cop to approach met with a worse fate. He too sought to end the situation with a gun. He squeezed the trigger, and the bullet screamed out of the chamber toward the advancing girl.

Celia stopped.

She raised a hand.

The bullet's path came to a sudden end as icicles shot from walls on either side, icy strands holding the lead shell in place. The force traveled back along the strands where it met the walls, resulting in hairline cracks that appeared in the cement and threw spouts of dust into the air.

Celia lowered her hand, and the icicles broke off and dropped, taking the bullet with them. The cop, astonished but determined, charged the girl with his fists, the gun dropping to the floor beside him.

Celia reached out a palm and smacked him in the chest. She could *feel* the water in his organs turning to expanding, cell-shredding ice. The cop hit the ground in an instant, clutching at his heart. His life faded away in seconds.

As she neared the end of the long hallway, an older man, white-haired with a beard, burst from his office wielding a shotgun aimed at Celia's left side. Without even looking at him, she raised her left hand, and a wall of ice appeared between them, trapping the cop in his office. The shotgun went off, and the shell embedded itself in the glassy barrier. An intricate web of cracks shot out in every direction from the bullet's entry point.

Celia exited through the front door.

The last fluorescent bulb in the hallway—the one right above the exit sign—popped out. The light-sensor on the exit sign saw darkness and it came to life, shrouding the hallway in electronic red as the door closed behind a quiet, unassuming girl, who now knew where she must go.

22

TRENT WALKED TOWARD THE GLASS kitchen door, beyond which the black-eyed angels stood, staring. As he approached, one of them reached out and opened the door.

"Whoa!" Ramón shouted at the angel. "You just step back there, buddy."

Trent asked, "I thought they couldn't enter?"

"I said there were *rules*, not laws. They're not forced to follow 'em, but they should." He glared at the angel, who smiled and let go of the door handle.

The angel took a step back from the door. "My apologies." His voice came out steady and unnaturally pleasant. "We simply wish to talk with Mr. Hawkins."

"Bullshit," replied Ramón. "Why don't you go ahead and take a few more steps back. I'd say twenty yards'd be good."

The two blonds looked at each other, shrugged, and then walked backwards. They stopped twenty yards from the door. The drifting snow swirled about the base of their long, gray coats.

Trent looked at Ramón, seeking some sort of acknowledgment of his next steps.

"Go ahead," Ramón answered. "It's your job now, not mine. Best you learn how to deal with guys like this."

"We've already met once today. Fucking cocky angels."

"Minor angels. Cherubim. Minions, really." Ramón raised his voice to make sure the angels could hear him over the howling winds. "They're just low-rank spooks, sent to give humans a good scare. But don't underestimate 'em too much. They can kill just the same, though taking out mortals is generally frowned upon."

Trent glanced at the angels. One of them smiled disingenuously. "Mr. Hawkins is not entirely a mortal," shouted the angel, his voice cutting weirdly through the storm winds, as though it had some special privilege to do so. "He is tainted, like the girl."

At the mention of Celia, Trent rushed the door, but found himself caught by Ramón's outstretched arm.

"Whoa, there. Hold up, son."

"They took Celia," Trent said through gritted teeth. Then, over Ramón's barrier, he shouted, "What the fuck did you do with her, you bastards?"

The other angel, who had been quiet up to this point, raised an eyebrow. "We simply set her on her rightful path. The Prophecy must be fulfilled." His gaze drifted from Trent to Ramón. "You know this as well as we, Ramiel Doom-Sayer."

Ramón shook his head and grinned. "You've read it all wrong. All you managed to do is ruin a little girl's life, and trash an old man's fate. And you call *me* the 'Doom-Sayer.'" He removed his arm from Trent's path, implying that the wait was over. "You want to deal with my boy here, then go right ahead. But I think you're making a big mistake."

Both angels grinned maliciously. "No mistake, Ramiel. Zamagiel has used his last favor with the Prince. Whether he wipes this place clean or not is irrelevant to us. The Bringer of Nightmares is already upon this coil. All that matters now is the ascension of the girl."

"Not if I get to her first," growled Trent, as he took his first steps out in the swirling blizzard.

Both angels pulled gleaming silver daggers from inside their coats. The one on the left spoke: "That, Mr. Hawkins, is what we are here to prevent."

Trent glanced back at Ramón, who made a head gesture that indicated that now was the time. He put a hand on the glass door. Before closing it, he said, "Remember, minor angels. Nothing to worry about." Then, he shut the door and walked over to the counter to refill his coffee cup.

Trent turned to face the angels standing twenty yards away. Between them, intermittent blasts of snow and ice whirled through the dark night. He was reminded of a scene in an old western. He half-expected frozen tumbleweeds.

"Angels, huh?" he ventured.

"Yes," the one on the left responded.

"Where's your halos? Or did you forget 'em?"

The one on the right smiled. "We can't let you continue this course of action, Mr. Hawkins."

"I don't think that's your choice, anymore."

The angel on the left replied, "This is a war that has been long in the coming. And it is time for it to begin."

The one on the right picked up where his twin left off. "The child must become the Frozen Queen. And then the War will begin. If you interfere—"

"—then the war will be postponed."

"And we cannot let that happen again."

Trent raised an eyebrow. "Then why don't you just start it yourself?"

The angel on the left frowned. "We can't. There are rules."

"Rules," Trent repeated, nodding.

"And the demons refuse to fight. They're content with the level of control they have gained over your kind."

"I thought we had free will."

"Free will?" The angel on the left shouted, increasing his volume to overcome the howling winds. "Have you seen this place?" He raised both arms and gestured to the sky. "You watch television that someone else has made for you, read news that someone else has written, eat what someone else has produced. Every day, you invent new medicine to keep yourselves alive even longer, apart from the Light of God that awaits you in death. You pretend that God doesn't exist, or that He is just a metaphor. You live your lives by rules written on stone tablets, by letters in books and words on the screen. Those who consider themselves among the faithful are little more than script-readers, content to pay their dues to a self-made club, and in return receive metal icons—a golden calf—to display on their vehicles, a symbol not of God, but of ignorance and blind faith in a God that they no longer understand!"

The angel on the right finished the tirade. "What sort of 'free will' do you believe that the race of Man *has*, Mr. Hawkins?"

Trent considered this for a moment. When he had been a rich gambler, he had lived by chance; he had lived the life that everyone else had expected of him. He had watched old friends disappear in the shadows behind the glaring lights of his own fame and fortune. And for what? For a feeling of control in his life that amounted to little more than blind faith that the life he was living was just the way it was, the right path.

And then it had all fallen away, leaving him broke, tired and dead inside. But, through it all, Susan had hung on tight—the one person who refused to give up on him. Susan, who had always known that he could choose to live differently, who had known that the money and the luck did not make the man. He balled his fists, remembering the final look in her eyes as she fell limp into his arms.

"I have free will!" he shouted back, his voice strong and loud despite the screaming blizzard.

He gave the angels the finger, then turned his back to the angels and headed through Ramón's frozen, dead garden, toward the archway and his waiting Ducati. He felt both pride and cold death in his heart. He knew that if he did this work tonight, ended Zamagiel's foul work, that his path would be one of vengeance, of retribution, of divine wrath. He felt as Ramón had described, divinely inspired to attend to God's wishes, no matter who might stand in his way, demon or angel alike. This was his path now. This was the way forward.

He was only steps from the bike when the angels hit him. He tumbled to the snow-covered ground, twisting his body to look up into the unblinking eyes of his attackers, both wielded their mercurial knives menacingly. The three of them grappled as they attempted to pin Trent to the ground. They were strong, and he realized that he wouldn't be able to fight off their murderous intent for long.

He thought about what Ramón had said: *Cherubim. Nothing to worry about.*

With an outstretched hand he grabbed a stone from the edge of Ramón's garden and brought it up in an arc and smashed it into the head of the angel on his right. The flesh and bone crunched soft like any other. Angels, maybe, but mortal bodies still. The blond tumbled backwards and came to rest in a crouched, knee-down position, head oozing blood onto the snow and his gray suit jacket whipping violently in the blizzard gale.

The angel on the left continued to stab at him, but Trent found that he had the strength to deal with one of them at a time. He threw the angel off and it slid onto its back in the snow, a few feet away. Trent scrambled to his feet.

Both of the angels glared at him, their mouths twisted into sneers. The three of them faced off. Snow and ice and the distant sounds of emergency sirens screamed in the dark. Trent analyzed his opponents—two men, medium build, about six feet tall.

Mortal bodies, he thought. *Mortal goddamn bodies.*

He made up his mind and rushed suddenly backwards, retreating back through the stone archway that marked the entrance to Ramón's garden. Both angels followed. The intense feeling of deathly calm welled up once more in Trent's chest and he could feel the miasma seeping over him. He wasn't sure if his plan would work, but he would damn well give it a try, and as the first angel passed under the arch Trent tensed and summoned the painful chest-pounding sensation that always made him wonder if he was having a heart attack. Except now he didn't wonder anymore. He knew what was happening. *Walking doom*, he thought. He gritted his teeth, yelled, and felt a black rush of emptiness pour out of him, tearing invisibly across the landscape toward the sneering cherubim.

A sudden gust of blizzard wind descended suddenly upon the yard, bringing a burst of snow that blew the gray Stetson off Trent's head and blinded the advancing angel with an unexpected spray of ice. He clawed at his face to wipe the snow away, finally cleared it, and looked up just in time to see the archway crumbling down upon him. The heavy stones crashed into his skull, shoulders, arms and chest and pinned him fast to the ground.

Trent knew the angel was not dead, but in a mortal body he only had so much strength. Trent expected the heavy stones would keep him busy for a while. He turned to face the other cherubim, feeling strangely naked without the hat atop his head.

"You can't stop this war, Trent!" the angel shouted. "It must come to pass! This feud must be settled! Leave the girl be! Let her find her true fate!"

Trent began advancing on the shouting angel. As he walked past the fallen archway, he absently kicked a small stone onto the pile.

"No. Not on *my* watch," he shouted back. "The demons might have us under their control, but you—" He aimed a finger at the angel, who took hesitant steps backwards. "You and your little friends are jealous. You're nothing but minions, cherubim, the bottom of the ladder, and you always will be, won't you? You want a war because you think it will bring back the days in which Heaven ruled supreme. But if God wanted Heaven to be the ultimate law, He would have kept things that way. He didn't give us all free will so we could use it to kiss His ass. He gave it to us so we could choose our own path, make our own choices. His glory is in our choices, not your Heaven, not your Prophecies, not any of that."

The angel trembled. With a sudden, snap decision, its long coat burst open in the back and wings unfurled, yellow and white feathers shimmering in the glow of Ramón's porch light. The angel took to the air, flapping twice to push itself into the sky.

"You won't go to Heaven when you die, Trent Hawkins," it screamed from above. "You won't go anywhere."

"Die?" Trent laughed as he stared up at the angel silhouetted against the snow-shrouded neon lights of the city. He could see that the cherubim's all-black eyes were filled with fear. Trent snarled. "I'm already dead."

With a thought, he infused the angel's body with the foulest of luck, blackened its fate, and another massive gust of storm wind swept across the yard, bringing sprays of snow drift with it, an unseen attacker aimed at the hovering angel. The gust slammed into the angel's wings, crumpled and twisted them in an instant, sending the creature back down to the ground. Its flailing body punched through the monk statue in Ramón's garden. The monk's snowy cap burst off in a cloud of powder and the monk itself crashed backwards onto some flagstones, where it shattered into a heap of rubble with the angel at the center.

Trent strode over to the broken angel, his boots crunching in the snow. He stood above the moaning man and looked down. The angel looked up, utter sadness in its black eyes. Trent felt guilty, but only for a moment.

With a quick right hook, he caught the angel in the side of the jaw. The man clutched at his bloody face and curled up beneath some of the cold-withered garden plants.

Trent reached down and picked up the silvery dagger. He marveled at it for a moment; he had never seen anything quite like it. It had a perfectly polished blade and an ornate, gilded handle and even the slightest motion made it sing quietly. He glanced at his haggard reflection in the mirror-perfect metal and then slid it into his belt. He found his cowboy hat, replaced it atop his head and walked out of Ramón's yard.

The angels, too scared to move, watched the mortal mount the Ducati, gun it to life and roll it off into the howling night, one hand on the handlebars and one holding down the Stetson against the furious storm.

23

THE LUXOR HOTEL, AT THE southern end of The Strip next to the gaudy towers of the Excalibur, rose out of the windy, snow-filled gloom ahead as Trent motored north. He did not want to return to The Strip, but his task had become clear: he would destroy Zamagiel, once and for all. Not for the demons, or for Ramón, or even for himself. For Celia. Too many had already died today, some in Trent's name, and some in hers. He would put a stop to it all, end the carnage, and clear the storm from the face of Sin City. If he had to give up his own life to do it, so be it. If he had become the Bringer of Doom, then he would bring it to Zamagiel.

Driving the motorcycle through the thick blanket of snow on the roads proved to be difficult, but Trent took it slowly. It gave him time to consider the days events, his new knowledge of self, and the path he had chosen. He thought about what Charlie had said to him and wondered just *who* the old Russian actually was; he knew a lot more than Trent would ever have expected. He thought about the detail given him by the demons, and by the old Mexican who was really a monster, and even the strange statements from the angels about a 'prophecy' and an 'ice queen' and he worried, for just a moment, if maybe he was inadequate for his mission, if this were a suicide run that would amount to nothing at all. But as the bike crunched along slowly through the snow, he brought a hand down to caress the intricate features of the silver dagger at his belt, and he felt confidence renewed. He could do this.

Ahead, the neon of The Strip grew brighter and then suddenly seemed *very* bright in contrast to the darker urban streets down which he passed. It was then that Trent realized that the city was blacking out. Through the low visibility of the storm, he could see lights winking out in the distance in every direction. Other lights came back on just as suddenly, as the waves of dead power rolled past. Las Vegas was dying, moaning under the weight of the storm, and its neon—its lifeblood—was quickly losing its potency. It was a sight that Trent could scarcely imagine, even as he watched it happen. He had to move fast. There was little time left for Sin City.

He hit the corner of Las Vegas Boulevard and Russell Road, with Mandalay Bay's trees hanging limp with ice just a few hundred yards north, and brought the bike to a sudden halt. Glowing amidst the dark storm he could see a series of spotlight beams traveling up and down The Strip sidewalks. He stepped off the bike and peered into the swirling snow and saw men carrying the lamps. Searching. Men in gray suits.

"Fuck," he swore quietly, though the storm's roar muffled any sound he made. "Fucking angels, again."

From the lights, he counted seven or eight searchers, and knew in an instant that he would not survive a frontal assault. And if there were this many all the way down by Mandalay, he figured there'd be plenty more around the base of the black pyramid. He had to find another way inside.

He stood, watching the distant search beams, and stretched his aching neck from side to side. He exhaled and tried to calm his thoughts. The last thing he wanted was to head back into the tunnels. But now, they seemed the only choice. He shook his head, left the bike parked in the snow, and headed off the road and into the ditch.

It took him a few minutes in the chaotic, black snowstorm, but he finally managed to locate one of the flood channels that invariably led down into the tunnels. He padded carefully down through the channel, trying not to slip on the thick ice that had formed on the concrete. Up ahead, a light pierced the blizzard veil at the twelve-foot diameter entrance to a flood control tunnel, and Trent panicked for a moment. Was he about to be discovered? They had actually sent angels to guard the tunnel entrances?

But then he looked again. Not a searchlight, but a lantern, battery-powered with a dim yellow glow. Not moving, not searching. This was the light of a tunnel-dweller.

Still, he found himself wary. "Hey!" he called out, hoping the storm would keep his voice from traveling any further than the drainage channel. "Who's there?"

"You Metro?" came a voice, barely audible over the din of the storm.

"No, just moving through," Trent yelled back, as he advanced on the light and the voice.

"We ain't leavin'. Nowhere else to go up there."

"I said I'm not a cop." Trent approached the light source and found it to be a small Coleman camp lantern sitting just inside the tunnel entrance atop an old wooden picnic table. Nearby, a crude camp had been setup, complete with a blue tarp tent and shelves made from stacked shipping pallets. Two men sat at the picnic table, one black, one white, both haggard looking and dressed in rags. Trent could see that they were shivering.

"Whatchu want?" said the black man, menacingly. He had a beer in one hand. The white man was smoking a joint.

Trent reached to his belt and gripped the dagger handle, ready for anything. "Just need directions."

"You comin' in here?"

"That was the plan."

"Why?"

"Need to get to the Luxor."

The white man took the join from his lips and pointed up to the street above. "Up there. Just go north a couple blocks. You're almost there."

"I need to use the tunnels." Trent walked closer, until he could see the men's faces. He smiled and held out the dagger to show them he was armed, but not prepared to use it. Then he slid the blade into his belt.

"No," said the white man, shaking his head. "Ain't smart. It's not far, but this part of the tunnels got lots of twists and turns. In this weather it's gonna be black as hell in there. You'll get lost and die of cold."

The black man nodded, grinning. His teeth shone in the lantern light. "Its too dangerous right now."

Trent looked around at the screaming blizzard. "It's better out here?"

"You got a point," said the black man. He lifted the beer can to his lips and, with shaking hands, slurped some of its contents.

"I just need to get up there. You guys know the way?"

The two men looked at each other for a moment. "You sure you ain't Metro?"

"Does it matter?"

"We send a cop up in there, and Mary goin' be pissed at us," replied the black man.

"I'm not a cop, I promise. Cops carry guns, not knives, right?"

The white man looked at his companion and nodded, then turned back to Trent. "Take your second right, then your third left. You'll hit The Church. You best treat them with some respect. They're good people. Better than most."

"The Church?"

"Yeah, Virgin Mary lives down here. Got her a little church in one of the overflow chambers. Even got a congregation from time to time. You find her, she'll show you the way to the Luxor. Tunnel comes up right in the basement."

Trent smiled and tipped his hat. "Thanks."

"How you gonna see in there, man? Pitch-black most of the way, ya know."

"Yeah," said Trent, frowning. "You guys wouldn't have a light I can borrow, would you?"

Both men glanced at the lantern on the picnic table. The black man shook his head. "Uh uh. No way. This is ours. You goin' up in there and get killed, we never get our light back. You gotta find your own."

Trent shrugged. "Fine." He walked past their small camp and headed into the frozen black. He stopped a few feet in. From the dim light of their lantern, he could make out a couple lines of text spray-painted on top of several layers of graffiti:

A dungeon horrible, on all sides round
As one great Furnace flam'd, yet from those flames
No light, but rather darkness visible
Serv'd only to discover sights of woe,
Regions of sorrow, doleful shades, where peace
And rest can never dwell, hope never comes

He stared at the lines for a minute, taking in the oddity of such educated verse spray-painted inside a flood control tunnel. It was beautiful. Beside it glowed a painting of a woman's face wreathed in flame, ornately done, detailed and perfect in its execution. Trent shook his head, astonished by the artistry. He turned to look back at the two men.

"Hey, did one of you guys paint—"

He saw a dark movement amidst the shadows under the picnic table, and a strange sensation crawled up his spine. He recognized that telltale motion, that impossible repositioning through open space. The shadow creature. What had the demons called it? A Render? Why wasn't it dead?

"Shit!" he yelled, and charged towards the men, knife suddenly, reflexively drawn.

The two men misunderstood his intent and both jumped up from the picnic table and rushed to grab crude weapons from a nearby stack of equipment. The white guy came up with a rusty steak knife; the black guy an old golf club with no head and they began to advance on Trent.

"Stay back, man!" the white guy shouted, his voice trembling.

But Trent did not slow. He knew that the Render would end their lives in passing, if he didn't get to it first. Beyond the light of the lantern, he saw now the telltale black glow, the dripping of smoke that was darker even, than the darkest patches of shadow cast by the storm clouds raging overhead, eclipsing the city from the night sky and the glow of the moon.

He rushed past the men, who watched him sprint by, perplexed, still holding up their ersatz weaponry. In the black of night, the Render moved even quicker than it had before, and Trent could barely see it as it came on. But now he knew something about himself, something different. He understood.

As the black, geometric points of its legs rose up in front of him, Trent blinked, and saw the world behind the world. He watched the multitude of possibilities as they danced across the dead bleakness of that place, all of them bad luck for the Render, and he chose one and brought doom to bear.

The white bum, panicked, stumbled backwards and bumped against the picnic table. The battery-powered lantern tumbled off and hit the ground. Its light fell across an old, cracked mirror leaning against some of the bums' stuff. The reflected beams hit the Render, sending it screeching past Trent, cutting legs waving in pain. It dropped out of the light and slid past Trent and into the tunnel darkness.

Trent spun on his boot heels and positioned himself at the tunnel opening, feet apart, ready to move at any second, with the dagger in his hand. He and the two bums had moved back farther from the tunnel, back into the chaos of the storm above the drainage ditch, where none of them could see or hear the others for the blizzard-force snow tearing at their faces. The snarling winds were the only sound, at least until broken by the voice of the black bum.

"What the *fuck* was that, man?" he shouted, his voice muffled and nearly inaudible.

Instantly, the Render reappeared, hurtling out of the blackness like a cannon shot. It threw itself at the bum who had just spoke, and Trent suddenly understood. It was blind, in a way; it could only see those things that reflected light and cast shadows. Here, in the chaos, in the black of night and storm, all were equals, all were creatures of shadow. But the Render could still *hear*.

Trent dove across the tunnel to put himself between the Render and the bum. With a quick swipe, he brought the dagger across the creature's abdomen. A thin beam of gray light burst across the flesh, glowed for a split-second, and then faded. The spider dropped to the floor and slid away from them, back into the darkness.

Trent reached out, found the bum's shirt in the dark, and pulled him close, until he could see the man in the light. He put a finger to his lips, indicating silence. Then he grabbed the other bum and did the same. They both nodded, and crouched perfectly still, like frozen statues in the ice-cold drainage channel.

Holding the dagger out in front of him, Trent moved quietly across the tunnel to the other side, then started back toward the opening, toward the camp with its fallen lantern, still casting dim light across the floor.

As soon as he had reached a semi-lit area, he said, quietly, "Okay, let's play."

On cue, the Render burst from a nearby shadow, slid up the tunnel wall, then leaped at Trent. Another blink, another change of the creature's luck, and it came down awkwardly in the wrong place, legs inadvertently slipping into the pool of lantern light. It screeched. Trent dove onto it.

His whole body felt numb as he landed atop the Render. The spider writhed and thrashed, but Trent was able to dig his fingers into the black with one hand. With the other, he brought the dagger down fast. The point stabbed into the shadow-flesh, sending up a momentary burst of light and even louder shrieks from the thing. It pulled forward then, taking Trent with it, a strange, disconcerting ride as it moved inexpertly through the dark space toward the paralyzed bums.

Fear overtook one of the men and he turned to run, his sneakers clomping loud against the concrete floor. Trent could feel the Render's sudden awareness. It changed direction immediately and headed for the escaping bum.

"No— you— don't—!" yelled Trent, straining to drag the blade back through the Render's mass. It felt like trying to cut through rubber.

The Render came within a few steps of the fleeing man, then jumped into the air. Trent knew that it was trying to shake him off by slipping into the bum's shadow. He pulled the knife free and let go of its flesh with his hand. The creature lurched wildly, throwing Trent free. He blinked.

In the black, he saw many possibilities, but only one that mattered. He focused on that one, focused with all of his willpower. He opened his eyes.

The creature sucked down into the man's shadow as Trent fell to the floor, arm outstretched, dagger gleaming in the dull light. He gritted his teeth and stabbed, point-down, toward the floor. The blade punctured two shadows then, the bum's and the Render itself. The bum lost his footing immediately, as though he had hit the end of an invisible leash.

The Render, half-in and half-out of the man's shadow, twisted violently, but could not seem to pull itself free. The angel's dagger had pinned it halfway between this world and the black. Trent's arm trembled as he struggled to hold the dagger tight.

"Get the lantern!" he yelled.

The white man looked down at him, confused and terrified.

"The light!" he screamed. "Get the fucking light!"

The man blinked twice, then ran back to the table and scooped up the lantern. He brought it over and held it above the conflagration.

The black man, face down on the tunnel floor, screamed in pain. "Get it out!" he shrieked. "Goddammit, get it out of me!"

Trent held out his free hand, received the lantern, and then shoved it, bulb first, into the place where the two shadows thrashed. He could feel a certain resistance, but then the lantern burst through into the dark and vanished. The tunnel was cast into pitch-black once more.

His arm was buried in the thing, numb yet buzzing with pain. He could still just barely feel the lantern's handle in his grip, somewhere in the place beyond.

The creature's shrieking came loud then, easily eclipsing the sounds of wind and storm. The shrieks, as before, had human undertones, the sounds of men and women and children crying out in unison, screaming, moaning, yelling; and somewhere in there, Trent knew for certain that he could hear Susan.

Then the shrieks stopped. The light reappeared, dim at first but then it came back suddenly, making the three of them blink. Trent lay there, outstretched on the floor, his fingers still gripping the lantern, white-knuckled. He took a deep breath and laid his head down on the concrete and listened to the blizzard howl.

"Can— can we talk now?" whispered the white bum. The black man lay on the floor nearby, whimpering.

Trent rolled over onto his back and absently read the lines of verse again, though upside-down now. "Yeah," he said, after a moment. "It's gone."

"What the hell was it?"

Trent thought for a moment, and then said, "Nothing."

"Well it sure ain't look like nothin'." The white bum helped his friend up. "Look, man, if you need the light you can keep it—"

Trent thought about it for a moment. "Nah," he said, finally. He tossed the lantern back to the bum. "It's yours." He turned and started walking back into the tunnel.

"But what if there's more of those things in there?"

"It's your light," said Trent, without turning around. "You need it more than me." And then he passed into the darkness of the tunnel.

24

THE STORM SCREAMED FURIOUSLY AS Celia moved through the unyielding night. A trail of devastation and horror lay in her wake. Her mind refused to consider what she had done— The Book made sure of that from its place within her jacket. She could feel it playing her mind like a puppet, pulling her strings and guiding her through the frozen wastes that had, only a day before, been the City of Las Vegas—now a barren realm, covered in ice and snow, its inhabitants scrambling for safety, food, and clean water.

In the devastation, The Book sensed a power vacuum and knew that its young thrall would now do her part. She felt it moving through her brain like a thief, searching for the big score. She felt all of The Book's foul desires, but found herself unable to resist its voice.

She moved toward the black pyramid on the horizon, with its brilliant beam of light still unbroken above it, a sharp contrast to the dying light of all the other buildings around. She felt her steps guided by The Book's invisible hand. The Book wanted revenge against Zamagiel, and Celia was only too willing to obey.

So great was the fury instilled in her psyche that all things seemed to make haste to avoid her. The snow ahead drifted quickly away from her feet, leaving clean, dry pavement beneath her ice-encrusted tennis shoes. The winds whipped around and past her, but no gusts struck her in the face or chest, giving her free passage through the crippling blizzard. Even light was unsure in her passing; street lamps winked out as she moved beneath them. Darkness marked her journey through the streets of Las Vegas, accompanied by howling winds and the unyielding fury of a thin, leather-bound book.

As she walked, she observed the changes that Las Vegas had undergone in only a day's time. Nearly every building she passed bore damage: façades ripped free by swirling winds and glass windows shattered and broken, admitting snow that whipped through the now-ruined lobbies. Looters had clearly broken some of these windows, and a part of her mortal mind found a small voice with which to register its complaint. As foul and greed-ridden as it was, Las Vegas belonged to Celia, and Celia to it. She felt angry with any who would take advantage of the city during a natural disaster.

In the distance, she could hear sirens and the occasional panicked scream or bloodcurdling yell. Along the streets lay tractor-trailers, delivery trucks, cars, bicycles, SUVs, and bodies, all frozen into the snow. The blizzard had ruptured arteries in Las Vegas. The City of Sin was suffocating beneath blankets of ice.

A different voice—an older voice—spoke up inside her head. It wasn't loud, but it drowned out her own monologue nonetheless. *But then, this storm isn't natural, is it?*

Her anger toward Zamagiel deepened.

What faith do you hold, child?

Lost in her emotions, she was struck by the sudden peculiarity of the question. She didn't have an answer. Her family had never been extremely religious, but after the day's events, she at least had come to believe in many things that had simply been myth before.

Good. Belief spawns power. Power brings rule.

She didn't want to rule anything. She just wanted to be rid of Zamagiel once and for all. She was tired of being the prey in a fallen angel's foolish hunt.

Rule will follow his death. Wars will be fought and my freedom will be assured.

Part of her thoughts—the part that had receded to the farthest recesses of her mind—grew frightened. She did not want rule, or wars. She remembered her parents.

Forget them! They were merely vessels for power. They gave you birth and nothing else.

But her imagined memories of their slaughter danced in her thoughts. She screamed into the cold, dead night.

Yes! If you must remember them, remember that for now! Oh, how you hate the grigori! How you seek his utter destruction!

She did, in fact, seek his demise. Every fiber of her being screamed out for revenge, for destruction of the one thing that had taken her life away.

He will die. And then you will rule.

Yes, she thought. After Zamagiel's death, she would take the power and control to which she was entitled. This world had done nothing for her. There was no one who cared about her anymore. But then, for the first time in an hour, Trent's face surfaced in her thoughts.

No. Ignore him. He is a useless mortal.

But he wasn't useless. Trent had saved her life. He had pulled her from the writhing hands of The Book itself. Celia found herself wishing to see him again, wishing to see that rare smile that sometimes broke across his lips that suggested everything was going to be alright. Trent cared about her. Trent was her friend.

He's nothing, child. Nothing!

The argument was broken by a commotion ahead in the darkness. It sounded like other people, and part of her wondered if Trent was among them. She rushed forward to see.

She rounded the corner past an abandoned shop, and then witnessed a stomach-wrenching sight. Trapped in the raging storm, a woman had stopped her car along an empty side street, abandoned by the city in the dead night hours of a blizzard. Alone and scared and tired, the woman, wearing only nurse's scrubs, had found herself suddenly surrounded, dragged from her car by a trio of whooping twenty-somethings with ragged clothes and baseball caps.

The young woman lay on her back in the swirling ice now, her clothes torn asunder as she desperately fought back the advances of three groping young men, clearly high and owners of a stack of looted electronics nearby. They had found another pastime on the now-lawless streets.

The nurse screamed, but little more than a stifled shriek escaped her lips. The men's hands darted in and out, clawing at items of clothing and tearing away with unchecked ferocity. They yelled things like, "Come on, baby," and "Don't worry, girl, we'll be gentle," even as they laughed and whooped and complained about the bitter cold.

Celia stopped dead in her tracks, watching for a moment as the trio clawed at their victim. She imagined the nurse as Susan and hatred welled up inside her.

The men were like animals, she thought, not humans. There was more desperation there than true desire. This is what the storm was doing to the city. Beyond the cold and the winds and the snow, Zamagiel's foul storm was stirring up the sin and greed into malevolent, hateful energies amidst the chaos. These men were the worst example of the collapse: men whose lives had been so irreversibly altered by the City of Sin that, without police, they no longer knew right from wrong. Or at least they no longer had a reason to.

"Hey!" Celia shouted, her voice just barely carrying above the din of the storm. "Leave her alone!"

All three men looked up then, night animals caught in the act.

"Get outta here, kid," yelled the tallest of the three, a young man whose face was covered in blemishes and sores.

One of his compatriots turned to him then and explained something that she could not hear, but had already guessed at. Sore Face turned his gaze back on her.

"Actually, honey, why don't you come on over here?"

Celia glanced at the woman on the ground. Her eyes were squeezed shut and she was shaking violently from a combination of cold and fear.

"Gladly," muttered Celia.

The three men smiled as she approached. One of them rubbed his hands together for warmth. Another, whose pants were already unzipped, reached beneath his waistband to fondle himself. His face bore an expression of imminent pleasure that did not disturb Celia so much as it enraged her.

"Enjoying yourself?" she asked. "It's going to be the last time."

None of the men moved as she came close. Like animals, they could smell danger. Had they known what was approaching them, they would have run in a heartbeat.

Celia glared at the man with his hand in his pants. He screamed and his eyes went wide. His hand stayed where it was, trapped and frozen against his own flesh. Doubling over, he dropped to his knees, still screaming, trying desperately to both free his hand and not move it at the same time.

She stopped only a few feet away and realized that the young nurse had a large, bloody gash on her forehead and her left eye was ruined. One of the young men was wielding a blood-smeared piece of metal rebar.

"You like hitting women, huh?" She glared at the guy with the rebar in his hand.

Shaken by their companion's terrified screams, the men shifted from animalistic lust to raw survival. The guy with the rebar charged, raising the rusty metal rod to strike her across the face. He never came close.

The old voice in her mind spoke up, and Celia discovered that she had become far more connected with the ice and snow than she had previously realized. In an instant, her right arm transformed.

Where fingers and flesh had been, a jagged two-foot length of ice formed, transforming her limb into a sharpened weapon. Fueled by The Book's lust for vengeance, Celia thrust the frozen shard forward, piercing the man's shoulder. Blood sprayed down his right side and his arm jerked spasmodically, causing him to drop the metal bar. She quickly withdrew the icy spike and the man stumbled backwards. He clutched at the damaged shoulder with his left hand.

The tall man with the sores on his face seemed to be the smartest of the bunch. Faced with something out of his nightmares, he turned and ran.

Kill him. He has sinned.

Celia's countenance was calm and dead as she turned and whipped her arm toward the fleeing man. The crystalline spike slid off, leaving her normal forearm and hand where it had always been. Whistling through the air at high-speed, the icicle slammed into the man from behind and pierced straight through the back of his neck. He stood for a second in shock and then dropped to his knees before finally slumping to the ground in a pool of steaming blood.

She stared at the death she had just delivered. Some part of her mind rebelled against the behavior, but the voice of The Book fought it off. Behind her, lying in the snow, the other two men writhed and twisted in pain.

Kill them both. They do not deserve life.

She shook her head. No, she couldn't do this, could she? She had already killed so many. As monstrous as these men were, she was not going to degrade herself further by slaughtering the fallen.

No! They must die!

She screamed. "I am not a murderer!" She reached into her jacket pocket and pulled out The Book. Steam lifted from the pages as she gripped the yellowed paper. The skin of her hand bubbled and seared.

You cannot toss me aside. Without my protection, they will find you. They will kill you!

"I don't care!" she bellowed. "Let them find me!"

Conjuring up all the willpower and strength she could muster, Celia hurled the paperback into a nearby storm drain. The old voice in her head, though it still lingered for a few seconds, became increasingly quieter. Her mortal voice came back to the forefront. The Book's voice finally departed as she watched the two injured men hobble off into the black night.

When they had finally left her sight, she turned to the downed woman. The men had bruised and bloodied the nurse, and her face bore even more damage than Celia had originally thought. Her blonde hair—dyed with red highlights—was now more blood red than dye-red. The guy with the metal bar had beaten her nearly unconscious before they had started in on removing her clothes. The gash in her forehead shone with deep, dark blood, and the massive damage to the left side of her face had left her eye bloodied, swollen shut. But she had survived. With her right eye, the nurse looked up at Celia with fear. She tried to open her lips to speak, but couldn't make any noise.

The woman was very pretty and probably in her early thirties, Celia estimated. She was clad in aqua-colored scrub pants and a white blouse, spotted with cartoon-style sports players. The blouse had been torn nearly in half and her bra had been ripped clear, revealing part of her right breast and most of her stomach. Her pants and underwear were around her knees.

Celia bent down and carefully rearranged the woman's blouse as best she could, pulled up her pants, and then tried to help her stand. She noted that the nurse's nametag read, 'Anna.'

Anna trembled violently as she stood, relying on the teenager for balance. Tears streamed down one side of her face.

Celia helped her to the open car door, brushed the accumulating snow from the seat, and helped her sit. She looked up and down the street. The streets here seemed reasonably clear.

She turned back to the nurse. "Anna, you need to get out of here, okay? Go home. If you can get the car started, I want you to follow me."

Anna, still sobbing, just nodded. With a shaking hand, she reached over and turned the key, still in the ignition. The engine of the small, white two-seater grumbled to life. Celia shut the car door as the woman gripped the steering wheel and eased the car into reverse. Celia walked around behind it.

Without The Book, Celia wasn't sure if what she was going to try would even work, but a part of her suggested it still would. She closed her eyes and imagined the pages in the old paperback, with their strange flowing script of lines and tiny circles. Celia felt a cold shiver make its way up her spine—a shiver that she knew was not due to the blizzard. She opened her eyes and, to her surprise, the snow beneath her feet was once again shuffling away, leaving dry pavement beneath.

The woman's car began to back toward Celia and the tires found purchase as snow edged its way out from beneath the rubber. She raised an arm for the woman to see in her rearview and pointed in the direction she had come.

"That'll take you towards a Metro office," she shouted. Memories of her escape from the police lockup buffeted her thoughts and stirred her guilt, but she fought them back.

The young nurse turned the steering wheel slowly as she backed up. Celia hoped that if the woman got far enough into the safer part of the city, she might find some roaming police officer that could take care of her.

The thought made her remember again what she had done in the police station. Images of dead cops flashed through her mind. She fought off the memories. She had too much to do to worry about that now.

She walked around the car to the driver-side window, which the Anna was in the process of rolling back up. She stopped as she saw the teen approach.

"Look," Celia said, frowning. "Just keep going straight and try to find a cop or somebody who can help."

The woman nodded.

Celia remembered something and reached inside her jacket pocket. She pulled out the apple Snake had given to her.

"Here," she said, and handed it to the nurse. "Something to eat in case you get stuck overnight. Things should be better in the morning. The storm will be over."

She thought about Zamagiel. Even without The Book, she hated the fallen angel for what he had done, and this woman's near-rape was yet another example of the pain Zamagiel was bringing to everyone in the city.

"I promise," she said, with a determined frown. "The storm will end tonight."

The woman took the apple, then rolled up the window and put her hands on the wheel.

As Celia moved, the snow parted beneath her feet, letting the front-wheel drive car behind her catch traction. As soon as it seemed to be moving at a decent clip, she trotted out of the way.

Facing south, she watched as the car finally disappeared into the blizzard mist. Behind her, she could feel the dark, inhuman presence of the city lurking in the night. The three men she had just witnessed were only a sample of the kinds of horrors that were only just beginning as the city crumbled. She turned around to face those horrors and found she was standing face to face with the worst of them all.

Salvatore smiled, his face broken, bone visible beneath bloody gashes in his cheek. His breath didn't form steam, despite the cold.

"They told me you would come back to me," he said. "You're too strong for Raziel's silly book, aren't you, child?"

Before she could respond, Celia felt the cold sensation of water rising in her throat. She began to gag. Her eyes felt as though they might explode from their sockets, as if water was pressing on the back of her eyeballs in an attempt to force them from her skull. The intense pain brought on swirling black and star-like fireworks that rushed into her vision from every direction. Her body went limp, her eyes closed. She fought to stay awake, fought to think about something—anything—that would remind her of the waking world, and her last mental image, before a deep sleep washed over her, was of Trent.

25

TRENT MOVED THROUGH THE TUNNELS as Las Vegas shut down around him. Sometimes he would pass drop inlets, where orange beams of light cast down from sodium lamps above. But after an hour of walking, even those went dark. Trent could only feel his way through the tunnels by touching the walls. Sometimes his feet would strike bodies, bums or tunnel druggies, most likely dead from exposure to the fearsome cold. In the distance, somewhere up above, he could, for a while, hear store alarms ringing as looters braved the storm. But as the lights blinked out, so did the alarms, dropping the blizzard-devastated city into an eerie, howling nothingness that seemed even more ominous down here in the dark.

The cold, he realized with a start, had grown so intense as to be near paralyzing, or at least it would have been for a normal man. Trent considered that maybe more had changed about him than just the ability to impart bad luck on others. What other traits had he stolen from Ramón. He felt the cold seeping into his skin, painful and panic inducing, but yet...

He marveled at his own resilience.

Soon, a light appeared faint in the darkness ahead. At first, Trent thought it might be someone with a flashlight, though as he approached, it grew larger and brighter. A series of battery-powered lamps, all hanging from the wall of a much larger, more open chamber.

He heard voices, and the sound of a radio, as he came closer, he started to see people, a dozen or more. He held the dagger tight, hoping that this was 'The Church' he had heard about, and not some gang or worse. A woman appeared out of the darkness, the lamplight casting her face in a striking pattern of light and shadow, outlining all the crags and wrinkles in her aging face.

"Oh my," she gasped. "Come in, come in. You poor man. Join the group, please."

Trent followed her into a large chamber, an open space filled with beautiful graffiti, much of it comprised of religious symbology. One wall had been turned into a shrine, with a picture of the Virgin Mary and the Christ. A beat-up old wooden crucifix leaning against a concrete pillar. The blue-white light from the lanterns danced on the face of the life-sized Jesus. Nearby, a half-dozen cracked panels of stained glass, salvaged from some church topside, had been placed against the tunnel wall and backlit with candles that cast multicolored glows across the chamber.

The woman, probably not far past fifty, gave Trent a wink and a smile and brushed her gray hair back from her face. She seemed to be taking the insane weather fairly well.

Trent looked around the cathedral and realized why. She had set the place up as both shelter and triage. It was her job to be cheerful and positive.

"No worries," she said. "You come inside, I'll get you a cup of coffee, and we'll wait this thing out together." She gestured toward the unorthodox congregation. "All of us together. I'm Mary, by the way."

Trent tried to fake a smile, but there were more pressing issues in his mind than desires for coffee and company. "No coffee, thanks. You really think this is gonna pass?"

She squinted and laughed. "'Course it is! Come on in, sit for a while. You'll feel much better, I promise. It's only snow. We just have to wait on the Lord and wait on the weather."

"I'm not sure the Lord is the guy responsible."

Her cheerful demeanor dropped in an instant, her façade discovered and tossed away like so much garbage. She leaned closer to Trent. "Mingle for a few minutes. Then we'll talk."

She strode away, rushing to help an old man who was trying, unsuccessfully, to get up from a rusty metal folding chair.

Trent took the time to do as she said and wandered around the ersatz shelter. Metal chairs, camp bedrolls, and dingy mattresses filled the chamber. A small table off to one side bore a stack of leaflets and a stovetop coffee percolator atop a burning can of Sterno. The residents were mostly middle-aged, and primarily men, though there were a few women too. Some were sleeping, while others sat in the chairs, talking or listening to the nearby radio.

"Despite meteorologists' insistence that this is an unprecedented weather phenomenon, the blizzard over Las Vegas and outlying counties continues to worsen. Winds as strong as ninety miles-an-hour have been reported in some areas and, as of this time, the

entire city is without power. Residents of Las Vegas watching this broadcast via emergency feed should be aware that the city is under complete police curfew and the Governor, in cooperation with FEMA, has ordered the National Guard mobilized immediately to the Las Vegas area. FEMA is advising all residents to seek shelter immediately and carefully ration food and clean water, as meteorologists have been unable to determine when the storm might end. Due to potential pollutants, snowfall should not be used as drinking water, and traditional city water may also be contaminated. FEMA advises that you boil all water—"

Trent turned away as the voice droned on about emergency procedures. The looks in the eyes of the men and women listening were enough to tell him what was happening. They were scared. It was the end of the world, they had decided. It made Trent sad to think that, this time, they might be right.

The notion gave him pause and he remembered the gift that Vladimir had granted him. He wondered idly if it still worked. He moved around the room, brushing a hand calmly over the shoulders of the sleeping and the sick. To his surprise, not only did the strange mode of sight still work, but he became aware that the cathedral played host to a handful of demons in old bodies, their twisted, hideous forms curled up in fetal positions beneath sleeping bags and blankets. Trent found it sad to look at them: once-powerful creatures reduced to hiding inside withered mortal forms, aging and arthritic, their life ebbing from day to day.

He was startled when Mary tapped him on the shoulder from behind. "Okay, young man. Let's talk."

Trent nodded. "I've got some questions."

"I'm sure you do."

Mary walked away from the chamber, back into one of the nearby tunnels. Trent followed until she stopped, a good distance from the others, in the pitch-black again.

"I think I can stop the storm," he said, not knowing why he trusted this woman, but figuring he might as well tell her the truth.

"I hope so, for the sake of all those people out there. If someone can't stop it, I don't think it's going to stop."

"It won't," he said. "There's a bad guy behind all this."

"I know. I've been watching them for months."

"Months? Them?"

"The others, the blonds in gray suits. And the old man that commands them. I think he goes by the name—"

"Salvatore," Trent interrupted. "Or Zamagiel, if you're a friend. Yeah, we've met."

Mary raised an eyebrow. "And you're still here?"

Trent shrugged. "Apparently."

"Then maybe you *can* stop it."

"Maybe."

"Sure you don't want some coffee?" She held out one of two cups that she had brought with her.

Trent frowned. "Why does everyone want to keep giving me coffee tonight? I don't think I'm in any danger of falling asleep."

Mary chuckled. "Don't be so sure."

"What does that mean?"

"There's more out there than just a *grigori* and a bunch of his thugs. There's dark things; things he's brought with him from beyond."

"You mean the Render? I don't think it was his." Trent shrugged. "But it's gone now."

"That's not what I'm talking about. Your Zamagiel has something else. Something far worse."

"What?"

"A nightmare. I've seen them walking the streets together this very evening. It's a dark thing, terrible to look upon. A little boy, ruined and sewn shut, with shadowy smoke that follows in his wake."

He recalled his memories from the plane crash. He remembered the creature that he had seen in the darkness only moments after waking in the burning cabin. He thought about what Ramón had told him about the Bringer of Nightmares. It all came together. Zamagiel had somehow trapped that thing from the plane inside a child.

"I don't know how he brought it here," Mary continued. "And I don't exactly know why. But this storm has something to do with it. Killing Zamagiel may not be the end of things."

Trent shrugged. "Then I guess I'll have to take out both of them."

Mary made the sign of the cross. "May Jesus and Almighty God smile upon you, young man. Is there any other way I can help you tonight?"

"Yeah," said Trent, scratching at the stubble on his chin. "I need to know how to get into the Luxor. I hear there's tunnels into the basement."

"Sure. There's a tunnel beneath the pyramid, but it's probably filled with Zamagiel's men. It comes up right near the elevator shaft. Been there since they built the Luxor."

"How do I get to it?"

"Entrance to that tunnel system ain't far from here, though Zamagiel's men bricked it up. No way in now, except to go up."

"Up?"

"There's an abandoned building right above that tunnel entrance. I see them go in and out of there sometimes. Probably have another way in from inside the building. But it's locked. You'll have to be real lucky and hope they left it open for a change."

Trent grinned. "I think my luck will hold. You know a lot more than I could have hoped for. You've made my job tonight a hell of a lot easier."

The priest frowned.

"Oh, sorry. 'Heck' of a lot easier." He grinned. "Mary, how do you know all of this? Who are you?"

Mary reached out and put her hand atop Trent's. In the flickering of generator-powered lights, Trent saw Mary's true form. She was radiant, breathtaking, a brilliant form unlike any he had ever seen. The cherubim seemed ugly, simple in comparison. Mary was a true angel, and for every bit of hideousness that Ramón had displayed, she was that much more beautiful. Trent barely managed to suppress tears as he gazed upon her.

After a minute, he finally worked up the courage to remove his hand from hers. He felt a wealth of gratitude in his heart. Standing before him, he realized, was the one person he had met all day long whose motives were nothing more than pure goodness, through and through. If he could, indeed, defeat Zamagiel, he thought, he would do it not only for Celia, but for Mary, the angel in the dark, and for all of the people huddled around the radio in her 'church.'

When the demons had steered him down this path over a game of poker, Trent hadn't had much inclination to do their bidding. Now, he had some good reasons of his own, and he was always more inclined to do something when it didn't just matter to someone else.

"Okay, so show me the way."

Mary shook her head and smiled. She gestured for him to follow. "You're either crazy, or brilliant. We got some of both down here."

"Don't think I'm either," said Trent. "Just lucky."

He followed Mary for a few minutes through the inky black. Without any jacket on, he could feel the deadly cold seeping through his dress shirt and into the flesh, but the pain—though intense—no longer bothered him.

After a few minutes of blind travel, Mary stopped. Trent could tell that she had walked this route many times before. She grabbed his arm and pointed at a ladder that led up to a closed manhole.

"Up there," she said. "That's the way. Cross the street and you'll see the building. Sometimes they keep guards there. You be careful, okay?"

"Thank you," he said. "If I survive this, I promise I'll come back and donate some money or something."

"Don't worry about it," she replied. "We got all we need down here, so long as it don't flood."

As soon as he emerged from the tunnel, the winds hit him hard. He pressed forward, across the street. His knees buckled, but he managed to remain standing. He kept his legs churning against the blowing wind and, for a moment, it seemed as though he might simply be running in place. It was hard to tell in the pitch-black. But then, the façade of the run-down building loomed only feet from his face.

He tried to stop, hit a patch of ice, and slid shoulder-first into the door of the building. He hoped there was no one on the other side, or at least that they would assume the noise was just flying debris. He looked around, checking the narrow street to make sure nobody was watching. With the storm scouring the sidewalks clean, Trent didn't see a soul nearby, though he guessed he wouldn't see someone in this dark even if they were ten feet away. He had expected at least a few of the angels out front, too, but no. No one. Quickly, he turned the doorknob.

Locked.

"Dammit!"

He couldn't even hear his own voice amidst the howling.

He groped at the door in the darkness. Solid wood, all the way through. This was no bedroom door—he couldn't just break it down with a swift kick. As his fingertips played over the fake wood, he came upon a small nodule in the upper-middle of the door. Peering closer, he could see light coming from it, so he pressed one eye up against the glass and tried to look through.

Though the hole was designed to be looked through in the opposite direction, it still worked. Inside, warped heavily,

Trent could make out a blurry form. It was growing larger as it moved toward the door. Trent knew it was someone coming to investigate the noise he had made. An idea came to him.

He took a few steps back from the door, his thoughts still focused on the person he knew to be behind it. Ramón had said that he was the "bringer of doom," right?

With a short charge, he slammed shoulder-first into the door again, at the precise moment that he willed the person's luck to change. Though it should have held easily, the door snapped off its hinges and came crashing down into the room beyond. Trent heard a man yell but his scream was cut off by the weight of the door bearing down upon him. It crunched down, with Trent riding shoulder-first on one side.

After a moment, he rolled off the collapsed door. A dead body with blond hair and a gray suit lay beneath the door in a pool of blood. Trent looked up and could hear shouting coming from other rooms in the abandoned building. It had once been a small office of some sort and he found himself standing in the entrance lobby, a small affair with a receptionist's desk in the very middle, surrounded by cracked glass divider walls. He saw old evidence of squatters scattered around the room: empty beer cans, broken furniture, crumpled cigarette packs. But he figured the angels and their mortal minions had cleared them out when Zamagiel moved in.

The shouting grew louder and Trent figured it would be a good time to draw his weapon. He ducked down in front of the reception desk that, because of the glass, gave him little obscurity. He fumbled at his belt for the blade. He heard footsteps coming around the corner. He pulled the dagger out, leapt up from his not-so-hidden hiding place, and turned to face his assailants.

Two men rounded the corner almost simultaneously, shotguns drawn. They had blue ski masks over their faces—the kind with only the eyeholes cut out. Trent threw the dagger with imperfect aim. It didn't matter. He understood now.

The dagger sailed just above the glass panel on the reception desk. Its target, surprised to see a tumbling knife coming his way, put on the brakes, but his luck went sour. The area rug at his feet slipped free and the thug slid sideways, catching the blade square in the neck. His momentum sent him cartwheeling backwards. His shotgun clattered to the floor.

The second assailant swore as he came to a halt and raised his weapon. The shotgun went off with a deafening bang, but Trent remained still, facing down the attacker. He saw no need to be subtle.

Shotgun spray blasted through the glass pane, sending shards raining down across the floor and over Trent's cowboy boots. A few pieces of scattershot and glass ripped through some of the loose fabric of Trent's shirt, but not a single piece pierced his flesh. Calmly, he advanced past the reception desk and walked toward the thug.

The attacker's eyes went wide with fear and he dropped his weapon. Trent bent down in mid-stride to pick the shotgun up, along with a handful of shells. He continued on toward his target, loading shells into the gun, not even looking up.

The thug screamed and backed himself into a hallway corner, directly beneath a still-working fluorescent connected to a generator on the floor. Trent looked at the generator. Then he looked up at the long lamp. Then he looked at the thug, and smiled.

The generator went dead in an instant and the light went dark. The thug looked up. The entire assembly snapped loose with a twang and came crashing, straight down. Trent cocked the gun as the fluorescent shattered onto the thug's upturned face. The guy became a broken heap in the corner, all blood and glass.

Aside from the roaring winds outside the now-open entrance, the office had grown unnervingly quiet. Trent could hear, and feel, glass shards and debris crunching beneath his boots as he walked around the dead office. He walked in turn to the two downed men and pulled back their facemasks. They looked normal, not beautiful like the angels. He touched one of their faces with his bare palm but the image didn't change.

Just regular guys, he thought, with a twinge of regret. Mortals. A part of him felt unnaturally calm about the killing. He feared that lack of panic and what it might mean about him.

He looked down at the man beneath the light assembly. He did not have to have a good aim or a powerful weapon. His targets just needed to be unlucky. He didn't even need bullets if the situation held the right arrangement. He understood that now.

A pack of cigarettes protruded from the dead man's pocket. Trent retrieved it and found a single smoke left, along with a cheap plastic lighter. He lit up and stuck the cigarette between his lips. He continued into the building and strode down the long hallway that ran the length of the office, along which hapless white-collar drones had once occupied too-small offices with inspirational posters and calendars and whiteboards on the walls. Trent wondered idly if they had ever expected their office would someday become a killing field.

As he rounded the corner, Trent's vision reeled. The walls of the corridor were not just damaged from years of neglect and squatters—they also bore writing of a strange and unknown quality, some painted on and some carved deeply into the drywall. Sharp lines and tiny circles filled every wall from top to bottom, some even scrawled upon the floor. The painted writing was a dark red, and Trent didn't have to guess what kind of ink it was.

Well, he thought, *at least I'm in the right place.*

He reached the end of the 'T'-shaped corridor. To the left, the hall ended in a pair of bathrooms. He looked right and saw that it ended at a barred window looking into the alleyway next door. Trent made a guess as to where this underground tunnel would start. He headed for the bathrooms.

By force of habit, Trent opened the door to the men's' room first, only to find that there really weren't two separate bathrooms anymore. The wall that divided the two rooms had been torn down, leaving a tangled array of dented and twisted metal piping and a series of crushed toilets scattered around the edges of the room.

At the far end of the women's side of the now-joined bathrooms, where the mirrors should have been, was a huge, man-sized hole, obviously blasted open with explosives. Trent took another drag on his smoke, checked the gun in his hand, and headed into the tunnel.

The narrow passage, barely wide enough for two people to pass each other shoulder-to-shoulder, snaked immediately down. The walls were strung with the occasional mesh-ensconced construction bulb, casting a dim pallor over the rough-hewn earth. The ground beneath Trent's boots was wet and muddy, and sucked at his feet as he trudged ever downwards.

Soon enough, the tunnel came to an end at an abrupt drop. Three feet below, Trent could see the lazily drifting waters of the sewer system, where it had apparently broken through at one point into the flood control tunnels. He wondered if the city new—or cared—or if the owners of the Luxor had kept it broken as an 'insurance policy' against interlopers in the tunnels. Either way, the sewers no longer routed here, so the muck below was old and static. With nowhere specific to go, the filth simply stood—a fetid mix of human waste, gray water, and filthy runoff from the streets above that dripped down through air vents and manhole covers.

Trent sighed and took a long, extended puff on his cigarette. He sucked it all the way to the filter and then let it drop from his lips into the muck below.

Here goes, he thought, and then hopped down into the rotten sludge.

The stinking fluid immediately rushed up around his ankles and slipped into the tops of his cowboy boots; an oily, greasy-feeling mass of ice-cold slime filled with bits of hard dust and gravel chunks from the streets above. Trent fought back the urge to vomit as he pulled his weary legs through the viscous sewage.

As he moved forward through the tunnel, darkness once again descended, the light from the broken bathroom wall behind him fading quickly into the distance. He mused that every step through these tunnels felt like miles of travel, and he wondered just how many of those miles he had traveled today. Hundreds? Thousands? He wondered about what a man might feel like living down here for half a lifetime, as many of the bums did. What would it do to you to live in the endless dark for so long.

And that thought made Trent think of Susan.

He had tried so hard for hours to avoid thinking of his wife, to avoid thinking of her fate, to simply continue with his stated goals. He had found the task easy at first, a numb sort of disinterest in himself and everything around him that made it easy to not care. But another part of him knew that it was just a sham, a distraction from reality.

Looking at Celia had made him think of Susan. Talking to Mary had made him think of Susan. Walking in the black made her smile inescapable. She had held his hand in the hospital. She had encouraged him even when she disagreed with his path. She had been the one to lead him out of the dark places after the crash and again after his second fall from grace. Susan was Trent's light in a world of shadow, and he had lost her.

His boots suddenly pulled free of the muck and started squelching against the damp, icy, but sewage-free, concrete of a normal drainage tunnel. Up ahead, from the light of an air vent overhead, he could make out a crude brick wall. In the wall, was a nondescript, gray steel door with a handle. Trent reached it, and stopped.

He put his hands on his knees and exhaled slowly, desperately trying to banish Susan's image from his mind, the picture of her on their wedding day, standing against the storm-dappled dusk sky beneath rays of new sunlight, grinning ear-to-ear, overjoyed at the site of colored ribbons friends had strung through the trees in the glade where they were to be wed. The image wouldn't go. Trent's heart collapsed. He fell against the brick wall and then slid down it until he was sitting upon the cold, concrete floor. He put his head between his knees and quietly cried.

26

It took fifteen minutes for Trent to compose himself. Fifteen minutes to wrestle with guilt and shame and anger, and he finally settled on the latter and let it pull him up from the floor. A permanent scowl settled on his face, a realization that the foul stench in his nostrils was not the sewer at all, but the entire world. His eyelids lowered. His brow furrowed. He turned and faced the steel door and knocked on it a few times.

He thought about the trick that he had pulled before, at the entrance to the abandoned office; but without a peephole to look through, he didn't think he could pull it off. And more than that, he simply wanted to face someone, to vent the anger that he had molded from his sorrow.

There was a noise and then a catch unlocking and then the door opened. An ordinary-looking man peered out in the tunnel, eyebrow raised, until he saw Trent.

"Who the fu—?"

Before he could finish, Trent was through the door, arm raised. His fingers closed around the man's neck in a choking grasp and he pushed him back through the door and into the basement hallway beyond and slammed him up against the wall, feet dangling. The man's eyes bulged and his skin had already begun to turn shades of purple.

Trent brought his face within inches of his victim's. "Where is Zamagiel?" he growled, quietly. He glanced down the hallway to see if there were any other guards here, but saw none.

The man only let out rasping cough and clawed at Trent's fingers.

"Salvatore!" Trent hissed. "Zamagiel! Where is he?"

The guard feebly lifted an arm and pointed up. "Penthouse," he croaked. "Under the beam."

"Elevators?"

The guard pointed down the hallway to a point where it took a ninety-degree turn to the left.

Trent nodded, then slammed the man's head against the wall. He went limp and Trent let the unconscious guard slump to the floor in a heap.

He headed for the elevators, boots clomping in a steady rhythm against the concrete. As he rounded the corner, he passed a doorway that led into a security room, presumably where the guard had come from. Trent peered inside and surveyed the bank of flat-panel monitors showcasing scenes from throughout the Luxor Hotel. One in particular caught his eye: the casino floor seemed to be the only place occupied by people, and all of them were on the ground, hands on the backs of their hands.

Hostages? Trent thought, and then saw a blond man in a gray suit walk into the frame, rifle in his hands. *Damned angels have taken hostages.* He realized then that the lights he had seen up on the street had been *police*, not cherubim. The

Metro had the Luxor surrounded. The angels had barricaded themselves inside.

"You've made a big mistake, Zamagiel," he mumbled to himself as he turned and left the security room. "Big fucking mistake."

The elevator doors stood mute before him. Trent stopped and pushed the silver button on the wall. After a few moments of motor noise, the bell rang out in the empty hall. He shook his head as he waited for the doors to open. "You picked on the wrong goddamn guy."

The doors slid open and Trent was surprised to see the diminutive figure of Salvatore, flanked by four angels in suits holding rifles. "No," said the old man. "You've made the mistake here, Mister Hawkins."

And before Trent could do anything, before he could even summon the fell energies inside him to darken the angels' fate, one of them raised a rifle and fired, blasting a hole in Trent's upper thigh. The bullet shredded through muscle and tissue and Trent saw a flash of red, then white, and then the leg collapsed and his view of the five men before him went sideways and he hit the ground hard, temple first. The sound of his skull cracking against the concrete ushered him into unconsciousness.

27

CELIA AWOKE, CHOKING AND COUGHING, in the ephemeral blackness of the dream world. Her throat felt tight, her lungs heavy, and her stomach burned with icy pangs of fear. She knew immediately that she resided in a dream, but the realization did not lessen the terror any. She could sense the things that haunted the shadows of her mind, and she knew that they had free reign over her current reality.

She glanced around her, confused amidst the furniture of her own bedroom. The single bed, with a blue comforter she had never seen, but nevertheless recognized. Her desk, strewn with school papers, pencils, and a set of plastic horses with nylon manes. She knew that one of the horses had a cowboy with a gray hat, but she could not find him. She looked beneath the desk and picked up the fallen figure. His hat had come off and his leg had broken in two. She stared at it for a long moment, trying to think of how she might repair it, and a sense of panic rose in her chest.

An eerie quiet lingered in the room.

Dusk broke on the horizon then, its arrival announced by a high-pitched squeal and the unending cries of emergency sirens. Celia moved to the window to look at it. The line where sky met ground burned a fiery orange, and the skyline of Las Vegas was silhouetted only in black. A low, thumping sound began to echo through the walls of her room, overtaking the pealing whines.

Just a dream, she thought. *I'm in a dream.*

A pair of eyes appeared in the window. Celia shrieked and took a step backwards. The eyes resolved as part of a gray, sickly face, lined with creases and crevices, the skin folded in on itself in various places. The eyes were sunken into a hideous, sagging face, and the mouth was little more than a black, bottomless well of howling. The creature's claws came up against the glass and began to scrape. Celia covered her ears with her hands and took a few more steps backwards. The thumping on the walls grew louder, as though something might burst through them at any moment.

The creature's claws began to melt through the glass like a blade through flesh. Celia screamed as it finally burst through, hit the floor on four withered limbs, and scuttled toward her, its face a mask of pure, unbridled glee. Instinct took over her actions. She thrust out a hand and the creature turned to an icy statue that lingered only a moment before exploding into a million shimmering shards.

The use of magic took Celia's breath away and she doubled over in unexpected pain. It felt as though something had reached into her chest, grabbed hold of her soul, and pulled. A fear of impending heart attack raced through her nervous system, but before she could steady herself, another creature appeared at the glass. And then another.

Both melted their way through the windowpane and dropped onto the floor. They howled in unison. Instinct again took over and Celia froze them in place. The draining sensation hit her again, twice, each time feeling successively worse than the last. She felt as though she might vomit up her own lungs and her exhalations came out in raspy, throaty gasps and she felt rivulets of water trickling out of the corners of her mouth.

She turned to run.

The bedroom door, her only visible exit, moved backwards as she approached it. Her room narrowed, lengthened, twisted like an image in a funhouse mirror. Behind her, she could hear the deafening pounding behind the walls, and the ripping sound of claws against carpeted floor. In the distance, from outside the window, the sound of police sirens mixed together in endless, cacophonous loops.

She reached out an arm for the bedroom door, but still it evaded her. She had run yards, maybe miles. Her legs began to strain, her muscles grew weak. She faltered, stumbled, clawed again at the doorknob. She fell to the floor, only a few feet from her target. She gripped the plush fibers of the carpet and dragged herself forward, willing her body to move, despite the pain, despite the noise, despite the overwhelming terror.

Claws grabbed her ankles and pulled. She sobbed, clawed her way toward the door, a handful of carpet at a time. The door refused to come any closer and, in fact, seemed to be taking the opportunity to move even further away.

She could feel the creatures' claws on her thighs, her buttocks, moving up along her back. She could see them squatting around her, picking, tearing, eating her sundered flesh. The pain was unbearable. She fought back the instinct to use more magic. She knew that if she did, it would likely kill her. Even in the dream world, she feared death.

And then, as sudden as they had come, the creatures stopped.

They stopped picking. They stopped tearing. Even their howls descended in pitch, becoming little more than low rumbles of dissatisfaction. The unending loops of police sirens dropped to a lower volume too. She could even hear the sounds of blizzard winds, and knew it was noise from the real world, not the dream one.

A voice, a soft woman's voice, broke the quiet. "Celia?"

Still sobbing, she tried to turn her face, tried to search out the source of the voice, but couldn't find it.

"Please, help me," she sobbed.

"Celia, you have to get out. You'll forget yourself here."

"Who are you?" Celia insisted. "Please, help…"

"I— I don't know. I've lost my name. But I know yours. And I know— I knew you, I think."

Celia suddenly recognized the voice. "Susan?"

Celia heard a door creak open and she looked up at the entrance to her bedroom. She saw Susan and recoiled at the hideous, deformed creature that she had become.

"Susan? My name was Susan?" Susan crept inside. The gray creatures backed away at her approach. Their growls changed pitch, higher now, an irritated, whining sound. She bent down and helped Celia to her feet. Celia noticed that she hands she reached down with were fading from a hideous, sore-infested gray skin to a more natural, pale and smooth flesh. She looked up and saw that the face that had horrified her had grown more normal too, more beautiful, like Celia remembered her.

"We have to get you out of here," said Susan, a fearful expression on her face. "You're not supposed to be here."

"Where am I?" Celia begged. "How do I get out?"

"You're in the Realms of Shadow. The Prince doesn't know yet. I've been hiding you from him." Susan grabbed Celia by the shoulders and began leading her backwards, away from the grumbling horde of monstrosities, toward the still-open bedroom door.

"Come with me!" Celia grew excited. "We can both escape!"

"No," Susan hissed. "I can't leave. But you can get out. Quickly!"

She took Celia's hand and led her through the bedroom door. Instead of the familiar hallway, Celia saw a long, empty corridor, lined with framed pictures. Each picture struck in her a chord of regret, a chord of happiness, or a chord of anger. Each picture a memory, or a nightmare, a discordant symphony of jumbled emotions. The images compelled her to stop, to analyze each and every one, to reflect on the events of her life, but Susan would not let her dally. She pulled the teenager along, yanking her hard by the wrist.

The gray creatures scuttled out of the bedroom behind them like rats.

"Close your eyes," Susan whispered.

Their movements seemed to go on forever in the darkness. Celia could hear the creatures behind her. She could smell the musty odor of dust, then mildew, then the foul stench of rotting flesh, then dust again. Susan squeezed her hand. She opened her eyes.

They stood before a massive wall that stretched an unidentifiable distance into the dark, starless sky. All around them were dusty spires of gleaming black rock and whirling vortices that meandered across the horizon. The wall was composed entirely of mirror materials, some silvery chrome, some polished panels of wood, a watery, vertical pool, a chunk of gleaming marble, a crystalline shard. Inset into the wall at its base was a small, person-sized door, made of uninteresting, gray-painted metal, without ornamentation or even a handle.

"Look at the door," Susan insisted. "Ignore the mirrors. Quickly. You must go."

Celia fought back a terrible urge to view her own myriad reflections. She leveled her gaze on the solid, uninteresting door. All around her, she could hear screaming, crying, the undying sounds of mad and imprisoned souls, left to fester in the unending, lightless realms of shadow. She wanted to stay, to help, to explore the shifting geometry around her, to revisit her own memories, to visit the memories of others...

Susan grabbed her wrist hard and dug fingernails into her flesh. The pain made her jump and snapped her out of the meandering thoughts.

"The door," Susan hissed. "Open it. Please! Go, Celia."

Her own name echoed in Celia's mind. She had nearly forgotten it for a moment as she gazed upon the mirrors. A wave of fear rushed over her and she sprinted for the door. Her fingers pressed against the cold steel surface and she pushed with all her strength. Finally, it budged, digging into the ashen dirt as it opened, clearly for the first time in ages. She paused and looked behind her.

Susan stood motionless, her face locked in a permanent expression of fear and sadness. In it, Celia noticed a glimmer of hope. But behind the woman, she could see the gray creatures advancing, their gleeful smiles reformed and howling voices merging into a menacing cry. They were rushing, moving fast, parting to avoid Susan, but hell-bent on capturing the fleeing teenager. Though she couldn't hear them, Celia read Susan's last words on her lips.

Don't tell Trent.

The gray creatures burst around the motionless woman like a flood around a crumbling dam. The leader of the pack leapt into the air and hurled its body at Celia, who panicked, screamed, and dove through the open door. The world around her twisted and distorted. Colors bled into each other. Shapes became warped, curved things that changed with every passing second.

Celia took a deep breath and found herself unable to draw in air. She panicked and pulled as hard as she could with her lungs, willing her body to draw in precious oxygen. The pain of inhalation burned through her chest and her vision began to swim. She tasted blood.

Susan dropped to her knees before the mirror wall. The gray monstrosities snorted and howled around her. She sobbed into her hands, alternately whispering her own name and Trent's.

"Susan," she said quietly. Then a little louder, "Susan."

Knowing her name gave her a new measure of confidence, a slight tinge of power. When Trent had last fought the

Render, she had seen his face through the monster's eyes, as had all the souls imprisoned in the Realms of Shadow. It was the Prince's eternal punishment upon them, that they might witness the real world, the world they had loved, punished and tortured by the vile shades. For every other soul, viewing the world through the Render's eyes had been torture, a punishment just like every other. But for Susan, it had brought a memory, a name, and with it, influence.

She could feel the mirror-wall dragging her back, calling her, not by her name, but by her soul. She said her name aloud again to silence its cries, and then "Trent" and "Celia."

Memories of Trent came flooding back. The time they went to the state fair and won seven bags of individual goldfish at various booths. The seemingly endless hospital stays, with Trent grasping her cold, thin hand while machines cycled adrenaline and antihistamines through her blood. Their worst fight, where he threw a dinner plate against the television, breaking the screen but not the plate. They had laughed for a full hour, drained of the will to fight. The silent journeys home from various reproductive counselors. Trent's smile when she climbed into bed with him after a late night shift as a waitress.

She felt the slightest wisps of power weaving a skein within her incorporeal being, and knew that she might soon have the power to make changes to this place, changes that would surely be discovered by the ruler of this black domain.

But how much had his plans for war consumed the Prince's attention? How long might her changes remain untouched before he became aware?

Even here, amidst the howls of vile, gray monstrosities and soul ending, screaming vortexes of the purest black, Susan ventured a smile. She had remembered what it meant to have hope.

Celia sat up, gasping for air. Tears streamed down her face and the sound of the creatures' howls ringing in her ears became the real noise of the blizzard outside. She was in the real world. She knew that for certain. She glanced at her surroundings.

She sat in an exquisite lounge or study of some sort, filled on three walls with bookshelves fashioned from expensive wood, bearing all manner of books and curiosities, all with an Egyptian theme. The fourth wall was mostly glass, and the shades were only partially opened, letting in a scant amount of dim gray light from the blizzard-ravaged world beyond. Las Vegas was mostly dark now, sputtering and gasping for life. The spires of the Excalibur next door shone only from the searing white light of the Luxor's generator-powered beam, the brightest commercial light beam in North America. Without the rest of the neon and spotlights, the city looked strange, eerie, dead.

Celia turned from the window to survey the rest of the room and then saw something else in the room with her. In the long, deep shadows cast by the dying light from outside, there lurked a form. A human's shape. A child's shape.

"W—Who's there?" Celia stuttered, whispering, still shivering from the terrors of the dream world.

Celia reached back and threw the drapes open further, that she might get a better look at her companion. The white light fell upon it, causing no reaction. The child stepped forward, a little boy, head bowed, arms hanging limp at his sides, his lips and eyes crudely sutured shut.

"Ohmigod!" Celia gasped. She wanted to rush toward him, but some part of her warned her back, some *deep* part that she did not favor, some voice that still lingered in the back of her mind, a voice she wanted desperately to forget.

The child took another step, and then he began to shiver and his legs gave out and he collapsed. His body went into seizure and the boy flopped and writhed like a fish on land. And then the sutures began to pop loose. With guttural screams from the boy's now-unburdened lips, the sutures on his eyes ripped free, and Celia saw that his eyeballs had been removed, leaving behind only black, empty holes. From those holes, a shape poured forth.

It was a ghostly shape, as black as the shadows themselves. When looking at it directly, the thing seemed to nearly vanish, but she found it was still visible at the corners of her periphery. She could feel its presence, could somehow taste its thoughts and intentions, and she began to understand. It was a thing that brought nightmares, a creature that served entirely to pollute dreams. And it was Zamagiel's siphon, made solely to drain the power from her.

Zamagiel had kidnapped those children, she thought. *He was looking for one who could contain this thing.* The notion horrified her. One of the ruined children had been a friend at her school. Zamagiel had done this to get his power back. From Celia. All of this—the kidnappings, the attacks in the tunnel, everything—everything to get at her.

Celia realized then that the draining sensation she had felt in the dream world was the Nightmare Bringer's gift to his new master, a transfer of ancient power that had given Zamagiel the ability to raise the blizzard that held the city in its grip. The Nightmare Bringer had taken some from her the night before, when she'd awoken from a terrible dream only to find herself in the midst of anaphylactic shock.

She felt a rage rising inside her, and the powerful magic of her ancestry rose with it. Her escape from the dream world had left her with much power still. More than enough, she decided.

She scrambled to her feet and glanced around the room, searching again for the ever-shifting Bringer. Her fingertips tingled with an icy sensation.

"It's time for this city to wake up," she hissed, drawing the Bringer's attention.

She could see it moving toward her, leaping from shadow to shadow as it crossed the expanse of the lounge. She waited.

It occupied, for a split-second, the shadow of one of the sleeping children, then the shadow of a broken table, then her own shadow. Then, for the first time since she had awoken, it came to life in its own form, appearing directly in front of her eyes. It was a reptilian thing. Its beady shadow-eyes locked with hers. It darted forward, seeking to bury itself in her sight and claw its way into her mind. But Celia was ready and had no intention of going back into the monster's foul nightmares.

She reached out and grabbed it.

As her shivering hands plowed into the shadow-stuff that formed the Bringer's flesh, she remembered the last magic The Book had tried to teach her. It was the thing that had caused her revolt, the spell that had forced her to throw the foul manuscript away in terror and disgust. It was the spell that The Book had wanted her to use on the fallen rapists, but she had refused. She hesitated to use the magic even now, though she knew the Bringer could not be killed by normal means.

It was a secret so foul that only the mad angel Raziel had been given it and only Raziel had written it down and Celia had learned its entire history in that moment in the street before the horrible men and their victim. It was an incantation learned by none who had possessed the tome in pre-history— not Noah, not Solomon. Only Celia had been entrusted with this secret, and its horrifying nature made her head swim. For a moment, she hesitated, terrified to use it.

The Bringer of Nightmares twisted and writhed in her grasp and she staggered backwards, still holding it, knowing that it would soon overpower her. Tendrils leapt out from its form and wormed their way into her eyes and mouth and ears and she knew she would soon be like that boy, a tool of power to use against a hapless world.

"No," she said out loud, her voice quiet with sudden calm.

Celia gritted her teeth against the pain sure to come, and pushed down her fear into a pit in her stomach, and then uttered but a single word in a language long forgotten by man.

The Bringer of Nightmares stopped its forward motion and shuddered violently. The tendrils of black that had already begun to crawl into the corners of Celia's eyes came thrashing out. She held the black shade aloft as it struggled and squirmed to escape her grip.

"You like nightmares?" she said, her voice a gritty growl. "Then live in mine."

She pulled her hand back fast and jammed her palm against her chest. With a quiet hiss, the spell birthed itself upon reality, tore a miniscule hole in the fabric of the world, and sucked the creature deep into Celia's soul. The Bringer of Nightmares disappeared.

Celia's eyes went wide, her fingers spasmed with shock and pain, and she was thrown backwards by an invisible force. She landed hard on her butt on the floor of the study. Her back and head slammed against floor-to-ceiling window, making the glass ring with the impact.

Inside, Celia could feel the creature clawing at the confines of her soul, at its new, immaterial prison. She tried to stand, but the pain forced her to drop to her knees. She knew that she had made a dangerous choice. The Bringer was not a thing of weakness, and only the strongest will could hold it at bay. She knew that it would be an unending struggle for her, even far past her death.

Shaking with concentration, she finally picked herself up, stood straight, and faced the window. With every passing second, the pain inside her dulled, as if the soul-caged creature had begun to wither in its attempts to escape its new cell.

As she looked out over the snow-encrusted landscape, Celia thought about all the death that lay beyond the window, in the dying city of Las Vegas. She could just make out the sounds of sirens in the far distance. She thought about the police she had slaughtered at the lockup. Suicide entered her mind. Too many people had already died for her sake. Her own death would take the Bringer of Nightmares back into the places of shadow. Only she would have to face it then.

She reached out her hand and, with a gesture, blew apart the glass in front of her. The new hole screeched with blizzard winds, surrounding her with ice and swirling snow and blowing lightweight Egyptian curios from the bookshelves around her. She looked down and saw light glinting off the smooth black side of the pyramidal hotel. She would fall, smashing over and over as she tumbled down the side until she hit the concrete below, removing her from the mortal world. And she would take the Bringer with her. She tensed and extended her arms against the buffeting winds, and prepared to jump. *No one*, she thought, *can survive a fall like this.*

A bloodcurdling yell cut the freezing air, echoing through the howling storm. The yell had come from the rooftop.

Trent's yell.

She had forgotten about Trent! Her mind cleared instantly of suicidal thoughts. If Trent was still alive, if he was in trouble, she owed him her help. She loved him too much not to.

28

TRENT WOKE TO THE SEARING vision of the Luxor's beam, the brightest light in Nevada, visible, on a clear night, for hundreds of miles outside of Las Vegas. But it was not a clear night tonight, and the beam illuminated only the metal maintenance platform atop the Luxor's point, the blizzard clouds and snow swirling above it, and the limping, corpse-like old man that stood interposing between the beam and Trent.

He had been tied to a metal pole. That much he gathered quickly. One of several tall lightning rods on the roof of the hotel, he surmised. He glanced up at the swirling, churning storm clouds, and saw electrical arcs dancing in the black, highlighting the snow and wind with random flashes of white. He wondered how long he had before the next bolt struck the pole to which he was bound.

"I don't suppose you have long, Mister Hawkins," said the old man before him. "The last bolt struck nearby," said Salvatore (*Zamagiel*, Trent corrected himself), "and caused you quite the shock. Your scream was impressive. I'm glad it woke you up." The old man limped closer and Trent could see the sunken features and dead-white skin that hung, sagging, from his face. "Now, at least, you can witness the cleansing of this place of its filth before you die."

Trent tried to shout again in anger, but found he had exhausted any suitable amount of air in his battered lungs. He could feel blood running down his torso, falling in frozen droplets to the ground below. His feet dangled pitifully.

The fallen angel walked closer to Trent and waved off the four nearby angelic guards. "You have caused me a great deal of pain today. A great amount of difficulty." Zamagiel sneered, an expression that looked to Trent more like a puppet moving the lips of a corpse than like an actual expression on a living face. "You quite nearly cost me my victory, my ticket back into Heaven."

"You'll never get into Heaven," Trent growled, his voice hoarse and broken. "You're a monster, Zamagiel."

The fallen angel winced at the mention of his true name. "To the contrary," he said, forcing an irritated smile. "I believe that God will reward me greatly for returning his Garden to its prior state." He took a few steps back and gestured with open arms to the blizzard howling around them. "This is ten thousand years of waiting, Mister Hawkins!" he shouted. "This is the Flood reborn in snow and ice! This is the rectification of my sins against the Almighty!"

"You're insane," Trent said, and then spit out a mouthful of blood that had collected under his tongue. "You're a murderer, not a saint."

The old man's broken, corpse-like body whirled back around to face him. He advanced on Trent, his motion a leg-dragging limp punctuated by a near-collapse with every footstep. The snow and ice swirled around him, avoiding his dead, rotting flesh as he moved.

"You're the murderer," he hissed. He gestured with broken, bloodstained fingers at his own chest. "You destroyed him, Trent. Look upon this tattered old wreck, this man. He was a father, a husband once, like you." He looked at Trent and sneered. "You destroyed him. He is dead now, gone forever, his soul trapped. And I am left to shamble about, an angel in a corpse." He paced for a moment, collecting his thoughts. "And yet," he said, grinning, "I can make you pay for your transgressions, even ruined as I am."

He stepped closer, wrapped his aged fingers around Trent's neck and slammed his head against the post with a clang. "Do you know how *hard* it is to enlist a favor from the Prince of Shades? He has given me *two!*" He spit out the last word. "He nearly refused me this second chance because of you!" He slammed Trent's head against the post another time for good measure. Trent's chin dropped and his head lolled from side to side, blood drooling from between his lips.

"And now, you *dare* approach me directly? You dare believe that you—a *mortal*—can defeat an angel at the height of its power?" Salvatore laughed into the screaming wind. "Even inside a corpse, I am an *angel*, Trent, and you are but a lucky mortal, nothing more!"

Trent lifted his head a few inches. It caused immense pain to match the *grigorim*'s gaze, but he did it anyway. His voice came out quiet and ragged. "You're a *fallen* angel, Zamagiel," he said, using the creature's true name again, eliciting another wince of irritation from the old man's face. "You won't win. They'll take you out, even if I can't. Your storm will start the

War and the demons will come down on you with all the fires of Hell."

Zamagiel rolled his eyes. (Salvatore's eyes, Trent reminded himself.) "They have their ridiculous rules. They cannot stop me. They're not *allowed*, and have grown too complacent, too weak. It's sad, really, that they believed you to be their last hope, a pathetic mortal with some extra luck. But you don't look lucky to me anymore. Do you *feel* lucky, Trent, with your body broken and your spirit crushed?"

"I've never felt lucky," Trent said, his voice carrying an edge of resignation. "I just win sometimes." Even as he said it, a part of him worried that this would not be one of those times. He glanced up briefly, just in time to see a massive lightning bolt arc between two clouds directly overhead.

"Well not this time," Zamagiel said, and chuckled. "I believe that your luck has run out." He peered at Trent for a moment, his gaze punctuated by a low, rumbling thunderclap. He pulled the silvery angel's dagger from inside his coat and contemplated it for a moment. "What are you, exactly, that you wield the strength to best a cherubim?" he asked. "Baraqel's child? The Luckbringer? I thought he was quite older than you."

Trent did not answer. He gathered up another mouthful of blood and spit it in Zamagiel's withered face.

The fallen angel let out a guttural grunt of displeasure. "Filthy simian," he said. "Whether you belong to one of my siblings or not, it hardly matters. You will die tonight, along with all of this ridiculous *City of Sin*." He pulled back from Trent and stepped away. Two of the four blond angels moved closer to guard Trent, rifles held aloft.

With his back turned now, Zamagiel said, "Are you cold, Mister Hawkins?"

Trent's legs felt like distant stumps, disconnected from his understanding of pain. He could only barely feel them dangling below him. As he hung there, back against the frozen metal pole, with blizzard tendrils dancing over his icy skin, he thought of death and then of Susan. How many times had she watched him fall? How many times had she picked him back up? Was this how he would go out? A wave of anger rose in his gut and he struggled against the metal cord that tied his wrists above him to the pole. His legs and back banged painfully as he writhed and yelled, his voice cracking with pain.

Zamagiel still did not turn. His attention seemed focused on the dying city below. "No amount of luck will help you now," he said, almost absently. "You should be content with watching the Lord's work be done."

"Fuck you!" he roared in reply.

Zamagiel spun around, a malicious grin on his face as he gazed upon his trapped victim. Another thunderclap cracked the air, causing the metal platform to ring from the boom. Below, in the Luxor parking garage, a chorus of car alarms could be heard faintly, competing with the howling blizzard winds.

And that's when Trent realized that the thunderclap had not come from the storm. It had been something else, heralding a nightmare far worse than a bolt of lightning. Behind Zamagiel, in the long shadow cast by the Luxor beam upon one of the other lightning poles, Trent could see a dark shape rising. The Render, swirling and forming, its black legs pulling gingerly from the narrow line and touching down upon the dark platform. Trent's heart stopped with fear. He had not managed to kill it. The thing had survived, and had come back for him, and now he was an easy prey.

"Zamagiel," he said, quietly, "you've gotta let me down."

The fallen angel laughed, even as two of the angelic guards near Trent seemed to suddenly notice the new intruder. "And why would I do that?"

"Look behind you," Trent hissed.

Zamagiel seemed uninterested in the ruse at first, but then his guards all raised rifles, seemingly aimed at him, and he took the hint and spun on his heels. "No," he gasped suddenly. "No!"

The old man took a few dragging steps backwards, almost collapsing in the process. He held his hands out in front of him and a swirl of ice and snow swept down from the sky and slammed into the Render, knocking it back and stunning it, just for a moment. "No," he said again. "He promised me. The Prince promised not to betray me again. What is this?"

"It's a Render," said Trent, louder this time. "I know how to kill it, but you have to let me down."

The Render seemed to shake off the icy blast and its spidery legs began moving forward, carefully, one at a time, advancing on Zamagiel and Trent.

Zamagiel took another few steps backwards, even closer to Trent now, and summoned another blast of wind and snow, knocking the shadow creature back a few feet. He glanced around at the angelic guards, all of whom had their rifles raised, but had not yet fired. "Shoot it, you idiots!" screamed Zamagiel.

But the angels would not fire. One of them said, quietly, "I'm sorry, *grigorim*. The Prophecy must—"

"There is no Prophecy!" bellowed Zamagiel, as he brought another wave of ice to bear against the Render. Trent could see that every use of the magic weakened the old man further and his posture had already begun to slump. "The Prophecy is naught but Ramiel's lies! Clever stories and misdirection! You have all been fooled!"

"Let me go!" yelled Trent, adding his own voice to the chaos. "Give me the dagger! Let me kill it!"

The momentary pause told Trent that something inside Zamagiel had begun to fight. Salvatore, maybe? Was he still inside that corpse, trying to find his own voice? But as quickly as it had gone, the moment went.

"No!" screamed Zamagiel again, though whether to Trent's insistence or to the Prince's betrayal, Trent did not know. The old man raised his arms again and blasted the advancing Render with another burst of snow. He took another step backward, putting the back of his head within a few inches of Trent face.

Trent thought about what Ramón had told him, about being a Bringer of Doom. He had used his dead luck on mortals, and on cherubim, and he guessed that, given enough concentration, it might work on a *grigorim* as well. He closed his eyes.

The world behind his eyelids swirled with black and gray. Ash drifted from a starless sky, falling on an endless, dark horizon, and in that darkness he could still see the Render, its spider-like form advancing on him, front legs twitching, birthing black smoke as it came on. With a herculean effort of will, Trent pulled his mind away from that place and to a point somewhere between that world and this, and there he saw the endless varieties of luck and fate and chance, dancing like video captures in his mind's eye, every possible permutation a choice, every potential moment an option. With a bloodcurdling yell, he *shoved* the universe and felt the possibilities collapse, favoring one.

He opened his eyes in time to hear the metallic clang as the bindings around his wrists snapped free. His head lurched forward as he fell. The Render leapt from its perch ahead of them and hurtled through the air toward Trent and Zamagiel. Trent's forehead snapped forward, catching the old man square in the back of the skull. The impact send Zamagiel tumbling to the ground in an instant, and the Render dove over him and toward Trent, who fell to the ground, just far enough to avoid the creature's piercing spikes.

The Render slammed into the metal pole, lost its balance, and tumbled over the platform's safety railing and onto the sloping black side of the Luxor pyramid. The shadow creature's bladelike appendages dug into the building's metal panels, leaving ragged slices as it slid a few feet down and then stopped and hung there. Lightning crashed through the sky, bathing everything in bright white for a moment, and the creature let out a horrible shriek and slipped further, but still managed to hold on. After a moment, it began, slowly, to claw its way back up the pyramid wall.

Trent stood, battered and broken, over the corpse-like frame of the old Italian man. "Give me the knife!" he yelled, holding out his trembling hand.

But before Zamagiel could even look up at him, the angelic guards raised and trained their rifles on Trent. "Stand down!" one of them yelled.

"Fuck off!" said Trent, irritated.

"Stand down!" replied the cherubim again. "You must let the Render take you. It has been written."

"Fuck your Prophecy!" But for a moment, Trent did consider the angel's words. In the constant shrieks of the Render, he could again hear Susan's voice, louder now, more obvious, screaming his name over and over. If he let it take him, would he go to the Realms of Shadow, to Abaddon? Would he see her again? He looked around, and in the distance below the Luxor, he could see the blinking red and blue of police cars and he thought about all of the people down there; living people, people with jobs and families and children. The children. Celia. Susan would never forgive him for letting Celia die. He turned to look directly at the cherubim who had spoken to him.

"You stand down!" he commanded, pointing an accusatory finger. "Do the job God gave you and let us make our own choices, angel!"

The four guards glanced at each other nervously.

Trent opened his mouth to say more, but the Render's terrible, high-pitched hum silenced him. He turned to see it cresting the safety railing. In an instant, it slipped into a nearby shadow cast upon the metal platform by the Luxor beam.

Trent roared and sprinted after it. When he reached the place where it had gone, he thrust his hand into the shadow and felt the burning sensation in his chest and then, to his surprise, his hand passed into the black, beyond the metal-grate floor. He felt unending cold and the buzzing, painful sensation of shadow-stuff between his fingers. He yanked as hard as he could, and the Render came billowing up from within the shadow. As it did, Trent thrust his other hand into its core and lifted it aloft.

The Render struggled awkwardly, throwing shadowy smoke like ink into the dark, howling night. It screeched, and the bulk of its sound was Susan's voice, screaming Trent's name.

Trent hobbled backwards, his balance compromised by the creature's writhing motions. The muscles in his arms strained, aching, as he moved towards the light beam. His heart banged against the inside of his ribcage as he tried to ignore the voice emanating from the Render's shrieks.

"Die!" he yelled, competing against the noise of the monster. "*Die, goddamn you!*"

He took a lurching step forward and thrust the Render down upon the face of the lamp that projected the Luxor's iconic beam into the sky. For the first time in years, the pyramid's beam went dark. Even light curling around the edges of the creature pulled unnaturally toward it, sucking into the black, smoke-like shape, and its howling grew more intense than ever before, a crescendo of howling voices that burned into Trent's eardrums, with Susan's voice at the helm, screaming his name.

"*Give me the dagger!*" he bellowed, using one hand to gesture towards Zamagiel, who still lay on the ground, stunned and confused. The light was burning the Render with unmatched ferocity, but Trent knew that he could not hold it for long. Already, his arm was giving out and he could feel the thing slipping from his grasp. If it came free, it would leap into the shadows again and regain its strength, and he knew he did not have the energy to fight it any longer. He had to end it now, had to use the dagger to pin it to the lamp face and let it burn away.

"No!" screamed Zamagiel, from his place on the ground. "Let him die! He has ruined us, taken the Garden from us!"

"I will not kill another!" screamed a slightly different voice from the same lips, and Trent realized in an instant that it was the voice of the old man, Salvatore, arguing with the rider that controlled his body.

"You will do God's will! You have always done His will!"

"I will not kill again!" screamed Salvatore, his voice gaining strength over the fallen angel's. He reached beneath him and retrieved the silvery dagger and held it aloft, but his arm strained and trembled.

"You are weak, little man. Let go! Let him die as we will. The Prince has betrayed us all!"

"You have betrayed *me*," replied Salvatore's voice.

The fallen angel spoke then, his voice coming out lower and meaner, gravelly and dark, "You have betrayed everyone you ever loved, Salvatore Cortina. You killed your own wife, your own child. You have not the strength to resist this."

Trent could feel the Render tearing itself from his grasp and he had to retract his outstretched hand in order to hold the thing with both hands, lest it pull itself free. His head still turned, though, he watched as the fallen angel struggled with the man he had usurped from his own body. At the mention of his wife and child, Salvatore's face went dead, impassive, no

longer empowered by the fury and anger that it had held
before. Trent knew that the old Italian had lost, and soon, his
own strength would give out and the Render would burst free
and end them all.

Salvatore shook his raised arm one last time, the dagger
gleaming in the light of a sudden flash of lightning overhead.
The cherubim raised their rifles and pointed them at the
fallen *grigorim*. Trent heard the metal clicks as they pulled
back the triggers. He knew that, even now, the cherubim were
following the rules. They could not shoot Zamagiel, for he
was one of them, an angel, albeit fallen. But if Salvatore—the
mortal—won out...

Salvatore's deadened expression drooped even further. "I
killed my wife and child," he said, quietly, resigned to the
sudden and irrevocable memory. His head lowered and his
arm fell and the dagger slipped from his grasp. It clattered to
the metal platform.

The cherubim visibly relaxed, and lowered their guns.
Crisis averted. The Render would take Trent and the
Prophecy would come to pass.

Trent's heart sank as he pleaded with the old man, but
Salvatore would not look up. The Render squirmed more
forcefully in his grip, and he knew he had only seconds left
before it came free. All of the muscles in his body were
shutting down, overwhelmed by pain and stress and blood
loss. He stared at the old man, defeated.

And then, Salvatore did look up. "I killed my wife and
child," he mouthed, silently. "And for that, I ask forgiveness."
He lifted one hand a few inches from the floor and, with a
flick of his wrist, a gust of wind poured down from the sky

above and caught the dagger and flipped it, end over end, towards Trent and the Render. It landed, wavering, point down in a square hole in the metal grate.

In a flash, Trent used his last bit of strength to reach out and grab the knife. Spinning it in his hand, he brought it forward in a ragged motion and jabbed it viciously into the shadow-flesh of the Render beneath his grip. Instead of piercing the glass of the lamp, as Trent had expected, the blade buried itself to the hilt in the black mass of the creature.

The Render's scream overpowered even the cacophony of the blizzard around them. Its unearthly wail, fronted by Susan's tortured, dulcet tones, shook even the platform they stood upon. The cherubim, for a moment, were stunned. Salvatore looked up, bloodless eyes wide with terror. Trent watched, head lowered, inured somehow to the horrors of the thing, as its shadow-stuff peeled off, in long strips first that glowed orange at the edges as though heated by rays of the Luxor beam. Then, the strips became irregular fragments, then dusty particles of ashen black that leapt into the air and were pulled apart by the swirling winds, and as the Render came apart, so did its howl. The voices dropped out, one-by-one, then en masse, and the scream became a hum and then a whisper, and the last thing that Trent heard was his name.

He turned on the stunned cherubim guards, rifles raising now, confused as to whom they should fire upon. Had Salvatore won out? Was the Prophecy broken? They seemed to suddenly arrive at the same conclusion and turned their guns on Trent.

Trent did not slow. He hobbled towards Salvatore's fallen body, paying no heed to the angels' guns. Bullets sprayed forth, punctuated by explosive pops and the clicking sounds of the guns re-chambering over and over. Trent's gut burned. The bullets zipped past him in all directions, ricocheting off the metal platform floor and railings and lightning rods. Four fleshy thwacks, then grunts, followed by blood that sprayed onto Trent on all sides as he reached down to help Salvatore to his feet. Four guns clattered to the metal catwalk.

"It's over," said Trent, whispering into Salvatore's ear as he helped the old man stand. "It's over." He looked into Salvatore's eyes and saw an immense sea of pain dancing in the light of Luxor beam behind them. But he saw happiness there, too. A sad, contemplative sort of joy. And already the storm above them had begun to subside.

"I remember now," croaked Salvatore Cortina. "I should have known. It was her favorite spice."

Trent looked at him, confused by the delirious ramblings.

"Her recipe. I remember..." A genuine smile burst across the old man's face. "Always an extra pinch of—" But he never finished the sentence. His eyes went wide and his mouth formed a surprised 'O' but no further sound came out. The old man's ruined body convulsed. Blood spewed from his lips.

Trent jumped back, surprised and alarmed, and saw what had happened. A glistening spear of ice now protruded from the front of Salvatore's chest, already dripping, melting, the ice water running to the ground in red-stained rivulets.

Salvatore locked gaze with Trent, eyes still wide with surprise and panic. Blood dribbled from the corners of his mouth, and then the Italian fell. Behind him, at the far side of the maintenance platform, Trent saw Celia, standing firm, her face solemn, arm extended.

29

WHEN CELIA REACHED HIM, TRENT noticed for the first time that she was wearing his cowboy hat. He reached up with an aching arm and felt his own hair and thought it strange that he had not noticed the hat missing. He had always assumed it to be the source of his luck at the poker table. He thought now about how it had once belonged to the demon, Ramón, and mused that, indirectly, it had been.

Trent looked down at Salvatore's dead body. His emotions roiled and collided with one another and a part of him insisted on burying the thought of what Celia had just done. The teenager scared him, more even than the Render. He imagined for a moment that her future could not possibly hold much beyond nightmares.

He pointed at the hat. "Where'd you get that?" he asked, forcing a weak smile.

"Found it in the stairwell."

He looked down at Salvatore again and thought about another of Ramón's tips. "We've gotta burn the body," he said, almost whispering due to the pain that had begun to flood him as the adrenaline wore off.

Celia nodded, and then helped him to his feet. With Salvatore's body fully dead, the angel was trapped and could no longer control the storm. The winds were already dying down, the temperature rising fast. Trent could feel the tendrils of arctic air slipping away from him, letting warmth move back into his muscles. His legs and arms still felt wooden, but he managed to lift the old man's body, with Celia's help. The returning warmth had set off painful tingling throughout his flesh, and he grimaced as he walked. Celia helped to steady his steps.

Together, they made their way down the access stairs and back into the hotel, Salvatore's bloody form slumped over Trent's equally bloody shoulder. Even as he limped along with the corpse, Trent could feel Zamagiel's will probing and pushing, trying to find some purchase inside Trent's body, trying to find a way into Trent's soul.

"I don't have a soul", Trent said aloud. "You're out of luck, asshole."

As they moved through the building, they could hear children crying and people yelling and saw a few blond angels run past them as they, too, headed for the secret exit in the basement. The cherubim only shot Trent nasty glares as they went past. Outside, Trent could tell that the howling storm winds were beginning to abate.

They reached the bottom of the stairwell and pushed through the door that led into the basement. Behind the door stood a surprised man, a mortal, standing only inches from Trent's face. He had a ski mask on and a rifle slung over one shoulder. He was clearly confused, now abandoned by his angelic overseers. He scrambled to right his gun and aim, but before he could do anything useful, Celia kicked him square in the crotch. The kick sent the guy into a crumpled heap, where he lay clutching himself and moaning pitifully.

Trent looked over at the teenage girl and raised an eyebrow. She smiled back at him.

They wandered the basement for a few minutes until they found a large, concrete-floored, equipment storage room. Inside there were a number of facility golf carts, some wheeled plastic serving carts, metal folding chairs, broken tables, and other assorted items. At the far end of the room were a series of gas-powered backup generators, now chugging along noisily. Beside them was a metal shelf housing a series of red plastic gasoline containers.

Trent stumbled over, grabbed a wheeled cart, and loaded it with Salvatore's body and an assortment of gas containers. Then he motioned to Celia and the two of them pushed the cart down the long basement hallway, past the now-empty security room, and through the nondescript, unguarded door at the end, which opened into the tunnels.

Once in the tunnels, with the door closed behind them, Trent pushed Salvatore's body onto the concrete and then doused it with the gasoline.

He sat down on the end of the rolling cart and faced the soaked corpse. Celia stood beside him.

"Well, don't know what to say, really," he intoned, his voice echoing through the concrete tunnel.

Trent looked down and saw the remains of a cigarette lying in the dust on the floor. He picked it up, lit it with the silver Zippo lighter from his pocket, and took a long drag.

The warmth from the fire had sent his body into aching convulsions. His mind and vision swam.

"You made this a really shitty day for me, angel," he said finally. "But Salvatore didn't deserve this. Anyway, I'm not much good at eulogies, and I didn't really even know you. But I guess I feel bad. You were a father once. A husband, I guess." Trent took a deep breath to clear his thoughts. His head throbbed. He could not stop thinking of Susan. He thought about Zamagiel's taunts. Trent had been a husband once. He still was. "That thing really took you for a ride, didn't it, Sal? Sorry, I—"

Trent stopped talking and took the cigarette out of his mouth. He stared at the glowing tip as it burned away, ashes dropping to the floor. He could feel tears coming on and hated the idea that he might be crying over his own misfortune while a man's body lay dead before him.

"Shit," he said, and tossed the cigarette onto the corpse. "Rest in peace, old man."

Trent and Celia sat in the darkness of the tunnel for a few minutes, watching the flames dancing on the concrete walls as they consumed Salvatore's body. At one point, Trent believed he heard Zamagiel's voice scream out his name in anger, but he pinned it on his imagination or the fast-wavering delirium brought on by the frostbite.

When the body had come to a pretty solid burn, they got up to leave. Trent stood, looked at Celia, took two steps, and then collapsed. His hand and leg and head all throbbed. It felt like a bubble had burst inside his brain.

I wish Susan were here, he thought.

There was a sudden wash of pain and then nothing but shadow.

30

TRENT'S CONSCIOUSNESS WAVERED IN AND out as the ambulance bounced along the snow-crusted streets. His pain-riddled dreams smashed hard into his subconscious—terrifying, monstrous, filled with blood. When his eyes finally blinked open, he realized that he was not alone. To his right sat Celia, concern painted across her face. To his left sat Snake, who looked as though nothing out of the ordinary had happened. In fact, he looked almost bored. The sound of the ambulance radio echoed through the cab:

"...disappeared as quickly as it arrived. The freak weather, which is being called the Great Vegas Blizzard, is responsible for two hundred reported deaths, including a number of police officers, as well as numerous injuries and property damage. That damage has yet to be assessed. The Mayor's office has issued a statement indicating that casino losses alone may be enormous, especially the Luxor, where opportunistic criminals took a number of hostages and caused significant damage to the gaming floor. For more on that, we'll be talking with reporter Martin Jones, in just a few minutes. But first, the dramatic conclusion to the serial kidnapping case. The

body of the kidnapper was found, burned, in tunnels beneath the
Luxor, apparently connected somehow to the criminals..."

Between flashes of pain, Trent considered the news story.
All that damage to regular folks' homes, all those homeless
and desperate living in the flood control tunnels, and all the
news could talk about was the damage that the casinos had
suffered. Trent wondered if he had really even saved anything
at all. He looked up at Celia, who met his gaze with a smile.
She still wore his Stetson.

He smiled.

"Celia," he said finally, breaking the silence. "You okay?"

She nodded, but before she could answer, Snake cut into
the conversation.

"Everybody's fine, Trent. You're fine, Celia's fine, I'm
fine. You did some good shit tonight. Don't worry about your
injuries. We're heading to a clinic now."

Trent wondered who would pay the hospital bills. It
worried him that he might be indebted to the demonic cabal
for the rest of his life. He closed his eyes and let darkness
wash over him again. "I'm tired," he mumbled.

"Yeah, me too," Snake replied. "After that poker game
last night, after sitting next to that hot succubus—" He wolf-
whistled. "I was up all night—" He stopped mid-sentence and
turned to Celia. "So kiddo, you like that apple I gave you?"

Trent opened his eyes to watch their exchange.

Celia looked a little guilty. "I didn't eat it."

"Really?" Snake seemed genuinely surprised.

"I gave it to someone else."

Snake's demeanor shifted in an instant and a worried frown graced his lips. "Yeah? Who?"

Celia shrugged. "Some woman. She was hurt, so I gave her the apple in case she got stuck in the storm."

"Oh."

A long, awkward pause lingered in the air between them. And then, as if nothing had been said, Snake returned to his usual irritating, but smiling, self again. "Yeah, okay. Well that's just fine."

"Snake, what are you doing here?" Trent mumbled.

"Came to make sure you two were doing alright, get you to the hospital. Can't have our new boy out there crawling through the snow with a bullet in his gut."

"Thanks, I guess."

Snake shrugged. "Everything's taken care of. Consider it payment for a job well done."

"Everything?" Trent hadn't thought about the police in a while, but suddenly wondered what was going to happen when they got to their destination? Had the demons somehow fixed that, too?

"Yeah, if you mean the cops, it's all straightened out." Snake shot Trent a wink. "Besides, after those guys held up the whole Luxor, one missing kid—" He gestured toward Celia. "—well, she didn't seem so important anymore."

"They know who I am. I was famous, remember?"

Snake shrugged. "We have ways of making people forget." He frowned and glanced at Celia. "At least, those who aren't dead."

Celia's eyes filled with tears.

"So," Snake continued, changing the subject. "What are you gonna hunt down next, after we get you rebuilt and all? After we make you stronger, faster..."

Trent shrugged.

"Yeah," Snake replied, as if a question had been asked. "Just watch your back. You really pissed off some folks." Snake gestured toward the ceiling of the ambulance. "Old feathers and halos don't exactly think highly of you anymore."

"Did they before?"

Snake grinned. "You know, there's others like your niece out there. Not many, but some."

"She's not my niece."

"Yeah, whatever. Point is, there's others like her. You gonna save all of them? I promise this won't be the last time you'll have to choose."

"I'll do what I can, I guess."

"You can't always be the savior, Trent. Keep that in mind." He paused. "Oh, I almost forgot. Celia actually *is* your niece now. I set that up. All legal and shit."

Celia's tears dried up in an instant. "What?"

Snake turned to look at her. "Lucky-boy here is your uncle. Legally speaking, of course. Story is he came into town to care of you after your parents died in that car accident."

"But there was no—" She shook her head and squeezed her eyes shut. "I can't—"

Snake cut her off. "Where else you gonna go, kid? Besides, just 'cause Zammy's gone doesn't mean someone *else* ain't gonna come looking for you. Trust me, this is the best setup for you both."

"Why are you doing all this?" Trent asked.

"Jesus, you just can't figure a hint, can you, fuckbag?"

Snake began making nonsensical hand gestures in a mockery of sign language. Each word he spoke came out with exaggerated enunciation. "You. Did. Us. A. Favor."

He shook his head and started messing with some of the medical equipment in the ambulance. He stopped when a button he had pressed let out a loud electronic alarm buzz. His hand snapped back and he turned to face Trent again. "So now, we're doin' you one back. Christ, we might be lying, manipulative assholes, but we're not rude."

Celia spoke. "Are all the other kids— You know, like me— Are they all— Can they all do stuff like—?"

"Powers? Nah. Most of the little bastards just have crazy dreams for the rest of their lives or nasty skin rashes or whatever."

"Are there *any* like me?"

"Oh yeah, there's some. There's always a few in the world, one for every grig that worked his mojo on a human broad. There's a chick in New York who can set things on fire. Or this kid in Canada, right? Asshole can steal cars by just touching the door, then touching the steering wheel. Can mess around with electricity or something. Dunno what we're gonna do about him, but he's causing a lot of trouble. They'll probably make *me* go up there and rein him in or whatever—" He put air quotes around 'rein him in.'

"What exactly do you *do*, Snake?" Trent asked.

"Me? I'm just a messenger." Snake smiled.

Trent didn't trust the guy at all. He knew that demons lied, and he suspected Snake had made a career of it—thus the name.

He looked at Celia, whose face had suddenly screwed up in pain. She held her gut with both hands and Trent could tell that she was breathing heavily. "What's wrong?" he croaked, punctuating his question with a bloody cough.

Celia lifted her gaze suddenly and stared at him, a hand lingering on her stomach. She looked to Trent like a pregnant woman surprised to feel the first kick. Her lips moved and her eyes widened, as if she might tell him something terrible, but then her countenance softened again. "Umm," she mumbled, then forced a smile. "Nothing. I'm just hungry."

Trent closed his eyes again and let his head fall back on the cushion. "Me too," he said, but the pain of his injuries had drowned out most of his hunger. He inhaled deep, then let it out, trying to calm his mind, to wipe the images of Salvatore-turned-Zamagiel, the blizzard-wrecked city, the thoughts of Susan, smiling, laughing. The memories of their wedding day. He felt a knot tighten in his stomach.

Her voice, in the dying screams of the Render. He had heard her voice mixed into the cacophony and was absolutely certain she still existed somehow, somewhere. He pictured her in his mind and imagined where she might be. Lost, he suspected, somewhere in the dark, walking in the corridors of black, the realms Ramón had described, the realms he had felt with his own hands, had seen in the darkness behind his eyelids, if only for a moment.

I'm going to find her there, he thought, as the ambulance bounced painfully over a curb. *No matter what.*

No matter what.

ABOUT THE AUTHOR

M. E. Patterson is the award-winning author of
the Drawing Thin series. He lives with his family in Austin,
Texas. Devil's Hand is his first novel. The second novel in the
Drawing Thin series, Burning Cards, is now available in
paperback and ebook.

Get the latest news about Mr. Patterson's novels, stories and his
favorite cocktail recipes at:

http://mepatterson.net

Catch up with Mr. Patterson on Twitter at:

http://twitter.com/mepatterson

MORE BOOKS BY M. E. PATTERSON

Burning Cards

In the second book (after the award-winning Devil's Hand) in this Kindle bestselling series, the world moves ever closer to Armageddon, as old friends and new foes turn against Trent, while his new charge, Celia, spirals dangerously out of control.

Song and Signal

Experience a bold new science fiction universe. Can a teenage boy change the fate of the universe? Or will a high-tech killer reach him first?

Song and Signal is the first book in the new "Post-Helix" universe, a dark future where alien machinations spiral around ancient Helix Gates. A future in which humanity faces an uncertain fate.

www.ingramcontent.com/pod-product-compliance
Lightning Source LLC
Chambersburg PA
CBHW020330180626
46812CB00001B/131